"Learning the truth could be dangerous if we continue," Mitch said.

"If?" Laura shook her head. "There's no 'if' for me." She was climbing out of her fatigue, fueled by a new desperation. "I deserve the truth and I intend to ask for it."

Still, she was afraid. But she couldn't give up now. "I can understand if you don't want to get involved any deeper," she went on. "I can continue alone. There's no need for you to put yourself in danger."

"I *am* rather fond of my neck," he replied. "But you really don't think I'm going to let you continue alone, do you?"

Relief was trickling past the fear, diluting it. "I'm letting you off the hook," she said, though even to her ears her resolve sounded weak.

Somehow his arms were around her, pulling her near. "I've always been a sucker for a damsel in distress."

"Damsel? I'm no—"

But his lips were cutting off her indignation. And suddenly her protest didn't seem at all important. Not nearly as important as the warmth of his arms holding her tight and the sanctuary she was finding there.

Closing her mind, she
bells that had been rin
night, she told herself. Ju

D0816147

Dear Reader,

I was drawn to write *Family Found* because the landscape of today's family has changed so much. And I believe each family, from the typical mom, dad and kids to single- and blended-parent families, is special. This is particularly true of families with adopted children, children of the heart.

Mitch and Laura have both been searching for roots, but it's love that brings them together and love that will cement the roots of their own "family found."

I wish you happy reading and joy in your own special family.

Bonnie K. Winn

Family Found
Bonnie K. Winn

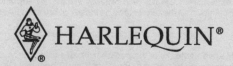

TORONTO • NEW YORK • LONDON
AMSTERDAM • PARIS • SYDNEY • HAMBURG
STOCKHOLM • ATHENS • TOKYO • MILAN • MADRID
PRAGUE • WARSAW • BUDAPEST • AUCKLAND

ISBN 0-373-70964-1

FAMILY FOUND

Copyright © 2001 by Bonnie K. Winn.

All rights reserved. Except for use in any review, the reproduction or
utilization of this work in whole or in part in any form by any electronic,
mechanical or other means, now known or hereafter invented, including
xerography, photocopying and recording, or in any information storage
or retrieval system, is forbidden without the written permission of the
publisher, Harlequin Enterprises Limited, 225 Duncan Mill Road,
Don Mills, Ontario, Canada M3B 3K9.

All characters in this book have no existence outside the imagination of
the author and have no relation whatsoever to anyone bearing the same
name or names. They are not even distantly inspired by any individual
known or unknown to the author, and all incidents are pure invention.

This edition published by arrangement with Harlequin Books S.A.

® and TM are trademarks of the publisher. Trademarks indicated with
® are registered in the United States Patent and Trademark Office, the
Canadian Trade Marks Office and in other countries.

Visit us at www.eHarlequin.com

Printed in U.S.A.

ACKNOWLEDGMENT

To Laura Shin and Paula Eykelhof, for embracing
this story with such wonderful enthusiasm.

For my son, Brian Thomas Winn. I blinked and you
grew up. I blinked again and you are a man serving
his country. And my eyes continue to fill with pride.

PROLOGUE

THE OXYGEN WAS being sucked out of the very air, certainly from Laura Kelly's lungs. Instinctively, she clutched her eighteen-month-old son, Alex, closer. It was an effort to protect, to deny and certainly to disbelieve. If what the physician said was true, Alex might have only months, even weeks, to live.

Dr. Fletcher gentled his voice. "Mrs. Kelly, I realize the news is a shock to you. However, you must know exactly what you're facing."

"But when you talked about treatment for Alex, you said I was a likely donor candidate!" Laura exclaimed, her mind racing through the possibilities. She'd never considered that as the child's mother she wouldn't be a match. She stared at Dr. Fletcher, silently willing him to produce a miracle. It was now the twenty-first century, the beginning of a new millennium. It seemed impossible to believe that a cure for acute leukemia wasn't within the doctor's ability. Houston boasted one of the most advanced and respected medical and cancer research centers in the world. If the cure wasn't within reach here, where would it be?

The frown line between Dr. Fletcher's eyes deepened, and Laura felt her heart clutch. "That's part of the problem, Mrs. Kelly. As we discussed during your last visit, the most effective course of treatment is a bone marrow transplant. However, your genetic makeup isn't adding up.''

Alex fussed, and automatically, Laura ran a soothing hand over his plump legs, then handed him a set of plastic toy keys. ''Not adding up? What do you mean?''

''I've run some preliminary tests on your potential donors. It's more than the fact that no one's a match. Genetically, it appears that they aren't blood relatives.''

For a moment Laura was speechless, and when she did speak, she had to struggle for words, for some sense of what the doctor was telling her. ''My aunt and my mother's cousins—of course they're blood relatives.''

Dr. Fletcher shook his head. ''I'm afraid not. Is it possible you're adopted, Mrs. Kelly?''

''Of course not!'' Then Laura paused. It didn't seem feasible, yet... People had often commented that she didn't resemble either of her parents. Her mother and father had always jokingly replied that the dissemblance was Laura's lucky chance of fate.

Meeting the doctor's troubled eyes, Laura realized her luck had just run out.

CHAPTER ONE

A WEATHERED SIGN identifying the office as belonging to Mitch Tucker, private detective, was just this side of shabby. As was the rest of the small building's exterior, Laura decided critically. Really not in keeping with the expensive commercial land it was situated on; but then, she wasn't shopping for a spotless houseboy. She wanted a first-rate detective, and despite outward appearances, Mitch Tucker came highly recommended by several adoptee search organizations.

Taking a deep breath, she knocked on the door, making herself ignore the chipped paint.

A hawkish, high-pitched voice ordered her to enter.

Now, that was a voice that would grate steel, Laura decided as she obeyed the order. The interior was dim, nearing murky. Having just come in from the glare of bright sunshine, she found focusing difficult. But even with the disadvantage, it was rapidly clear that Mitch Tucker was nowhere in sight.

So who had spoken?

"Hey!" the voice screeched again.

Startled, Laura whirled around. A bright-green parrot eyed her balefully.

"Hello," she replied cautiously.

"Hello," the parrot mimicked as he lurched sideways in a scooting motion across his perch.

Laura glanced at an ancient desk covered by disorganized piles of seemingly neglected papers. Immediately, she wondered if the man's detective methods were equally sloppy.

The phone rang, startling her anew and making the bird squawk. "Hello," the parrot repeated, swinging from side to side.

An answering machine clicked on. A husky male voice invited the caller to leave a message.

Laura listened while the female caller ended her one-sided conversation with a suggestive kiss. Strolling closer to the desk, she saw that a light on the answering machine indicated several other messages.

"Probably all women," Laura muttered in disapproval.

A masculine voice from the doorway surprised her. "Then maybe we'd better listen."

"That's not necessary."

He met her gaze. "And you're Miss...?"

"Kelly," she replied shortly. "Laura Kelly."

He glanced at his caller I.D. "You're right. Practically all women." There was an indiscernible note to his voice and Laura couldn't tell if he was serious or simply needling her.

Then he motioned for her to take one of the chairs angled in front of the desk. After she was seated, Mitch pushed himself back in his own chair, propping boot-clad feet on the scarred edge of his desk. "So what's your story, Laura Kelly?"

Laura didn't care for his casual demeanor or neglected office. She crimped the handles of her purse together as she started to rise. "I'm obviously wasting your time."

He didn't answer right away, instead studying her again. "Depends. What's your problem?"

"My *problem?*" Without warning she was shaking—with fury, fear and an inescapable sense of injustice. "Is that what you reduce the agonies in people's lives to? Their *problems?* Sarcastic, insignificant—" But she couldn't speak any longer as the pain assaulted her.

"Oh, hell," Mitch mumbled, swinging his legs off the desk, his chair scraping the wooden floor as he pushed it back. His boots thudded as he crossed over to her, a dull but distinctive sound in the echoing room. Awkwardly he shoved a box of tissue toward her. "Didn't know you were going to get all weepy on me."

But Laura had not given in to tears. The fear was too great for that. And she was all out of retorts.

Mitch's sigh reverberated in the soulless office. "Divorce? Hey, it's rough. You marry someone, expect picket fences and champagne. Instead you get barbed wire and beer. But, trust me, you aren't the first."

The pain in her chest was multiplying. Suddenly she was dragging in big gulps of air; yet they didn't seem to be reaching her lungs.

"Oh, man, you're really freaking." Mitch rapidly looked around the office; his eyes landed on the remains of yesterday's lunch. After dumping soggy French fries, onion rings and the remainder of a cheeseburger, he popped open the white paper fast-food bag. Without hesitation, he pulled the smelly, grease-stained sack over Laura's head.

In a few minutes, her breathing returned to normal and she pushed the bag off her head, ignoring the fragrance of onions that lingered in her hair.

"You okay?"

Not quite meeting his eyes, she nodded.

His gaze was sympathetic. "No need to be embarrassed. Divorce isn't pretty."

"That's not why I'm here."

He poured coffee into a disreputable-looking mug and handed it to her. "No?"

She drew in the warmth of the mug, feeling the coldness that had accompanied her since she had learned that she might lose her son. It was a chill she couldn't shake. "It's worse."

Mitch paused as he poured his own mug of coffee. "How much worse?"

"It's a matter of life and death."

His voice gentled. "Why don't you tell me about it."

Laura knew she couldn't conceal the pain that possessed her. She didn't even try. "I need your help to save my son's life."

"What's he in danger from?"

"Being related to me." She took a deep breath. "Because I don't know who I'm really related to. That's why I need your help. I need to find out who I am."

SHE WAS EITHER a ding-a-ling or a mental case. Mitch wasn't sure which, but he didn't need this kind of complication in his life right now. He'd lost months of work after an investigation had left him laid up in the hospital. The fact that his client had failed to pay the huge bill he'd racked up on the case had only further compounded his problems. He was close to losing the small building that housed his office, along with the valuable land it sat upon. He had already lost his condominium, and had been forced to move somewhere less expensive. And he'd been forced to trade in the sports car he loved for an annoyingly practical SUV that made him cringe each time he climbed inside.

He didn't have time to waste on an unbalanced woman. Maybe he could find a number for some sort of help hotline.

But then she raised large, deep-blue eyes and he paused. It wasn't instability he glimpsed there, rather an immense pool of pain.

"Why did you come to me?" He had noticed the distaste in her expression as she'd glanced around his neglected office. It was hardly the indication of someone who believed in his work.

"I've been told you're the best."

An arrow of ego pierced his armor. "Oh, yeah?"

"I understand your success rate with finding birth parents is phenomenal."

He nodded in acknowledgment. Before his extensive recuperation it had been true. "But that's not usually considered a life-and-death matter."

"It is when your eighteen-month-old son needs a bone marrow donor to survive."

"You're not a match?"

She shook her head.

"What about your husband?"

"We're divorced." She met his gaze. "I contacted him. He was tested, but he wasn't a match, either. Nor were any of his relatives who agreed to be tested. So, of course, I looked for potential donors in my family. That's when I learned they aren't my blood relatives. To cut to the chase, since my parents are both dead, I confronted my aunt Rhoda, and she admitted I had been adopted."

"Any reason your adopted parents didn't tell you the truth?"

"Such as?"

"Perhaps they knew the birth mother, had promised to keep the adoption secret."

But Laura was shaking her head. "No. My aunt Rhoda contends that at first they didn't know how to approach telling me, then they decided there was no point in risking my happiness. And, she said, deep down they were afraid of losing me. They were older when they got me and I guess they weren't completely comfortable with the entire parenthood thing."

She stood suddenly, crossing to the window, presenting her back. Waves of long, dark hair cascaded over her shoulders, glinting in the few rays of sunshine that struggled through the murky panes. She crossed her arms and rubbed at her elbows as though chilled. Yet if anything, the office was too warm.

"Have you tried looking yourself?" he asked, ignoring the appealing picture she made.

She turned to face him, visibly arming herself with determination. He guessed he must have imagined that glimpse of vulnerability.

"Of course. But I've come up empty. I'm told the

records are sealed. End of story.'' An even fiercer determination seemed to possess her. ''But I refuse to accept that answer. I'm assuming your familiarity and methods can open doors closed to me.''

''It usually works that way,'' he acknowledged.

She pulled out a check. ''I'm prepared to pay you a sizable retainer so you can devote your time solely to this case.''

Considering he had been back to work for only a week, exclusivity wouldn't be much of a problem. Clients palming ready cash weren't exactly lined up at the door. ''With expenses, my rate isn't cheap,'' he warned. ''In fact, the bill can escalate—'' he snapped his fingers ''—like that. And I don't want to be burned. Can you afford an all-out investigation?''

Her face registered mere annoyance. It mingled with the distaste that had never completely disappeared from her expression.

''My parents left a comfortable inheritance. Your bill won't be a problem.''

He should leap at the offer, but despite not knowing where his next client was coming from, he still didn't like the disdain in her expression. ''People *think* they want to find out all about the past when they start looking. But the truth can be pretty ugly.''

She raised those deeply blue expressive eyes. ''Nothing's uglier or less acceptable than the alternative. I don't care what you learn about me—as long as it saves my baby's life.'' For a moment he saw a flash of something else in her face, something she used the disdain to camouflage. It was desperation coupled with a healthy dose of fear. And, he guessed, like a protective mother bear, she would claw and scratch to safeguard her young. Grudgingly, he respected the quality—even more than the impressive check she had allowed to drift onto the desk in front of him.

She held out one neatly manicured hand. ''Do we have a deal?''

He accepted the handshake, refusing to acknowledge the softness of her skin, the betraying tremble. And especially the pull of her beckoning eyes.

CHAPTER TWO

How ODD, Laura decided, as she sat across the living room from her aunt Rhoda. With Mitch Tucker seated in the wing chair between them, it seemed strangely like the days when she had been a teenager and she had brought a boy home to meet her parents. There was the same sense of inspection, skepticism and uncertain approval. But her mind raced past the comparison. Could her aunt Rhoda give Mitch any information that would help?

They had been talking for hours and Mitch had diligently taken notes the entire time. In many ways, though, his questions were similar to the ones Laura had asked herself. True, he inquired about many things she hadn't thought of, but she wondered if that would be enough. Wouldn't he find some of those same avenues of pursuit relentlessly closing up? Frustrated, she wanted to jump in and help—to rush the process.

However, her aunt Rhoda was echoing some of her very concerns. "I've already told most of this to my niece. What makes you think you can learn any more than she has?"

"Because I'm a professional investigator, Ms. Johnson. No disrespect intended, but I know the ins and outs of the system, where to probe and poke."

Rhoda sighed. "Of course. I wasn't discounting your ability." Her shrewd gaze swept over him. "It's just that I don't want Laura's hopes raised on a wild-goose chase."

But he didn't back down. "Isn't that Ms. Kelly's choice to make?"

A grudging look of approval crossed Rhoda's face. "I suppose it is, young man."

Although Laura didn't comment, silently she acknowledged that he had just raised his esteem in her own book sizably.

Yet there was a more nagging question, one she hadn't been able to put to rest since Mitch had posed it. "Aunt Rhoda, can you think of any other reason Mom and Dad didn't tell me about the adoption?"

A shadow flickered over Rhoda's face and she answered slowly, her voice strained. "I've already told you. They thought you were happy. Why rock the boat?"

Laura glanced over at Mitch and saw the skepticism on his face. She wasn't sure why, but she sensed that Rhoda was concealing something. Still, her aunt had insisted she would do anything she could do to help in the search. "And there's nothing else?"

A dart of something resembling fear surfaced in Rhoda's eyes, but she shook her head. "No." Then she looked at Mitch. "But you're supposed to discover things mere mortals can't, aren't you?"

Mitch lifted one side of his mouth in a wry grin. "I haven't heard it put that way, but yes, I suppose so." With the words he rose.

Automatically, Laura did so as well, but she

reached out to snag his arm, not ready to stop her questions. As she started to speak, his gaze cautioned her to drop the inquiry. Startled by the insistence in his eyes, she followed him, absently bidding her aunt goodbye as they left.

Once outside, though, she wasn't as acquiescent. "Why did you stop me? We need to find out everything we can about—"

"Pushing people isn't the way to do it. We got enough for today."

Frustration borne of worry seized her. "You don't seem to understand. We don't have time to waste. My son's life is at stake!"

He met her gaze, his deceptively easygoing manner not concealing the intelligence in his tigerlike eyes. "I understand perfectly. Which is why we don't want to alienate your relatives. Right now they're our strongest source."

Sobered, Laura had to agree. And that frightened her even more.

OBLIVIOUS TO THE alteration of cells that threatened his life, Alex was an extraordinarily happy baby, whose world was decorated with smiles and chortles of joy. Laura hadn't realized such pure love and utter happiness could be found on this earth. She had made her share of mistakes and bad choices, but everything about Alex was both good and right.

Seeing her approaching the nursery, he stood in his crib, stretching out his arms, and shrieking for her. "Mama! Mama!"

Laura's answering smile was instant and huge.

"How's my boy?" she asked, bending to lift him.

"He's an absolute peach," Mrs. Plummer replied affectionately.

"Not that you're prejudiced," Laura told the older woman as she hugged Alex.

Mrs. Plummer continued picking up toys, stacking them in the padded toy box. "I am and I don't mind admitting it."

Once again Laura thanked the fates for Mrs. Plummer. A widow whose only daughter had died before she could marry, Mrs. Plummer had no grandchildren of her own. And she treated Alex like the grandson she'd never had. She was dependable to a fault.

Laura had struggled through the first days of single parenthood, terrified about leaving Alex in the care of strangers. And then she'd discovered Mrs. Plummer. Terror had receded, replaced by a growing dependence on the older woman. While she provided Laura with invaluable security, Laura believed that she and Alex filled a place in Mrs. Plummer's lonely life. And although Laura had a good relationship with her, it was Alex whom Mrs. Plummer had fully connected with. But that was only natural; they spent the greatest amount of time together.

"The restaurant called," Mrs. Plummer told her as she continued straightening the room.

Laura sighed. "I guess they don't know what leave of absence means."

"My thoughts exactly," Mrs. Plummer agreed. "They take advantage of you."

"The good and bad of being the manager." Laura paused to nuzzle Alex's cheek. "I'm relieved to know I'm missed, but on the other hand I'd like to leave the worries behind.''

"Then stop taking all their calls!''

"It's not that easy. I'd like to know my job's still there when—'' she paused, her hold tightening on Alex "—I'm ready to get back to work.''

"You've got your inheritance,'' Mrs. Plummer reminded her. "And D'Beti's isn't the only restaurant in the city.''

Laura sometimes wondered about the wisdom of confiding all the intimate details of her life to her baby-sitter, but Mrs. Plummer had been determined not to accept any pay while Laura was on her leave of absence. Unable to allow such a sacrifice, Laura had disclosed the source of her funds.

"So, has the hotshot detective found out anything?''

Grinning, Laura shook her head. It was a good description of the man. "Not yet. He wants me to be patient.''

Worry settled over Mrs. Plummer's features. "But we don't have time to be patient.''

Laura patted the older woman's arm, knowing Alex couldn't have asked for a more devoted surrogate grandmother. "That's what I told him.''

Mrs. Plummer sniffed suspiciously, then ducked her face for a moment, no doubt hiding a trace of tears. "Good for you.'' Then as abruptly, she headed out of the nursery. "I'd better check the chicken, or it'll be spitting dry.''

Laura took advantage of the quiet to settle into the well-worn rocker. The gentle creak of the wood against thick carpet soothed. Alex was content to snuggle in her arms, his fingers latching onto hers. Laura smoothed back the baby-fine hair on his forehead, feeling her heart clutch. What if she couldn't save him? Couldn't unlock the secrets to her birth?

He kicked chubby legs and she stroked his soft skin. "Somehow I'll find out, Alex." Briefly, she closed her eyes. "I don't care how it affects me." And Laura knew it was true. Mitch Tucker could learn she was the child of criminals and she wouldn't care—as long as it brought her closer to a cure for Alex.

HER EYES WERE definitely blue, Mitch concluded. An intense blue, one that evoked thoughts of a stormy Irish sky. Emphasis on stormy, he acknowledged. Laura Kelly was a woman possessed. And it was getting on his nerves.

"What are you doing here?" he asked, pushing still sleep-rumpled hair from his forehead. "It can't be much later than six."

"Seven-fifteen, Tucker. We don't have time to waste."

"I never consider sleeping a waste of time," he retorted, seeing the bluish haze of dawn on the Houston skyline through the living room windows. He shook his head in continued disbelief, wishing he hadn't provided her with his home address and phone number. "And if we're going to talk while I'm still in my boxers, you might as well call me Mitch."

Her face flushed, not two petite, delicate spots of color but a tidal wave of embarrassment. "Don't you own a robe?"

"Tell you what, Laura. Next time I show up at your house before breakfast, I'll be sure to call the fashion police, too."

Laura's gaze collided with his bare legs, then darted away. She lifted her chin. "I think we have more important things to worry about than your wardrobe."

"You brought up the issue," he replied easily, enjoying the way she emotionally scrunched herself up into a tight knot. He guessed there was a lot of inhibition trapped inside, just waiting to bust loose. Then again, she could be one of those eternally rigid fusspots.

She ignored the rebuke, her single-mindedness vaulting back to her initial purpose. "We need to go over what you've learned." As she spoke, Laura trailed behind him through the apartment.

At the door of his bedroom, Mitch turned around, leaning one hip idly against the doorjamb. "It's not that I mind sharing my shower, but I draw the line at discussing business at the same time."

If possible, Laura flushed even darker.

Unable to resist needling her, Mitch let one hand drift toward his waistband. "I'll leave the choice up to you."

Laura whirled around and retreated into his living room.

Chuckling, Mitch padded into the bathroom and turned the shower on full blast. He suspected he would need the bracing wake-up to face the morning.

Ten minutes later he was sure of it. Strolling into his kitchen, he found that Laura had commandeered the space. Blissfully, he inhaled the aroma of freshly brewed coffee. He grabbed a mug and filled it to the brim. After sipping the strong brew, he tipped the mug toward her in a mock salute. "I'll give you this—you know how to make a decent cup of coffee."

But her eyes were doing some sort of strange dance that didn't seem to have anything to do with the coffee. "Don't you get completely dressed before noon?"

He glanced down at his jeans. "Didn't know we were going formal today."

She waved in the direction of his bare chest. "I don't think anywhere we go today will be *that* informal."

"We?" He lowered his mug. "Look, you hired me to do a job. I work solo."

"But I can help you. There must be some grunt work I can do that will free you up for the more difficult things."

"So, you're going to be my gofer?" he questioned skeptically. She didn't seem like the sort to take orders well.

Laura met his eyes evenly. "I would clean sewers bare-handed if it would help my son."

Sobered by the reminder, Mitch lowered his mug. "Our methods may not be the same, but I know how serious the situation is. You don't have to dog my steps to make sure the investigation's being conducted the right way."

"That's not the point."

He guessed it was, but let the comment pass.

"I can't just stand by doing nothing." Laura

paced toward the window, yet she didn't seem to notice anything beyond the shuttered panes of glass.

Mitch studied the fierce determination in the set of her shoulders, the earnestness in her eyes. And sighed in defeat. "If I let you help—"

"You'll—"

"I said *if,* Miss Kelly. And let's get one thing straight. *I'm* in charge of the investigation. I won't put up with you second-guessing my methods."

"What do we do first?" she asked, choosing to ignore his warning.

"First, *we* put on my shirt." His gaze took another unhurried appraisal, enjoying the sudden jumpiness in her eyes. "Or do you want to be in charge of that?"

Instead of answering him, she turned her back and made a production out of clattering the mugs in the sink and yanking at the faucet, purposely adding the roar of the water to the manufactured noise.

"Oh, and, Laura—"

"Yes?"

"Next time you show up before breakfast and drag me out of bed—you'd better mean it."

LAURA FELT MORE in control with the width of a sturdy oak library table between them. And it didn't hurt that Mitch had donned a shirt. Papers and books surrounded them, but he didn't seem to mind the clutter. He had selected the library for the morning's work since it contained microfilm records he needed to probe.

"What is that you're doing?" she asked, impatient to cut to the chase, to find the key they needed to unlock her past.

"Finishing your personal profile," he replied. "We did the preliminaries before talking to your aunt. Now we need to dig deeper."

She frowned. "Why?"

The librarian strolled by, hushing them, her wrinkled face looking like that of a pug dog's—set in permanent lines of disapproval.

Laura lowered her voice. "So?"

"Right now, we have an equation of the unknown, and the only known factor in the formula is you. I have to learn everything about you, Laura. From top—" he paused as his eyes drifted over her slowly "—to bottom."

Despite the fear gnawing at her, Laura felt an unexpected warmth curling in her belly. Resolutely, she straightened up in the rigid, narrow-backed chair. "And we had to come to the library to do this?"

"I need to dig through their old records. Of course, we could have stayed at my apartment to complete your profile."

"No, the library's good." She tried to hide her discomfort. "I've told you I'll do whatever it takes to help Alex."

He had a way of blinking, a slow easy motion that seemed to mock and tantalize at the same time. "Then let's start where we left off."

And they did, including her memories of junior and senior high school. Patiently Laura recounted her past, balking only when they got to the choice of her senior prom escort.

She narrowed her eyes suspiciously. "Why do you want to know that?"

His answering smile was a lazy curl of his lips that seemed to reflect deep amusement. "Wondering if you hung out with the jocks, the geeks or the brains."

"What possible relevance can that have to finding my birth mother?"

Again the librarian hushed them.

Mitch's voice was low, but it reached her easily. "I didn't say it was relevant. I just wondered."

Exasperated, she was prepared to let him have it, albeit in a quiet tone.

But he was smiling fully. "That's better. You were looking entirely too serious."

"This *is* serious."

"Right. You won't be much help, though, if you burn out."

Realizing she must appear entirely humorless, Laura eased off a bit. "We have been at it for hours. I guess we could both use a break."

Surprise drew his brows upward. "You said it." Rising, he swept the papers into his well-worn leather portfolio. "Why don't we finish this over something to drink."

Sighing, Laura realized she'd brought this one on herself. Give a playboy time to play and of course he would do just that.

However, as they strolled from the weathered brick building, Mitch steered her not toward the car but toward a grassy slope. Perhaps the bar was within walking distance, she reasoned. Likely the detective would have picked a library close to his creature comforts.

They climbed to the top of the gentle incline. To Laura's surprise, a wooded park greeted them. Like many of the dichotomies of the cityscape, skyscrapers framed the outline of the trees. The park should seem like an encroachment. Instead the green sanctuary felt like a fitting oasis for the glass-and-concrete edifices.

Again Mitch took her elbow, then led her down the path to a coffee cart. "They've got everything from cappuccino to regular old sludge."

Suddenly the heat and flavor of a latte sounded immensely appealing, and she placed her order.

As the vendor handed her the steaming, foamy cup, Mitch pulled out a bill. "Just my usual, Pat."

The older man grinned. "None of that fancy stuff for you, eh, Tucker?"

"Simple man, simple tastes," Mitch agreed, tipping the man generously.

Then he turned to Laura. "There's a bench down by the water. Bound to be a few ducks doing a matinee."

Laura smiled, caught by the whimsy in his words. "You think they only swim for show?"

"Keeps the bread crumbs coming. It's steady work, not much chance for advancement, but no layoffs or forced retirement, either."

Once more, Laura smiled. The detective might needle her, but he could also be amusing when it suited him.

The bench curved as the shoreline did, a scallop

that placed Mitch and Laura together in the center of the weathered redwood structure.

Preposterously, the proximity made her nervous. Again Laura straightened her spine, but the gesture made her feel even more foolish. She wasn't a blushing teenager out with a man for the first time. Not that they were *out*—still, she felt ridiculously prudish. Just because she had been badly burned by one man, it didn't mean she couldn't relate on a nonpersonal level with the entire sex.

Frustrated with herself, she took a large sip of her latte, forgetting until it was too late that the liquid was still very hot.

"Getting burned?" Mitch asked.

"What?" *Had he read her mind?* Realizing she had advanced beyond ridiculous, Laura settled the lid back on her drink. "No, not really. It's just so good I got impatient."

"And a good thing shouldn't be rushed."

Laura glanced at him skeptically. "Really?"

"Yep." His gaze sidled over her face. But he didn't add anything else.

And judging from the reaction in her twisting insides, he didn't need to.

CHAPTER THREE

MITCH'S OFFICE appeared even more disreputable-looking under the latest pile of materials. He knew that Laura Kelly wanted answers yesterday, but in truth, investigations rarely moved quickly. And they seldom held the excitement portrayed in television and the movies.

An image of Laura Kelly flashed in his mind. Then again—

The phone intruded. Snatching it up, Mitch was disappointed to learn that a fairly reliable lead had been a dead end. Despite what Laura appeared to think, he had placed dozens of phone calls, while building her personal profile and creating a comprehensive search file. It was the plan, his blueprint. And despite his casual approach to many things in life, he never undertook a case without a well thought-out plan.

The door flew open and Mitch didn't need more than one guess to know who was behind it.

Laura's dark hair was thrown back like a banner, and her eyes glistened like polished lapis. She seemed to bring in the rush of the city streets, the whirl of incoming breezes and a touch of captured sunshine. He'd never seen so much contained energy in any other person. But having it all directed at him was a tad unnerving.

"Galveston," she began by way of greeting. "My parents never wanted to go there. Once, though, I remember coming in the house and overhearing them. They didn't realize I was inside and I heard them mention Galveston. But as soon as they noticed me, they stopped talking. Do you think that means something?"

"And good morning to you, too, Laura Kelly."

She waved away the greeting. "Do you?"

"It could be something."

Her eyes brightened.

"And they could have been discussing a clandestine meeting when they hoped to ditch you so they could be alone."

Deflated, she slumped into a nearby chair. "I suppose you're right. I keep replaying reels of my life like some sort of out-of-whack movie theater in my mind that I can't shut down. In the middle of the night, I'm sure I've come on some incredibly important memory and by morning I realize it's worthless." Easing back in her chair, she glanced around at the piles of books on the couch and coffee table.

"Phone books?" she questioned, flipping one open, then shoving it aside. "Isn't that kind of low-tech?"

"Depends on your point of view," he replied evenly. "Investigative tools range from low-end phone books to high-end computer databases. Don't discount what you don't know."

"Point taken. So, what are we working on today?"

Mitch creased one hand over his forehead. She was using the royal "we" again. And she was becoming a royal pain. As quickly, he remembered the reason behind her insistence and realigned his attitude. He'd be insistent, too, if his son's life hung in the balance. "I'm following up on some leads."

She leaned forward anxiously. "Ones that have panned out?"

"Not yet."

"Damn!" Laura rose in one hurried motion, frustration pouring from every gesture. "That's not good enough!"

"What do you suggest? You want me to lean on your relatives? Maybe your aunt Rhoda?"

"Of course not! I...I..."

Mitch gentled his voice. "You're paying for my expertise—trust it."

She hesitated for a moment. "I suppose I do. I'm just so terribly worried."

Mitch sighed inwardly, knowing she would feel no peace until they had some answers. And it wouldn't hurt him to fill her in. "I'm requesting a copy of your original birth certificate. With the sealed records law in Texas, we'll get a copy of your adopted certificate, but we need the paper trail proving our intent, showing we've taken all the steps. We'll have to have that once we request a court order to unseal the original."

A contemplative expression covered her face. "You mean I have two birth certificates?"

He nodded. "One filed with the information on your actual birth parents, another with your adopted parents listed."

"Will that one say I'm adopted?"

"No. That's part of the sealed records process. For all appearances, the second birth certificate looks like the real thing. Unless you know about the original information, you'd have no reason to suspect it's been changed."

"This is a whole new world," Laura murmured. "I feel like I'm in some sort of strange limbo and I'll wake up tomorrow and find out this has all been some sort of bad dream."

"Including Alex's illness?"

"Especially that," Laura agreed, the pain in her eyes surfacing.

"I don't suppose your ex-husband has been much help."

"As you know, he was willing enough to get tested for a bone marrow match." She shrugged, a forlorn movement. "But beyond that he acts as though Alex's illness really isn't his concern. It's *all* I can think about. I eat, sleep and live wondering how we can beat this. But Kevin acts as if—" Laura brought clenched fingers to her mouth, unable to complete the words.

"Maybe he doesn't know how to express his feelings," Mitch suggested.

"That wouldn't be a first," Laura commented bitterly. "But to ignore his son, to act as though it doesn't matter whether he survives—"

"It won't help to torture yourself," Mitch soothed.

"Why not? I'm the one who chose the worst possible father material as my husband. I'd have done better if I'd blindfolded myself, twirled in a circle until I was dizzy, then stabbed my finger in the direction of the first man I encountered.''

Mitch shifted uncomfortably. ''Maybe he feels impelled to hide how worried he is.''

''He never wanted a baby,'' she admitted, surprising him. For a moment even Laura seemed surprised that she had allowed the admission. ''Alex wasn't planned. In fact, I didn't learn I was pregnant until after Kevin and I had agreed to divorce. Still, I always wanted my baby. I considered him a great gift, a wonderful blessing after so much hurt. But for Kevin it was different. He seems to have divorced his feelings for his son along with our marriage. He's seen him only twice since he was born, and then only at my insistence. Kevin has made it clear he'd prefer to forget Alex altogether, to never see him again.'' Bewildered, she raised widened eyes to meet his. ''Do all men feel this way after a divorce?''

Staggered by the question, and far too aware of his past, Mitch hesitated. ''I can't answer for all men—and the truth is you could ask a dozen men and get a dozen different answers. I can only speak for myself, but if I ever had a son, I wouldn't let anything come between us. People get divorced every day. That's a fact of modern life. It's not often people can stick a marriage out forever—that's become kind of a myth. And people remarry, which is okay. But you have just one set of parents. You can't take that away from a kid.''

If possible, her face blanched even further.

Then it struck him. ''Hell, I'm sorry. I didn't mean the adoption thing.''

She waved away his apology. "It's all right."

But Mitch felt an urgent need to make amends, his own experience a painful reminder. "No. I was talking about a father's responsibility, not being adopted. A man ought to stand by his kid, no matter what. What sort of guy deserts his kid when he's sick?"

"The kind I married," she answered quietly.

Mitch realized he didn't have a spare inch left to cram any more of his foot into his mouth. He'd gone from bad to worse, then worse again. "You know, I was just thinking this might be a good time to do some of the legwork. You want to tag along?"

"Tossing me a bone, Tucker?"

"You up for catching it?"

Her smile was sad but accepting. "I opened this can of worms."

"And I poked the jagged edge of the tin into your feelings. So why don't we put a bandage on the morning and get the hell out of here?"

"You've got a way with words, Tucker."

"Does that mean yes?"

The sadness hadn't left her eyes, but a sliver of light penetrated the darkness. "I suppose so. Good to see you finally admit it."

He skirted the desk, crossed to the front door and opened it for Laura. "Admit what?"

Faint slyness edged the beginning of a smile. "That you need my help."

LAURA WASN'T SURE what she had expected. But the musty corridors of a genealogical library were a surprise. Floor after floor of books and records held a wealth of secrets.

Mitch quickly decided he needed the help of a librarian, rather than dig through hundreds of rolls of microfilm on his own.

"We need to see the birth records for March 1970," he was telling the woman.

"Harris County?" she asked.

"To start with." He lowered his voice a bit. "And then Galveston County."

Laura hid a triumphant smile as they followed the librarian to the section of the library with birth records. The helpful woman then explained how they were divided and how to find certain years.

"Are you tracing your family history?" the librarian asked.

"Actually, we're—" Laura began.

"Yes, we're working on our genealogy," Mitch interrupted. "I appreciate your help. After we find my sister's records, I'd hate to be searching all over the building for Grandma Tucker's birth certificate."

The graying librarian laughed. "That's why we're here. Let me know if you need anything else," she added, before moving away.

"Why did you cut me off?" Laura demanded in a quiet voice.

"Because telling people you're searching for your birth parents closes more doors than it opens. It's safer to stick to the story that you're researching family roots."

Slightly deflated, Laura studied his face. "You

mean people won't want to help if they know the truth?''

"This isn't a black-and-white issue, Laura. A lot of people believe that digging up the truth only opens buried pain and problems. They feel the birth parents have a right to their privacy." He held up one hand, anticipating her protest. "Some are even sympathetic to the reasons for a search like yours, yet at the same time are hesitant to cross certain lines. And most of them have heard stories similar to yours that have turned out to be ruses, so they're cynical. While some legislators advocate opening all the records, some are equally insistent they remain sealed."

"But the librarian—"

"May or may not be influenced by the debate. Why send up an unnecessary flag, though? In investigative work, it's always best to be low-key."

"No shoot-outs unless absolutely necessary?" she questioned dryly.

"Right, Watson."

She smiled. "As in your trusted assistant?"

He pointed in the direction of an oversize cabinet. "There's March 1970. When you're finished, we'll talk."

Laura felt her smile draining away. "You want me to dig through the entire cabinet?"

"You said you wanted to help."

"I do, but—"

"Then start digging."

MANY HOURS LATER, Mitch glanced at the interior of Laura's home. It was a modest, middle-income home. And much like her it didn't reveal a lot. It could be anyone's home, in Anywhere, America. It was light and airy, but with no individuality. It was so lacking in the personal bits and pieces that revealed the owner's personality that the living room could be one in a model house.

He had expected her to be tired of his company after a day spent digging through records and tracing old addresses. But she had insisted on bringing him to meet Alex.

An older woman appeared in the doorway. "Hello, Mr. Tucker. I'm Leona Plummer. I care for the baby."

He rose, extending his hand. "Ma'am."

She accepted his handshake, a faint light of approval entering her stern expression. "Mrs. Kelly would like you to come to the nursery to meet young Alex."

He followed, wondering at the austere woman. She seemed an unlikely choice for a baby-sitter. But then, nothing about Laura Kelly had met his expectations.

Entering the nursery, Mitch was struck by the burst of colors. Beautifully hand-painted murals covered the walls. A herd of cuddly stuffed animals populated the room, along with colorful blocks and an impressive collection of children's books. Unlike the bland living room, the nursery screamed with character.

Laura turned with the baby in her arms. Mitch had steeled himself for a sick child, expecting to see the ravages of disease.

He hadn't expected bright blue eyes, ones that

matched his mother's. Or chubby arms and legs that waved in obvious delight.

Alex squealed just then. "'Lo!"

"That means hello," Laura explained, smoothing the soft hair from the baby's face, dropping a kiss on his forehead.

Surprised yet mesmerized by the transformation in Laura, Mitch stepped farther into the room.

"Hello, little guy," Mitch greeted him awkwardly. Then he directed his attention to Laura. "He's looking good."

She studied Mitch, then responded matter-of-factly. "You can't see his illness yet." Again Laura smoothed back the baby's hair. "In time you will—if he doesn't get the bone marrow transplant, but for now he looks like any other healthy baby."

"Hey, that's good, isn't it?"

"I suppose so. But sometimes it's hard to convince people how desperate the situation is. They see a healthy toddler and think I'm ringing premature alarms."

"You don't have to convince me," Mitch replied quietly.

Laura met his eyes. "That's not why I brought you here. I just thought it might make the search more personal. More important."

"It was already important." Mitch took the baby's hand, smiling when Alex curled plump fingers around his. "But I don't mind meeting the client behind the client."

Laura finally smiled again, then glanced down at her son. "You haven't been a client before, have you, punkin?"

Alex squealed in answer when Laura nuzzled his cheek.

"This room is great," Mitch commented, still struck by the artwork. Characters from fables and ancient nursery tales coexisted with fantasy characters surely drawn from a very fertile imagination.

"Thanks, I had fun doing it."

Mitch pulled his gaze from the brilliant walls. "You painted this?"

"I wanted it to be special for him."

"It's that and more." Struck again by the variance between the nondescript living room and this dazzling nursery, Mitch whistled. "You must enjoy decorating."

"I used to."

"But this—"

Her laugh was a self-deprecatory sound. "This is the only room in the house I've decorated."

That explained it.

"When Kevin and I divorced, I left our house and everything in it."

"That's a rather unusual move, isn't it?"

"For the woman you mean?" Laura concluded accurately. "It's true. Usually men are the ones most willing to leave everything behind, to step away from any reminders of their past. But I didn't want anything from what we'd shared." Her grip tightened on Alex. "Except this one, of course."

Mitch grinned. "It's clear you got the best part of the deal."

Surprise and something else he couldn't quite decipher entered her softening eyes. "Absolutely."

Alex squirmed just then, craning his head in

Mitch's direction. It almost looked like the kid was reaching toward him.

"Seems he wants you," Laura said in surprise.

"I don't—"

But before he could protest, Laura was handing him the toddler. Warmth, the fresh aroma of talc and softness assailed him. Awkwardly, Mitch held the baby, not certain what to do with him. His experience with children was a total zero. He turned Alex toward him, positioning him so that he could hand the child back to his mother. Just then Alex smiled. Not one of those vacant, meaningless smiles. Their eyes connected, Alex's toothy grin one of delight.

And something warm crawled through Mitch's insides. Something that scared the life out of him.

CHAPTER FOUR

THE WEATHERMAN HAD predicted a thunderstorm, but it hadn't struck the city yet. The sky was graying and the air had cooled enough that the storm wasn't an empty threat. The wind picked up errant leaves and showered them over the streets like chocolate-colored raindrops. Even though Laura liked nothing better than a stormy, windswept day, she scarcely noticed the changing atmosphere. Her mind was too full.

Had she taken the right course in hiring this cowboy detective? Or should she have taken a more conservative approach? Filled with worry, she leaned a bit longer on the doorbell than she'd intended.

The door was yanked open suddenly and Rhoda stared at her. "Is the house on fire?"

Laura managed a wan smile. "Sorry. I guess my mind was on other things."

Rhoda studied her. "That's understandable with all the strain you're under. Come in, child. I'm brewing some chamomile tea."

Tea. Her aunt Rhoda's solution for everything. Yet there was comfort in the familiar. Laura recognized that the routine was as soothing as the actual liquid.

Trailing her aunt, she entered the kitchen, a large

high-tech room. However, despite a recent, costly remodeling the room was no longer warm and inviting. While the kitchen typically represented the heart of a home, this one needed just that. It had no heart. Before renovation, Rhoda's house had seemed cozy; now it looked as though it belonged on the slick pages of a glossy magazine. But Laura knew the house was a point of pride for her aunt. She had struggled for many years and only recently had been able to afford to improve her lifestyle.

Rhoda placed thin, fragile bone china cups on the oak table. Laura recognized them as the antique cups that had once belonged to her grandmother, cups that had been in her family for generations. That same familiar spurt of disbelief struck her. How was it that she wasn't the product of this family? It seemed the same blood must run in her veins. Otherwise, how could the connection be so intense, so real?

"Any news?" Rhoda asked her as she filled the creamer.

"No. Actually, that's why I'm here."

The crash and shattering china distracted them both. Laura jumped to her feet, then knelt beside the broken pieces. "Oh, Rhoda. The creamer that came by wagon train." Carefully, she retrieved the largest fragments. "I've heard about specialists who can repair broken china so that it scarcely shows a trace of the break." Gently she handed the pieces to her aunt. "I guess we're all feeling the strain."

"Uh, yes, of course. Don't worry about the creamer, Laura. It's just china."

Laura eyed her aunt in concern. Family heirlooms

rated near the top in importance for Rhoda. Apparently, her aunt was so worried by the seriousness of Alex's condition that the heirlooms had lost some of their importance. "Still, let's save them."

"All right." Rhoda rattled around the cupboard, before settling on a small silver creamer. "I guess I can use that tea almost as much as you."

"I've been thinking about what you said."

Rhoda stilled her movements. "What was that?"

"About how I should hire an attorney rather than a hotshot detective."

Slow and deliberate, Rhoda crossed the room. "Isn't he accomplishing what you expected?"

Laura shrugged. "I want him to have the answers *yesterday* and I know that's not possible, but I just want to make sure I did the right thing in hiring him."

Frowning, Rhoda studied her tea, adding a bit of sugar. For a few moments only the clink of the silver spoon punctuated the silence. "I realize I suggested a lawyer, but if you're satisfied with your young man's methods, then you should stick to your decision."

"He's hardly my 'young man,' Rhoda."

Thin eyebrows arched in inquiry. "You could do worse."

"And have," Laura admitted. "But that's not the point."

"I wasn't sure what I thought about him at first." Blunt by nature, Rhoda seldom minced words. "He seemed awfully sure of himself. But I remember once liking that in a man. Mitch Tucker could be a keeper."

Laura rolled her eyes. "I'm worried about saving Alex, not snagging a man."

"I'm not suggesting anything less, dear. But you don't have to blind yourself to the obvious."

"Dare I ask what that might be?"

"A handsome, confident man who knows his own mind."

"Right now I need to be sure of my own mind first. What if I've done the wrong thing in hiring him? Suppose I'm wasting time? Time we don't have to waste. Maybe I should meet with the attorney, at least talk to him—"

"Laura." Rhoda placed one hand atop hers. "You can't go off scatterbrained in a dozen different directions."

"But—"

"I know you want to do everything within your power, but going crazy won't help Alex. You'll be dividing your energies in so many ways, you'll exhaust yourself. Laura, trust your instincts. *And* allow yourself enough time to see if this will work."

"But we don't have time!" Laura reiterated. She heard the despair in her voice and lowered her head.

"Laura, don't give up on Alex."

"I'm not!"

"You have to trust that he can hang in there as long as it takes."

For a brief moment Laura considered her own denial and the quiet understanding in her aunt's expression. "You're right. I guess I just sort of panicked. I keep thinking that Alex's fate rests in my hands. If I don't make the right choices, he's the one who'll suffer."

"That's where you're wrong, Laura. His fate is in larger hands than yours. You'll just have to trust in that."

"I do. But I've always felt I had to be the strong one, in charge, sure of what I was doing."

"It doesn't hurt to lean. You just haven't had anyone strong enough to lean on. Maybe that will change."

Shocked, Laura drew back. "Surely you don't mean Mitch Tucker."

"It may be premature, but I'd like you to drop your defensive shields and be open to possibilities."

"That hasn't worked too well for me in the past."

"And this is today, Laura." Rhoda shrugged, but her hands moved nervously as her gaze appeared to settle on something far beyond Laura. "It's wise to learn from your mistakes, not to wallow in them."

Laura winced. "That was candid—and I appreciate the concern. But I can't allow myself to become involved with another ladies' man."

"Isn't that a rather quick conclusion?"

Laura's smile was tinged with wise regret. "I guess experience makes me a quick learner. But right now I don't need to worry about romance. I need answers."

"Then believe in yourself. The rest will follow."

Laura wanted to accept her aunt's words, yet she couldn't miss the betraying nervousness of Rhoda's manner, the subtle but skittish movements she tried to disguise. It seemed neither of them was all that assured. And that sent the fear spiraling.

MITCH INHALED the ripe smell of incoming rain. It would be another drencher. Houston didn't bother with gentle rain. Instead the skies opened, dumping water over the landscape, much like upturned buckets. The uninitiated were often shocked by the deluges. But the natives took it in stride. And Mitch was native to the skin.

Crossing the parking lot, he heard the squeal of an approaching car. Briefly closing his eyes, he emitted a groan. He could guarantee without looking who was driving the car. And it was too late for a clean getaway.

"Tucker!" Laura called out as she pivoted sharply into an adjoining parking stall. In seconds, she scrambled from the vehicle, then slammed the door and headed toward him.

Mitch had dealt with difficult clients in the past, but he'd never had one who had become glue. He wouldn't be surprised if she welded the bumper of her car to his so she wouldn't miss a move.

"Tucker!" she repeated as she reached him. "I almost missed you!"

"And that would be a tragedy," he replied, pulling keys from his pocket.

"What?"

He sighed. "Nothing. I'm on my way out, so if you don't need anything urgent—"

"Good! I was afraid I wouldn't catch you." She pulled open the passenger door of his car. "Where are we going?"

He withheld an additional sigh. It would be easier to rid himself of his own skin. "To hospitals."

She frowned. "What are we hoping to find?"

"First, how many females were born in each one on the same day you were. Once we learn that, we find out which doctors and nurses were on duty the same day."

"Ones who might know something about my birth mother?" Laura questioned. But her voice began to cloud. "How can they possibly remember something that happened so long ago?"

"We won't know until we try. And we need to explore the possibilities until we receive your birth certificate."

"What if we can't get my actual certificate, only the adopted one?"

"Even more reason to do this now. Because our next stop will be contacting each of your relatives to see what he or she might know."

She slumped in her seat. "The more I learn about this, the more overwhelming it seems."

Seeing her pain, Mitch ignored his usual reserve and covered her hand. "That's why I suggested you let me do this on my own. I realize you want to do everything in your power to speed things up, but for someone who's not familiar with the search process, it can be pretty overwhelming, especially when it's this personal."

He could see her struggle, then her face softened subtly. "I suppose so." She turned in the seat, leaning toward him, her body, face and voice all earnest. "But I can't just sit by. Can you understand that?"

"Too well. But you'll have to trust me to direct the investigation."

"Funny."

Starting the car, he glanced over at her. "What is?"

"That's the second time today someone told me to trust."

"Then maybe it's time to listen."

"Mmm."

But he could feel she wasn't convinced. Good thing that wasn't his job. It was one assignment he didn't think he wanted to tackle. Convincing Laura Kelly of anything other than what she wanted to believe would be a mammoth challenge. And one he didn't need.

HOSPITAL RECORDS departments all appeared similar to Laura. Dry, boring places with seemingly endless supplies of paper. To think that buried within those reams of paper might be the solitary document they needed frightened her. The task of finding it felt nearly hopeless. But that didn't deter Mitch Tucker. Efficient and capable, he didn't appear intimidated by the sheer volume of information or the red tape it took to wade through it.

Still, Laura couldn't ignore the ticking of her internal alarm system, one that was counting down the time they had left to learn the truth. Yet they managed to visit three hospitals.

Leaving St. Mark's Hospital, Mitch drew in a deep breath of the humid air. "Can't abide the smell of antiseptic. Don't know how people can work in it all day."

Laura shrugged. "They're probably used to it. A person can get used to most anything after a while."

Mitch didn't look convinced. "Mmm. Why don't we call it a day. We've—"

"What?" Halting, she pivoted to glare at him.

"Tucker, you don't understand. This isn't like some of your other jobs. We have a pressing deadline! One that's more important than your playtime."

He held open the car door for her, his expression and voice remaining even. "We've been at it all day. I thought you might like to go and check on that little deadline."

She blinked, then glanced at her watch. "It's after six o'clock. I didn't realize…"

"We covered a lot of ground today, Laura. It's dinnertime. Why don't you go home and I'll head back to the office."

"The office?"

"I want to check the national database search again, see if I missed anything. Then I need to follow up on some calls and go through the mail. Hopefully, there'll be some solid leads."

The breeze kicked up around them, straggling remains of the morning's storm. Wind tugged at Laura's hair and she pushed wayward strands away from her face. "But you need to eat dinner, too."

"I'll grab something."

"A hamburger, no doubt," she said, feeling guilty for her outburst. "That's not a proper dinner after a long day."

"I'm used to it." He drew his brows together as he cocked his head, studying her skeptically. "Don't tell me you're concerned about my dining habits?" He shook his head slowly. "Or my *welfare?*"

Uncomfortable with his scrutiny and her own harsh words, Laura tossed back her hair. "Of course not. But I'm the one demanding the long hours."

"Feeling guilty, Laura? That doesn't sound like

you. But then, I don't suppose I know you well enough to say, do I?''

Uncomfortable, she edged back a bit. Ridiculously, ever since her disastrous divorce she had unplugged her radar for dealing with men. It felt safer to exist as a sexless nonplayer than to deal with any more hurt. Mitch Tucker was probably so used to the male-female dance that the motions were as automatic as breathing for him. She doubted he was even aware he was doing them. Laura was certain he'd be amazed to learn how ill at ease she was.

Edging even farther back, she all but fell into the car. "You're right. We should be going."

He still looked skeptical. "Did I say that?"

But he took the hint, closing her door, then crossing to the other door and sliding inside the vehicle.

When they reached Laura's home, she hesitated. "Why don't you join us for dinner."

"With the formidable Mrs. Plummer?" He smiled. "Not really my style. But you and the little tiger have a good one."

Once in the house, Laura shut the front door and leaned against it. Mitch Tucker's presence was so intense she felt a moment's relief. Then, oddly, the relief segued into letdown. It was absurd, she knew, yet she couldn't easily shake the feeling.

Straightening, she gazed down the dimly lit hallway. While the house was as welcoming as it could be without the personal touches it needed, it had never seemed quite so lonely. Aggravated with herself, Laura shook her head. Her life was hardly lonely. She had Alex and even Mrs. Plummer. No, she wasn't alone.

An interior door opened softly and crepe-soled shoes quietly approached. "I thought that might be you," Mrs. Plummer greeted her. "I was checking on dinner—we have a nice roast."

"Just for us?" Laura questioned, realizing she had little appetite.

"I always had a small family, and let me tell you, roasts are not only for crowds. Just because a body doesn't have a dozen children, that's no reason to skimp on dinner."

"Did you ever regret having only one child, Mrs. Plummer?"

A bleak look flashed in the woman's eyes. "Despite what people think, the number of children isn't what counts. Like little Alex, one is perfect."

Laura couldn't prevent a smile. "Do you suppose all mothers of onlys feel this way?"

"I can't speak for all mothers, but I know my Linda was perfect, just like your Alex."

"You're right, Mrs. Plummer. And since we almost had company for dinner your choice sounds a lot better than a frozen diet dinner or a can of soup."

"Company?"

Laura half waved away the words. "No, I mean yes. Well, sort of. Just Mitch Tucker."

"That investigator?"

Somehow Mrs. Plummer made the name sound faintly repugnant, and disapproval flavored her tone.

"That would be him. I made him work late, so I felt a little obligated to invite him to dinner."

"A gentleman shouldn't ever make a lady feel obligated."

Laura held a twitching smile in place. The generation gap was showing. In fact, it was waving like a banner. "That's not exactly what I meant."

"Harrumph."

"I think I'll check on Alex. He's awake, isn't he?"

A warm smile transformed Mrs. Plummer's face. "Yes, the little angel. I'll put dinner on the table."

Smiling, too, Laura headed for the nursery. At first, Alex didn't hear her approach. His head was bent forward as he concentrated on the plastic blocks he held. A swatch of soft, dark hair fell across his forehead and his chubby face was furrowed as he tried to fit the plastic cubes together.

Laura's heart constricted with love and she tried to banish the fear that crept in, as well. She had once heard that no one could understand the depth and enormity of love for a child until it was experienced. Now she knew that to be true.

Alex, sensing her presence, lifted his head, his face immediately creasing into a smile as he awkwardly crawled forward, reached for the top border of the playpen and pulled himself up.

"How's my best boy?" she asked him, scooping him into her arms. She took his answering chortle as a greeting and bent to nuzzle his cheek.

After carrying him over to the rocker, she settled in, knowing it wasn't long until his bedtime. Each day, each hour, was so incredibly precious. That this time might come to an end was inconceivable. While she wanted to spend every second on the investigation, she didn't want to sacrifice one moment with little Alex. As the lump in her throat grew, she painfully acknowledged that she didn't want to ever look back on this period and regret having not spent it with her son.

It was always during the later hours, in the night, that the doubts were the strongest. They sneaked in with the shadows when the absent sun could no longer banish them.

The rocker's quiet creaking faded into the background as Laura recited a bedtime story. She had chosen a book from a nearby shelf, knowing it was one of Alex's favorites. He loved to hear about animals—especially the rabbit.

As she often did at the end of storytime, Laura plucked a stuffed toy from the same overhead shelf, delighting Alex as she made the bunny's ears wriggle. His laughter was pure joy for them both.

A wave of regret struck her, making her wonder yet again how her ex-husband could have simply walked away. Having such a child as Alex was like winning the greatest lottery of life, yet Kevin had dismissed him as though he were of no consequence.

She should almost have expected it, though. Kevin was an adventurous big talker, but a weak man. His charm had convinced her he was what she had been seeking all her life: a permanent connection, her soul mate.

That was why she had married him. She had wanted to believe him, wanted to think they would be together forever. But his actions had proved to be as empty as his words. Kevin was restless, easily bored. Seeking out "companionship" to relieve that boredom hadn't taken him long. Laura's marriage had been filled with humiliation and heartbreak.

The lesson had been hard learned, but she knew she would never trust another adventurer, especially one who attracted the ladies—like Mitch Turner. No, if there ever was a next time, she would find someone solid and reliable. Even then, however, she intended to keep standing on her own, not depending on anyone else again.

Laura gently rocked Alex, wondering anew how something so wonderful had come out of something so terrible. That it had made her feel eternally grateful. Alex snuggled closer, and if possible, Laura's heart melted even more.

Mrs. Plummer's sudden presence in the room seemed like an intrusion. "I have your dinner on the table," she announced, moving nearer. Before Laura could protest, the older woman plucked Alex from her arms. "I'll get this little one ready for bed."

"I appreciate the concern, Mrs. Plummer, but since I've been away all day, I'd rather do that myself."

The older woman sniffed. "That roast will be tougher than I am if we reheat it one more time."

"I'll risk it, Mrs. Plummer." Gently, Laura retrieved her son. "I know you went to a great deal of trouble, but I'm really not that hungry." She hitched Alex up a bit on her hip, brushing the top of his head with her chin. "And I don't want to miss a minute more with this one than I absolutely have to."

Mrs. Plummer's expression softened slightly.

"Can't say as I blame you, my dear." And she left them alone.

Laura treasured the moments with her son, even after Alex nodded off. She watched him for a while, enjoying the apparent normalcy. But finally she rose.

Unsettled and at loose ends, Laura roamed through the quiet house. Mrs. Plummer was staying late to use Laura's computer. Poking her head into the refrigerator, Laura saw the evening's meal tucked efficiently into plastic containers. But she didn't feel like heating up anything. Truth was, she didn't feel like eating alone. Impulsively, she glanced at her watch. It wasn't late…yet.

Refusing to question her motives, she pulled out the roast and a loaf of fresh bread. To prepare two roast beef sandwiches and wrap them in foil took only a few minutes. After spotting the moist chocolate cake Mrs. Plummer had baked, she cut two generous slices and wrapped them, as well.

The bounty tucked into a canvas bag, Laura trotted down the hall to her study. "Mrs. Plummer, do you think you'll be a while?"

The baby-sitter turned toward Laura. "Do you need to use your computer? I can finish this another time."

"No, not at all. Actually, I'd like to run out for about an hour or so, but I don't want to inconvenience you."

"Take as long as you want, Laura. This computer's a lot for me to manage and I'd like to get a good start on organizing my recipes. I can work for several hours if you don't mind."

Although the possible sacrifice pained her, Laura

smiled. "I can stay and help you with the computer."

"No. If I don't do it myself, I'll never learn."

"If you're sure..."

"I am," Mrs. Plummer replied firmly.

Unwilling to risk another offer that might be accepted, Laura retreated quickly and grabbed her car keys and purse.

Houston's streets were never empty, but now the cars were no longer crammed end to end on the unyielding concrete. The giant city sprawled over more than four hundred square miles, so it was lucky Tucker's office was located close by. That hadn't been a consideration in choosing him, but it had been an unexpected bonus. She remembered thinking that it was fate's hand that he was practically in the neighborhood. Now she wondered if fate was mocking her, sending her out in the night. Still, she didn't turn around.

When she pulled into Tucker's parking lot, the light was still on his office—as she'd suspected it would be. But she hadn't expected the door to be locked. Perhaps he'd simply forgotten to switch off the light when he left, she decided, preparing to leave.

Before she took more than a few steps, the door burst open.

Startled, she dropped the canvas bag.

"Laura? What are you doing here?" Mitch's exasperated voice washed over her.

Suddenly, she felt incredibly foolish. And beneath the glare of the overhead lights the white of the canvas bag gleamed between them.

Mitch crossed the threshold. As he passed through the doorway, she scrambled to retrieve the dropped dinner, but he was faster.

He held the bag out toward her, his eyes questioning her presence.

She accepted the bag, then swung it lightly. "This is going to sound really stupid, but I was worried that you wouldn't eat a decent dinner, so I brought you a roast beef sandwich."

He glanced at the oversize bag. "That must be one big sandwich."

Laura was grateful for the darkness that camouflaged the telling warmth in her cheeks. "Actually, I brought enough for two."

"Concerned about Morgan?"

"Who?"

His lips eased into an offhand grin. "My bird. He's not much on roast beef, though."

She strove for lightness. "No, but I am."

Surprise flickered over his features, then faded. "Saving me from a life of burgers and pizza?"

Laura shrugged. "Do you need saving?"

For a moment the silence pulsed between them, tension building in the quiet dark. Then a sudden screech broke the mood. "Hello," Morgan squawked.

Laura laughed, grateful for the bird's interruption. "I brought chocolate cake, too. Mrs. Plummer's finest. And a thermos of coffee."

"You've convinced me." He held open the door.

Self-conscious, Laura slid by, feeling the brush of hardened muscles, the taut measure of long legs. For an instant she considered lingering, then rushed on.

She'd only made him a sandwich, she reminded herself. Nothing to get so riled up about.

Still, her stomach churned as she wandered inside the office, and she felt uncertain now that she was here. Mitch, however, was as relaxed as she was uncomfortable.

He swept the papers from a scarred coffee table, which rested in front of an equally disreputable-looking sofa, and they both sat down.

She frowned. "I hope those weren't important."

"Not nearly as important as home-cooked roast beef."

Laura's expression brightened. "So, I'm not intruding?"

"I didn't say that."

Chagrined, Laura grabbed for her purse.

But Mitch's hand stopped hers. "I'm still misreading you, I see. I thought you could take a little joke. So where's this world-famous roast beef?"

Laura released her grip on her purse, realizing once again how badly she was out of practice in dealing with men. "I didn't say it was world famous, simply home-cooked."

"In my book, one and the same."

"Don't tell me you're lacking in attention," she scoffed.

His grin was again easy and mocking. "Depends on the kind of attention you're talking about."

Some of her humor faded. Yet she knew he was a charmer, a man who loved women as much as they loved him. It shouldn't prevent her from sharing a simple supper with him. Keeping that in mind, she shored up her smile. "I don't think you and Morgan lead a solitary existence. No doubt you have more attention than you need."

"You might be surprised."

The words startled her and for a moment she saw past the usual nonchalance in his expression. Within seconds, though, his easy smile was back in place, and she wondered if she had imagined the earlier change. Unwilling to explore the thought further, she opened the sack and pulled out the sandwiches, fussing over them more than necessary.

Mitch played along, digging into the impromptu dinner. "This beats the pizza I'd planned on ordering."

Laura nodded. "I guessed as much." Remembering the coffee, she took out the thermos from the bag. "Oh, I forgot to bring cups."

"I'm not completely without creature comforts. There should be something to drink out of around here." Mitch rose and searched for cups, tossing aside a box of petrified doughnuts. The mugs he retrieved looked a bit worse for wear, but Laura decided she needed the bracing warmth of some coffee. He sat down again and twisted off the lid of the thermos, and in an instant the tang of fresh coffee filled the small space between them.

Mitch poured coffee into the mugs, then sampled the brew. "I get so used to my own sludge, I forget how good coffee tastes. Mrs. Plummer must really be a treasure."

Laura shifted on the sofa. "Actually, I made the coffee. Mrs. Plummer's coffee tastes like it has part of the pot in it."

He laughed. "I should have remembered. I've had your coffee before."

Instantly Laura remembered the morning in his apartment. She also remembered his casual threat about disturbing him again before breakfast. Squirming, she shifted even farther down the couch.

"You keep that up and you'll end up on the floor."

Laura blinked. Then the absurdity struck her and she couldn't contain an embarrassed giggle. "I guess you could say I'm not real comfortable around men."

"No kidding."

So he'd noticed. Laura clasped her hands, stopping their nervous motion. Silent moments passed, but finally she spoke. "You know from what I've told you that my ex-husband was a jerk."

"That's a mild term," he commented. "I wouldn't be so generous."

She grimaced in agreement. "So don't take it personally."

Mitch abandoned his interest in the sandwich. "Don't take what personally?"

Laura gestured vaguely. She knew it wasn't an answer, but damn, how had she cornered herself this way?

"I don't read shrugs," he countered.

She sighed. "This is silly. I shouldn't have even said anything, especially since we're only working together." Meeting his eyes, she saw that he was waiting for further explanation. "I'm just not comfortable with certain types of men."

"Oh?" Although his voice was still mild, a new

note had crept in, one she couldn't completely decipher.

"It's just that because of my experience I'm not comfortable with men like…" From the expression on his face, Laura realized her words were a mistake, yet she couldn't recall them.

"Me?" he said flatly, completing her sentence.

Stomach sinking, Laura wished she hadn't broached the subject. "As I said, don't take it personally."

"You know another way to take it?"

Laura pushed her half-eaten sandwich away. "I'm sure you know a bevy of women who are far more than comfortable with you."

"Bevy?" he questioned in disbelief.

She squirmed anew. "I don't know about you, but I was really enjoying our dinner until I opened my mouth."

"It would be hard to enjoy the dinner otherwise," he commented, his light tone signaling acceptance of her proffered olive branch.

Laura smiled, noting again the wealth of charm the man possessed. No wonder so many women were interested in him. She ignored the lump in her stomach the thought caused. To find him attractive was natural, she supposed. After all, they were spending a lot of time together. And proximity was an influential factor in many male-female relationships. Laura nearly laughed aloud. As though she knew much about that. Then her gaze caught his and the laughter died away.

Busying herself with the remainder of the sandwich, Laura was startled when Mitch's hand closed over hers, though not nearly as startled by the movement as by the reaction it caused.

Catching her breath, she stared at his strong, tanned hand.

"Laura, relax. A man and woman can spend time together without anything more exciting than a sandwich between them."

"Oh," she managed to croak.

"Unless you count the chocolate cake," he added with a mocking leer.

Laura remembered to breathe, but she still felt shaky. "And Mrs. Plummer's cake is pretty darn exciting."

"Thank God. I thought this was a ploy to get me to work all night."

Sobered, Laura stared at him. "Did you really think that?"

"Hell, did you have your humor surgically removed, Laura? I'm trying to lighten the mood. In case you hadn't noticed, it got pretty heavy in here."

"Yeah, I noticed."

He tipped up her chin, meeting her eyes. "Then work with me. Laugh a little."

Once again, Laura had to control the nervous motion of her hands. "There hasn't been much to laugh about lately."

"Yeah, but that's what we're going to change, isn't it?"

Laura's throat tightened. "This has been a solo battle for so long, it's nice to have someone else on my team."

He saluted sharply. "And I'm a hell of a team player." His gaze roved around the run-down office.

"This place may not look like it, but you've got the best investigator in town."

"Humble, too, Tucker?"

"That's the Laura I know."

She laughed, a shaky but genuine sound. "I've been kind of pushy, huh?"

He paused, and a kind light shone in his eyes. "Not so that it shows."

Pleased, Laura again concentrated on her sandwich, and for the next few minutes they shared a companionable supper. She was surprised but pleased by the easy silences and the equally easy conversation.

"This cake is wicked," Laura declared, nibbling at the crumbs.

"Agreed."

Glancing up, Laura saw that Mitch was wearing some of the frosting on his lower lip. Giggling, she pointed out the errant chocolate. When he swiped at it and missed, she brushed her fingers over the spot.

Mitch's eyes met hers.

She froze.

It was a little thing, really. Just a dab of chocolate frosting on his lips. Lips that beckoned beneath her touch.

Mitch's head bent toward hers and she anticipated the taste of those same lips.

The strident ring of the phone made her bolt.

Mitch was cursing beneath his breath even as he rose to answer the call.

"Yes." Annoyance was clear in his tone as he answered. He listened, then passed a hand over his hair. ''Sorry, Christie. Nah, nothing's wrong. Just working late.''

Laura stiffened. Of course the caller was a woman. What had she expected? Mitch Tucker was a connoisseur of the opposite sex, and it wasn't wise to ever lose sight of the fact.

CHAPTER FIVE

CREPE MYRTLES LINED the streets, flowering sentries whose plump blooms spilled over wooden fences, dripping delicate petals over thick carpets of grass. But Mitch didn't have time to notice the natural beauty as he drove away from the residential neighborhood. Beyond the nearly tropical flora, skyscrapers dominated the skyline, and he was wondering just which one of those concrete beauties held the secrets he was seeking.

From the green crest just off the Allen Parkway he had a perfect view. Yet that didn't still the restlessness he felt. For an instant he longed for a smoke, even though he'd kicked the habit years earlier.

Instead, he pulled into a curved parking lot, scanning the other cars, looking for Laura's. They had agreed to meet here this morning to get an early start. After the strained ending last night at his place, it seemed like a good idea.

He flat couldn't figure out the lady. Just when he'd thought they were clicking, she froze. He couldn't remember ever knowing a woman as uptight as Laura. Of course, she had plenty to worry about, but it was more than that. It was as though she compared every male on the planet with her scummy ex-husband. Still, that didn't explain why she had jumped to her feet the night before when the phone rang, and dashed out as if intruding on an intimate moment rather than a mere phone call.

After all, he didn't exactly try to hide his lifestyle. Laura was right about him knowing a lot of women. He liked women. In fact, he loved women. Just not one in particular. That was a luxury he had never allowed himself. There had been no one serious. There would be no one serious.

Having grown up as the only male in an otherwise all-female household, he appreciated the sensitivity, beauty, humor, even the sense of mystery of women.

But growing up this way, coupled with his years on the police force, had caused him to lose most of his illusions, including his belief in happily-ever-afters. While he had no argument with anyone else wanting to grasp that brass ring, it was tarnished for him. And despite Laura Kelly's bad marriage, he suspected she still reserved a piece of her heart for a white knight. For her sake, he hoped one still existed.

As though his thoughts had conjured her up, she drove into the parking lot. With her usual energy she jumped out and then zipped over to the passenger side of her car.

Stepping out of his vehicle, he watched as she reached inside and unbuckled a child carrier. His stomach sank. The carrier wasn't empty. Little Alex was inside. She grabbed an oversize bag, as well.

Mitch stepped closer and took the carrier from her. "What's with the kid?"

"The *kid* is your client, too," she reminded him.

"Mrs. Plummer's coming down with a cold. Actually, she just sneezed a little this morning, but last night I was thinking about how I didn't want to wind up regretting that I'd spent too much time away from Alex, in case…" Her voice warbled before she got it back under control. "Well, just in case. I know we're going to be successful, but we can still be successful and have Alex along with us, can't we?"

Not allowing Mitch to reply, she walked over to his car. "The car seat buckles into any car and converts to a stroller. You're probably more comfortable driving your car, so I'll just hook this into the back seat, okay? Alex won't be any trouble. He's a happy baby and he naps, too, and—"

"Whoa! Don't you ever come up for air?" Exasperated, Mitch stared between Laura and her unblinking baby. "Look, I don't have anything against kid—uh, babies, but they don't mix with investigations."

"Pooh," she responded airily. "While people are oohing and aahing over Alex, you can dig into all kinds of records. He'll be better than a court order demanding the information."

But Mitch didn't share her enthusiasm. "Hey, I can understand your need to spend more time with him, but this isn't the way to do it. In fact, I think you should take Alex home and let me get on with the investigation."

"You'd like that, wouldn't you? Get rid of me just like that." She snapped her fingers.

"Not exactly—"

"It's not going to be that easy, Tucker. I still

intend to help you. I know you think Alex will slow us down, but I promise you he won't.''

Alex grabbed for Mitch's keys, his toothy little grin irresistible. Mitch felt himself losing the battle. It was only one day, he reasoned. By tomorrow Mrs. Plummer would be back to normal and Laura would have learned that a baby didn't belong in the middle of a tough search.

BUT A WEEK LATER, Mitch wasn't certain who had learned a lesson. He was easing the sleeping child from the car seat. Laura's hands were filled with the diaper bag, her purse and a portfolio of papers she had brought home to work on.

Her house looked shuttered as they headed up the sidewalk. Mrs. Plummer was at her place, her cold now a full-fledged case of the flu. Although Mitch suspected Mrs. Plummer hadn't really been sick the first day Laura had brought Alex along, now the woman was genuinely ill. He also suspected she had become ill from stress. She seemed to think that Laura was deliberately keeping little Alex from her.

Mitch admitted he'd lost the battle with Laura. He had tangled with his share of determined women in the past, but none to equal an obstinate, protective mother.

Alex snuggled closer in his arms and Mitch felt a now-familiar twitch that he'd been ignoring. It was the same twitch he felt when Alex smiled, chortled or reached up chubby arms to him. But then, the kid was a charmer, he acknowledged. And it wasn't as though he himself was a dog-kicking, baby-hating hardhead.

"It's been a long day," Laura was saying. "I can't promise one of Mrs. Plummer's home-cooked meals, but why don't you stay for dinner. We can order Chinese." She grinned, a flash of pearly teeth in the near dark. "Alex loves the fortune cookies."

"Szechuan?" Mitch bargained, not particularly eager to return to an empty apartment or equally unappealing office.

"Why not? I live for adventure."

Mitch smiled, even though Laura had turned away. He knew why she was especially cheerful. While researching the hospital records for births in Galveston they had stumbled onto a partial list of attending physicians. It was an unexpected bonus, since finding this information was unusual.

Mitch had cautioned Laura to not be too optimistic. The list wasn't complete and so many years had passed. Memories might be faulty; some of the doctors might be deceased or unable to be located. Yet secretly he was very pleased at even this minor breakthrough.

Laura flipped on lights as they entered the house. "I have a menu from a pretty good Chinese place," she remarked. "The food's great, and even better, they're fast."

"Mmm. I think Alex is waking up. What should I do with him?"

"Bowling's out," she replied with a grin as she picked up the take-out menu from a collection in an oak letter holder. "Actually, you can put him on the floor over here." She pointed to an area in front of the cabinets. "I keep some plastic containers and big wooden spoons in there that he can play with."

Mitch shot her a baleful glance. "Girl stuff? What do you make of that, big guy? Nah, we want tanks, toy soldiers, men stuff."

Laura burst out laughing. "There's no room to park a tank in the kitchen, but I guess we could make a play one out of blocks."

"A fort we can build out of blocks, but not a tank. You better buy him some appropriate male toys or I'll have to report you to M.A.S."

"M.A.S.?" Laura asked, frowning.

"Men Against Sissies," he replied without missing a beat.

"Very funny. Alex has all kinds of educational toys."

"Are they educating him to grow up like a real man?"

"As opposed to the imitation variety?" she retorted. "I could probably dress him in pink and have him play exclusively with dolls and he'd still wind up macho."

Mitch grinned, inordinately pleased. "You think so?"

Laura groaned. "You're missing the point. But I believe that being a man, you aren't able to grasp the concept."

Mitch lifted Alex onto his shoulders. "Come on, Alex. Let's go find a football game on the TV and leave this woman's work to your mother."

Laura lifted one brow. "Woman's work?"

"You know, all that complicated stuff—checking the menu, calling in the order. It's tough."

"I could order fried brains," she threatened.

"That must be some Chinese restaurant," he commented. "But Alex and I can take it."

Mitch carried Alex into the den, where he easily plucked the child from his shoulders. "Okay, tiger. You up for a game?"

Alex chortled in agreement, immediately reaching for the magazines spread neatly on the coffee table. Laura had wisely put the breakables up out of reach.

"You don't want to read *Cosmo,* champ." Mitch disengaged small fingers from the glossy pages. "Why don't we check out those blocks in your room."

In the nursery, Mitch could see no male influence at all. Although he'd been joking with Laura, it was glaringly obvious that little Alex didn't have a father. Having been raised without a father himself, Mitch knew the deficiency wasn't easy to overcome.

His mother and sisters had smothered him with love, but nothing could take a father's place. Mitch remembered the envy, the isolation he'd felt, when classmates and friends had gone fishing or hunting with their fathers. He still carried with him a sense of loss, one that had never gone away. He hated to think this little guy would share the same fate.

That is, if this little one survived to grow up. Mitch would do whatever it took to have that happen. The last week spent with Laura and Alex had made this case the most personal one he'd ever worked on. And although he hadn't admitted it to Laura, he wasn't going to stop until he found one of her relatives. He didn't care if he had to give up sleeping.

After they'd played with the blocks awhile and

were back in the den, Alex nestled against him as Mitch opened the pages of a soft book. When Alex spotted the picture of the puppy, he shrieked with glee. "Dog!"

"It sure is." A boy needed a dog, Mitch thought. One that could grow alongside him. He wondered how Laura would feel about the idea. "You like that puppy, champ? Real ones are even more fun."

"Don't fill his head," Laura warned, but she didn't sound particularly disturbed. "I think I've got all I can handle right now."

"I don't know. *I've* been thinking about getting a dog."

"You have?" she questioned in disbelief.

"Sure. I'd train him to guard the office."

"Yeah. Wouldn't want anyone to carry off that deluxe furniture or any piles of paper, not to mention a sterling collection of phone books."

Mitch sniffed. "You say that now. What if one of those piles proves valuable?"

Some of the humor in her eyes faded. "Then I'll take back every word."

Realizing that her feelings were dangerously close to the surface, Mitch picked up her hand. "We'll find what we need."

Acute vulnerability flashed over her features. "Really? I know what we found today is a lead, but do you truly believe it will pan out?"

"If I didn't, I wouldn't be putting in sixteen hours or more every day. Look, Laura, I joke a lot." Mitch tightened his grip on Alex. "But I understand what's riding on the outcome. In fact, after you put him to bed, I'd like to go over the lists we brought home."

She brightened. "Me, too. I just didn't want to push. I know you've been killing yourself on this case."

Mitch couldn't resist glancing down again at the child in his lap. "It's worth it."

To his surprise, Laura's eyes brightened as though with a sheen of tears. But she didn't say anything.

"Laura?"

She stood abruptly. "I need to set the table. Excuse me."

Before he could reply, she disappeared.

"Well, Alex. Looks like we're back to *Pal, The Puppy Who Makes a Friend*." His attention was divided, though, as he wondered why Laura had so abruptly vanished.

LAURA PUT THE take-out containers on the table, then added chopsticks as an afterthought.

Mitch secured Alex in his high chair and she couldn't help noticing how adept he had become at handling the baby. Perhaps he'd had younger brothers and sisters, she thought, realizing she knew little about him. Mitch never talked about his family or his past.

She was also surprised when he handled the chopsticks as though born to them. "You're a real expert with those."

He shrugged. "Spent some time in Asia. It's not that difficult."

Laura forgot her own struggle with the utensils. "What part?"

"Korea, Thailand, Hong Kong, a few other spots."

She studied him. "I didn't realize you were such a world traveler."

"Started with a stint in the army. But once I had a taste of traveling it was in my blood."

Laura tried to spear a mushroom with her chopsticks and missed. "I've always wanted to see the world."

"Then why haven't you?"

She shrugged, thinking of the excuses, realizing how lame they sounded. "Kevin wanted to concentrate on his career and I suppose I wanted to concentrate on him. And now I've got Alex."

"After Alex is better, there's no reason he can't travel. Does a kid good to know there's a world bigger than the neighborhood he lives in."

"I guess I've always assumed that once a person has children, there's not really any room for adventure."

"Depends on the kind of child you want to raise. Sure, they need stability, but there's nothing unstable about traveling, learning."

This man had many sides, Laura was discovering. "That's very perceptive. I hadn't thought about it that way."

"Think about it. Pick a place. After Alex has his transplant, go there as a celebration."

"Ireland," she decided instantly.

He raised his glass and clinked it gently against hers.

Touched by his vote of confidence, she smiled, trying not to allow her lips to quiver. "You sound so certain. I thought I was the only one who truly believed we could make this happen.''

''Haven't you been listening? I'm going to find out who you are, Laura Kelly. And soon.''

CHAPTER SIX

"IT'S A ROADBLOCK, LAURA. So we find another angle, take a different route."

Frustrated, she pounded her fists on the scarred desktop, making the parrot squawk from across the room. "But why would they deny me access to my original birth certificate?"

Mitch sighed. "We've gone over this. I told you we had to be prepared for this setback. That's why we've been creating a paper trail, showing that we have utilized every legal recourse. Now we petition the court, citing the 'good cause' clause. And there's not a much better cause than saving your child's life."

Disappointment and despair were stabbing through her despite his encouraging words. "But you said yourself that judges are fickle. Some grant any request and others deny them even in the face of extreme medical need. How do we know what kind of judge we'll draw?"

"We don't. But we also don't give up at the first sign of trouble. We just have to work harder."

Terrified that wouldn't be enough, Laura began to shake. Not a gentle movement, but more like the tremoring of a tree caught in a powerful windstorm.

"Laura, I thought you were made of tougher

stuff,'' Mitch admonished. Yet he drew her close, smoothing back her hair, lending some of his strength.

A few minutes passed and the shivering subsided. Although Mitch still held her, she drew away enough so that she could see his face.

Embarrassed, she sniffled a bit. "It just seems so unfair. Why Alex? And why did my parents feel they had to keep everything so secret? It's as though my whole world has turned upside down and landed topsy-turvy."

"Messy world you got there."

Surprised by his reply, she very nearly laughed, relieved that he had broken through her terror. She punched his arm lightly. "You're not being appropriately serious, I think."

"And I think this is a good time to get a grip on your sense of humor, haul it back to earth."

Laura recognized his attempt at levity and a small part of her appreciated the effort. "Are you suggesting I'm a little too grim?"

"No, I'm suggesting you're a lot too grim."

She took a shaky breath. "You have a way with words, you know that?"

He smiled, that lopsided grin that simultaneously mocked and charmed. And suddenly Laura realized she was in his arms and she was feeling more than just his strength.

Awareness jumped to life, a patent array of sensation. She couldn't recall ever experiencing anything like it. Not with Kevin. Not ever. It was as though every vein, artery and nerve had leaped to attention. Her blood seemed impossibly thicker, yet at the same time was a heated river racing through her body.

Throat dry, she couldn't think of anything to say. No mocking rejoinder, no casual laughter. Nothing. Only a blank silence heated the air.

Alex's quiet cry startled her more than a blast of dynamite could. She had completely forgotten about him. Disgusted with herself, she jerked away and hurried to the stroller.

"He's probably just hungry," Mitch commented mildly. "Aren't you, champ?"

Obviously, the embrace hadn't affected him at all. That realization was nearly as unsettling as knowing she had temporarily dismissed her child.

Laura gentled her hands with an effort as she picked up her son. "The answer to caring for a child isn't to stick a bottle in his mouth every time he cries."

Mitch's brows lifted. "I didn't suggest it was."

Laura knew she was overreacting and acknowledged as much. "I suppose I'm just disappointed by our news."

"Mmm."

She wasn't certain he was convinced. "So what do we do now?"

He pulled out a crumpled piece of paper. "You fell apart before I could tell you the good news."

Her peevishness forgotten, Laura brightened. "Good news?"

"I found the names of attending physicians for some of the Houston births."

Part of her exuberance faded. "Is that all?"

"This is probably the key to locating your birth

mother. People often reveal far more than dusty records.''

Laura realized she had insulted him, thrown his accomplishment back in his face. ''I'm sure you're right. I guess I'm still reeling from learning about my birth certificate. It's my right, not some court's, to see the truth about who I am.''

''That argument has been raging for decades.''

Laura shifted Alex, yet he still fussed. To her surprise, Mitch plucked him from her arms.

''What's wrong, champ? You need to run off some of that energy?'' He set Alex on the floor and the toddler immediately scooted toward the birdcage. ''That's all he needed.''

Laura frowned, uncertain she wanted her son scrabbling around the scruffy office. ''Actually—''

''He's not a hothouse flower. Let him be a boy.''

''I'm not stopping him from being a boy!''

Mitch shook his head. ''It's not the same thing. You have to raise him with more than just female guidelines.''

''Oh, please. What would you know about it?''

But Mitch didn't hand her one of his easy replies. Instead he turned away.

Puzzled, she studied his back. ''Mitch?''

''I really need to get on these leads.''

Distracted, she looked around for Alex's diaper bag. ''It will only take me a minute to get his things together.''

''I can get more legwork done alone.''

''But we can help.'' She continued to search for the diaper bag.

Mitch grabbed a slim portfolio. "I don't think so. Not today."

"But—"

The door as it closed cut off her words. Clearly, he had seen he could escape before she could gather up Alex and all his baby paraphernalia. What she couldn't understand was why he'd left so abruptly, what she'd said to upset him. And why that bothered her so.

MITCH PUSHED OPEN his apartment door. Immediately, the stale odor greeted him. Had it been that long since he'd cared enough to make the place livable? Flicking on the lights, he tossed a collection of flyers and advertisements on a dusty table.

He'd been on cases that had filled every waking moment. Yet none had ever taken this much out of him. Right now he felt as though someone had drained all the life from him.

Laura's comment the previous morning had sucker-punched him. And he hadn't been able to shake the feeling since.

When he had taken her case he had considered his chances of success to be about fifty percent. But after he'd met Alex, he'd decided to increase those chances.

Now he wondered if that was possible. Today had been immensely disappointing. Despite what he'd told Laura, the partial list of attending physicians had been a dead end. The few still in practice had refused to speak to him. At present, he had a fractured list of possibles who were likely either dead or relocated to another part of the country.

The phone rang and he stared at it for a moment. He didn't want an inquisition from Laura. And he certainly didn't want to admit how discouraged he was about her case. Yet he couldn't ignore the ring. He had forwarded the office phone. The call could be important.

"Tucker," he answered curtly.

"Been chewing on nails?" responded a familiar, slightly mocking, equally sweet voice.

"Hey," he replied, instantly relaxing as he recognized his eldest sister's voice.

"Hey yourself. You sound pretty rugged. Something wrong?"

"Always the big sister, aren't you?"

"It's a lifetime sentence, bud, and don't you forget it. So what's wrong?"

He sighed, then decided he needed to talk over the situation with someone he trusted. After he'd finished the tale, he waited a moment. "Karen? You there?"

"Yeah. No wonder you're bummed. It sounds like you're the little guy's only chance."

He didn't speak.

"I'm guessing you're shrugging on your end, Mitch, and I can't hear that. I'm also guessing you want support, an assurance that this isn't all your responsibility. Instead I just added more weight to your worry. Mitch, I know you'll do your best. That's all this woman can ask. It's all you can ask."

"And does little Alex get a say in this?"

Karen paused. "You're getting attached, aren't you?"

He pushed at his forehead, feeling a deep wrinkle of tension between his eyes. "I didn't say that."

"You didn't have to." Karen paused. "Is it just the child or his mother, too?"

"Don't you think I'm too old for you to be asking about my love life?"

"Nope," she replied cheerfully. "Now, give."

"She's attractive," he finally admitted.

"Are you holding out on me?" Karen demanded.

"Tell you what, Sis. When I know myself, I'll tell you."

The concern in her voice was audible. "And you're sure the ex-husband really is history?"

"Ancient history. Doesn't seem to care what happens to the kid. He's washed his hands of him."

"Mitch, you're thinking about Dad, aren't you?"

"He never was a dad to me."

Karen sighed. "I can't argue with that. You were such a little guy when he left. But he wasn't all bad."

"Can't prove that by me."

This time her sigh was heartfelt. "No, I don't suppose so. I think he just wasn't cut out for a family, for all the responsibility."

"Too bad he didn't consider that before he fathered six children and then deserted them."

"It's not always that black and white, Mitch."

He felt the tick in his jaw, one that had never disappeared. "For me it is. You have kids, you stick with them."

Karen sighed again. "I'm not excusing what he did—"

"Sounds like it to me."

"We'll never agree on this one, Mitch. What he did was wrong, and in a lot of ways I miss him more than you because I *did* know him. I miss the laughter, his incredible imagination. Mother's the best, but there was something about Dad..."

"Something elusive?" Mitch suggested bitterly.

"Perhaps." Her voice quavered a bit. "But I am sorry you had to grow up in a house full of only women."

Mitch felt a stab of remorse. "It wasn't all bad. I wouldn't trade you heathens for a pack of brothers."

She laughed finally. "Even though you grew up believing all bathrooms came equipped with half a dozen pairs of drying panty hose?"

He laughed, too. "Yeah. There were also advantages. I have a deeper appreciation of the female psyche."

"Translated, you know how women really tick, and you're not perpetually mystified like most men."

"You could say that, Karen."

"Then why the uncertainty about Laura?"

He paused, wondering himself. "I think this is one test where having a curve isn't going to help."

CHAPTER SEVEN

HOUSTON WAS A MYSTERY to all but her natives. Lush charm strugggled against seams torn apart by unholy growth spurts. To the outsider, the city was a steamy mishmash, a sprawling giant impatient to shed its ever-emerging wings. Insiders knew her bucolic orderliness. But the beauty was in the dichotomy. It surfaced among the rich, swept over the poor and lingered long after both were gone.

For Laura, her lifelong love affair with the city was filled with as many pitfalls as a rocky relationship, yet provided equal solace on lonely evenings.

That wasn't the case tonight, however. Two days had passed since Mitch had ditched her and managed to avoid her. With her determination that wasn't easy.

Apparently, he was even more determined. What she didn't understand was why. She admitted that initially he hadn't wanted her help, but he had given in. Now all traces of his easygoing manner had disappeared. As he had.

Restless, she roamed the hallway. Alex was asleep. Mrs. Plummer had finally left. The older woman had been thrilled that the baby had been home the past few days. The way she clucked over him you'd have thought he'd been in the care of a kidnapper rather than his own mother. Laura knew she should be grateful that the woman cared so much, but at times she was too intense, too concerned.

But then, everything these days was too intense. The ache that tied her stomach in knots; her desperate fear that somehow she wouldn't be able to save Alex, that despite everything he, too, would be lost to her.

Although she had been honest when she'd told Mitch she didn't care about her parentage as long as it helped Alex, she couldn't stem the feeling that she'd been cut loose. That now she was afloat, alone, not connected to anyone. Her adoptive parents were gone. She couldn't question either their reasons for not telling her the truth…or their love.

Her ex-husband had made it clear he was out of her life forever. The last time he'd seen Alex, he'd looked at him as though the child made him uncomfortable, almost ill. Kevin had no tolerance for the weak. She supposed she could now be included in that group.

The world that had once seemed so familiar had become alien. She had nothing secure to grasp any longer. And she was terribly afraid that what little remained would be snatched away.

Now that Mitch had distanced himself, she felt another blow, another disconnection. Laura glanced out the window, seeing the deep endlessness of the night. She had been foolish to depend on him, to count on him so much. Much like her ex-husband, Mitch was a man of the moment. And she needed so much more than a moment.

She cocked her head, hearing a soft knock. It was coming from the front hall, but that didn't make sense, because her doorbell was in working order. Feeling a shiver of uneasiness, she moved quietly to the door. Peering into the peephole, she was surprised to see Mitch's face in profile.

She stepped back, blinking before she opened the door. "Mitch?"

He turned toward her and she was staggered by the rush of relief she felt. But surely that was because she'd been frightened, she told herself. Not because she was so glad to see him.

"I realize it's late. I probably should have waited till morning."

She opened the door wider, her heart feeling as though it had lodged abruptly in her throat. "Do you know something?"

But he was shaking his head. "That's what I'm here to tell you."

"Then you'd better come in."

"Is Alex asleep?"

"Oh, yes. Mrs. Plummer has fussed with him nonstop for the past two days."

A flash of something she couldn't quite decipher crossed his face, but he didn't comment.

"Would you like some coffee?" Laura offered, suddenly nervous and not quite sure why.

"Sure. You make great coffee."

She met his eyes and recognized something there; something they had yet to speak of; something that hung in the air, waiting to be resolved. "It's fresh," she managed to say.

"Good."

"I was kind of restless so I brewed a pot."

Again the awareness pulsed between them.

"Laura, we have to talk."

For a moment her heart seemed to cease beating. So it was bad news. Bracing herself, she met his gaze. "Yes?"

"I'd hoped to have better news, but the list of doctors has been a dead end so far."

"Is that all?"

Mitch was puzzled. "All?"

"I thought maybe you'd come to quit."

"Why would I do that?"

She shrugged, sensing again that disconnection with the universe.

"I'm sorry about the past two days. I needed time on my own to track down some leads." He met her gaze. "Actually, that's not the truth."

She felt a desperation gripping her once more. "Are you so certain we're going to fail?"

"No!"

Startled, she stepped closer to him. "You're not?"

"No," he repeated more quietly this time. "I'm not through searching. I won't be until we find your birth mother."

She wasn't certain why she hadn't realized the tears were so close. But then they were escaping, streaming down her face, wetting her cheeks, drowning her voice.

"Laura!" But his exclamation was muffled as he pulled her near to shelter her against his chest. "I didn't mean to upset you."

She shook her head, uncertain how to stop her

tears, even more uncertain what to say to express her relief, her gratitude or, worse, her despair.

Mitch smoothed back her hair. "The truth is that the problem is with me, not you, not Alex. And I had to have a few days to sort through my feelings."

Laura willed her tears to stop, swiping at her face.

But Mitch captured her hands, easing his fingers over her cheeks. "You're so soft," he said in wonder. "You always act so tough, so independent. I never suspected..."

"What?" she questioned, her breath catching on the word. She didn't want him to draw away, to stop holding her.

"That you could be so soft. So touchable."

Laura was incredibly aware that they stood chest to chest, that they were scarcely a whisper apart. His scent wound around her senses, an inviting male aroma as unfamiliar as it was exciting. It had been so long since she had abandoned herself to the strength of a male embrace. She wanted to escape into the comfort, accept the sanctuary.

Mitch's head angled, his lips moving over hers, a gentle exploration. How was it that his lips fit so right, that his taste made her hunger for more?

The shudder rocking her soul had nothing to do with her lingering fear.

One hand cupped the back of her neck, the fingers of his other hand playing over the tender skin of her throat. Swaying even deeper into the embrace, she hungered for the heat he was creating. She'd put such feelings aside with her divorce, hadn't she?

Like a bucket of cold water, the thought reminded her of all she had painfully learned. Kevin had never been faithful and the wounds from his infidelity still ached. Pulling away, Laura knew she couldn't become involved with another man who played women like a game.

"Laura?"

She shook her head. "I'm sorry, Mitch. I guess I'm so scared for Alex that I got fear confused with…" She took a deep breath.

"With what?"

"Relief, I suppose. I'm just so glad you're not giving up the case, that you're not going to quit."

A mixture of emotions crossed his face, but Laura wasn't certain what they meant.

His jaw tightened. "No, I'm not going to quit." He turned to the door.

She laid a restraining hand on his arm. "Thank you."

His face seemed strangely closed, yet he met her gaze. "That's a bit premature."

"It is?"

"Wait until the job's done, Laura. Then you can thank me."

He pulled open the door and disappeared into the night, not saying any more.

Feeling strangely bereft, she slowly closed the door. And wondered why the house again felt so empty.

MITCH KNOCKED ON Laura's aunt's door. He could see the car in the driveway and was pretty certain Rhoda was inside. Working on a hunch, he hadn't called ahead. He wasn't certain why, but he had the feeling that Rhoda might not be eager to see him.

He wasn't sure that she had withheld information, but she hadn't volunteered anything, either. Instead he'd sensed that he was reluctantly pulling the information from her.

And her face when she opened the door only confirmed his intuitions. "Mr. Tucker?"

"Mitch," he replied, hoping to soften the suspicion he glimpsed in her expression.

She opened the door a bit wider. "Won't you come in."

"I hope I'm not disturbing you."

"I was about to have some tea. Would you care to join me?"

"Sounds good." Tea wasn't one of his favorites, but he'd learned early on, first as a cop, then as an investigator, that it paid to put people at ease.

After seating him in the living room, Rhoda returned a few minutes later with a loaded tray.

Mitch accepted a cup of tea, declining sugar or lemon.

They sipped for a few moments in silence.

Then Rhoda's razor sharp glance zeroed in on him. "So, what brings you here this morning, young man? As good as it is, I highly doubt it's my tea."

He tipped the cup in her direction. "But I appreciate the civility."

Her brows lifted. "I would think most young people consider this an outdated fussiness."

He met her gaze evenly. "I'm not most people."

"Touché," she replied, a bit of a smile lighting her eyes. "Still, you and Laura are in a headlong rush to help Alex. So what can I do?"

He was surprised by her directness. "You're

right. I'm hoping there might be something you remembered that could help."

"If there had been, I would have told Laura."

"I've been trying to run down the agency Laura's parents used. I'm hitting a dead end."

Rhoda frowned and looked away. "I don't really know anything about an agency."

Again, Mitch had the feeling she wasn't sharing the entire truth. "I know you told me that your sister didn't reveal the adoption to Laura because she didn't want to upset the status quo, but do you think there might be some other reason?"

Rhoda's hands trembled a bit and she grasped her cup more tightly. "What other reason?"

Mitch searched the woman's expression. "I'm not certain. That's what I'm trying to discover. We've been denied Laura's original birth certificate and I'm not having a lot of luck locating the attending physician at her birth."

Rhoda frowned. "I didn't realize that." A pained expression crossed her face. "I've been hoping that the national donor bank would come up with a match, that Laura wouldn't have to find her birth mother."

"Any special reason?"

Rhoda waved her hands in a seemingly casual manner, but Mitch sensed her ease had evaporated. "I'm just not certain any good will come of it." Then she met Mitch's gaze. "Despite what you believe, Laura's parents loved her very much."

"I don't have any reason to think otherwise."

"My sister didn't marry until she was older. And even though she and her husband were very involved in their careers and each other, their lives simply bloomed once they had Laura. There was never any intent other than her happiness. It's the legacy they left her, a legacy I don't want ruined.''

"And you think finding her birth mother may ruin it?''

Rhoda's face froze for a moment, before she again waved her hands dismissively. "Don't put words in my mouth, young man.''

Mitch sensed he wouldn't get anything else from her. Whatever she knew she wasn't telling. After finishing his tea quickly, he rose. "Thanks for the hospitality.''

She escorted him to the door. She opened it and then paused. "Don't you think there's still a chance that the national donor bank will provide a match?''

Mitch met her eyes. "About as much chance as finding Laura's birth mother.''

CHAPTER EIGHT

LAURA SECURED THE diaper bag to the back of the stroller. This time Mitch wasn't going to make a fast getaway. She guessed he still didn't want her help, but she couldn't stay away. Spotting his car in the parking lot, she wondered why he hadn't disappeared as he had the rest of the week. She had arrived early, hoping to beat him to the office and lie in wait. Finding him here seemed almost too good to be true.

Gathering her courage, Laura pushed open the door and entered. She wasn't sure what she had expected, but it wasn't to see Mitch sprawled across the couch, nearly buried by a pile of papers.

The parrot noticed her entry, swinging from side to side as he squawked out a greeting.

But her gaze remained focused as she walked to the couch. "Mitch?"

When he didn't respond, she placed a gentle hand on his shoulder. When that didn't have any effect, she shook him. "Mitch, are you all right?"

He opened groggy eyes. "What time is it?"

"Nearly eight."

"You say that as though it's noon."

She refused to be intimidated. "It is a business day."

"For you every day is business," he responded without any particular rancor.

"I brought coffee," she offered. "*We* brought coffee," she corrected.

Mitch focused on Alex. "Hey, champ."

Alex chortled and reached for him.

"See you've already had your coffee, big guy." In one easy motion Mitch rose from the couch and bent over to lift Alex from the stroller.

Laura watched uneasily. She hoped Mitch didn't intend to make sure she scattered her things around the office, then flee while she gathered them back together.

But Mitch was striding toward the door, carrying Alex as though he'd done so every day of the child's life.

"Uh, Mitch?" Trying to follow him, she tripped over a pile of phone books. Once she'd regained her balance, she glanced around the office, not seeing him. "Mitch?"

When he didn't answer, she hurried to the door. Mitch was at the far edge of the parking lot. After hesitating a moment, she approached.

Then he disappeared.

She had never noticed that the parking lot sloped downward on the western side. Her fast walk turned to a trot. But when she reached the slope, she stopped in surprise.

Peering down, she saw a small pond. It was scarcely more than an oversize puddle, yet a few ducks swam in it beneath overhanging wisteria.

Laura couldn't contain a smile. Alex was clapping his small, chubby hands in delight.

And to her surprise, Mitch appeared equally enchanted.

He glanced up just then. "You can join us."

Feeling as though she were intruding, Laura stepped down the embankment. "I never guessed this was here," she remarked.

"It was the first thing that attracted me to this property—a miniature slice of green amid the asphalt and concrete. A great place for an office complex. It provides aesthetic value. Even better, a spot for the nine-to-fivers to escape for a moment."

She nodded. "It's charming."

He looked around. "It's no Lake Tahoe, but it's my little dose of sanity."

Laura shoved her hands in her pockets. "Any particular reason you need some sanity today?"

His crooked grin emerged. "In case you hadn't noticed, most of us need sanity on a regular basis."

She smiled herself. "Now that you mention it, I guess so." Pushing her shoe against the grass, she eyed him. "This isn't just a way to divert attention so you can ditch us again, is it?"

He sighed, a heavy sound in the early morning. "You can come along if you'd like."

"I only want to help," she explained.

He met her gaze. "You're doing a good thing here, Laura. But rushing it…or me…won't help."

Laura couldn't hide her anxiety. "I have to rush. It's vital."

"This process goes one step at a time. And I'll do each as fast as humanly possible. But if I rush too much, I risk overlooking something vital—

maybe the missing piece that leads to your birth mother.''

"Can't we rush and be careful at the same time?"

His grin emerged again. "Don't ask much, do you?"

She recognized the weariness in his eyes and it hit her why he'd spent the night on the couch. He had been working into the early-morning hours on her case.

She glanced between this unusual man and her son. And her voice softened. "You know, Alex and I didn't have much of a breakfast. Let's start the day with pancakes."

He rubbed a hand across his jaw. "I need a shave."

Inspiration struck. "Why don't we meet at your place. I'll detour by the store."

"Afraid I don't have all the ingredients?"

"Actually, I was thinking you might like some time alone to shower and shave."

"It wouldn't go amiss," he admitted.

She smiled. "Then breakfast it is."

MITCH INHALED the hearty aroma of fresh coffee. Laura did have a way with the brew. And judging from the equally appealing scents of bacon and pancakes, she wasn't a slouch in the cooking department, either.

He had expected her to push him to eat quickly so they could zoom on to the search. Instead, she was preparing juice.

"Would you like some eggs?" she asked, still stirring the juice.

He glanced at the large stack of hotcakes. "I've missed a few meals, but I'm not quite starved to death."

Still, his appetite was sparking as he speared some bacon and a few pancakes and accepted a dish of strawberry sauce from Laura. He *had* missed more meals than usual. And since he'd already lost some weight while he was in the hospital, he didn't need to shed any more.

He took a few bites, then looked at Laura in surprise. "This is really good."

"You don't have to sound so shocked."

"I thought you didn't cook."

She chuckled. "You know I'm a restaurant manager."

"Yes." He frowned. "It doesn't follow that you can cook."

"I used to be a chef," she told him. "That's how I got into restaurant management."

He swallowed another bite. "It's the public's loss."

Looking pleased, she reached for a pancake and added strawberry sauce. "Thanks. But blintzes are my breakfast specialty. I wasn't sure you'd be up for something nontraditional."

"You really think I'm a Neanderthal, don't you?"

"Of course not! But I also don't assume that everyone has the same tastes I do. I like warmed-up spaghetti for breakfast. You'll notice, though, I didn't serve you any."

"Too bad." Sensing her uneasiness, he lightened up. "I love warmed-up spaghetti for breakfast, almost as much as leftover pizza."

"Great. Next time I cook you breakfast, I'll plan to clear out all my leftovers."

Laura's smile was still easy, but something else stirred in her eyes. She had mentioned cooking another breakfast as though she assumed it were a matter of course. Yet there was nothing matter of course about what they had embarked on.

And there was another taste he remembered.

One that had haunted him, tormented him as they spent more and more time together.

The taste of her lips beneath his, the sweet breath of her sigh as she had for a moment surrendered her past.

Meeting her eyes, he saw that she, too, remembered the moment. Then her eyes darted away as she pushed the pancake around on her plate, obviously too nervous to eat. Since she didn't want anything between them, there was no reason to make her feel uncomfortable. After all, they had to work together until they found a donor for Alex.

So he grinned, calling on the charm only his unique background could cultivate, a charm born of knowing and appreciating women. "If we're going to be burning the midnight oil, you need to eat a good breakfast." He glanced over at Alex, who was gumming a piece of pancake. "Baby food breaks only today. Right, champ?"

She relaxed a fraction, then took a bite of her pancake.

Mitch poured them both some more coffee, then quickly attacked the rest of his breakfast. Despite Laura's effort to not make him feel rushed, he felt the need to quickly get to work. The days were flying by too fast. And the more he was around little Alex, the more he knew he couldn't rest until he found a donor.

MITCH AND LAURA were tired. They had been at it since morning and *frustration* was the word of the day. Now, at the records department of LaSordia Hospital, they were coming up against one wall after another. Even though Mitch had faxed the hospital all the necessary letters requesting Laura's records, they hadn't yet received any information.

And Laura was beginning to appear desperate.

He and Laura were about to leave the most remote storage room. Mrs. Phillips, the records manager, who had accompanied them, was very strict in allowing them access only to one box of records at a time. Records that were mainly dry statistics—nothing with the confidential information they needed. She had been reluctant to even permit them inside this last and obviously oldest storage room.

It was then that Mitch spotted the dusty journals, perched on a neglected shelf that looked as though it hadn't been touched in decades.

Elbowing Laura, Mitch motioned with his eyes toward the shelf. He could have shouted with relief when she caught his meaning immediately. Approaching the small table they had been assigned, Laura leaned over the stroller. "Hey, punkin, what's wrong?" Deftly, she lifted Alex into her arms. "You're tired, aren't you?"

The records manager turned, her expression softening. "This is pretty boring stuff for little ones."

"It *has* been a long day," Laura admitted. "I

don't suppose there's a window we could see out of? He really likes that.''

''Certainly. There's a great view from my office.'' The woman walked away, beckoning her to follow.

Laura glanced back long enough to make eye contact with Mitch and confirm they were in sync. He winked and Laura felt her pulse race.

Once inside the other woman's office, Laura commented on the framed pictures on her desk, which elicited a proud description of each of the woman's grandchildren.

As though on cue, Alex cooed and charmed Mrs. Phillips, prolonging their stay in her office. To Laura's relief, the woman seemed inclined to spend the next half hour entertaining them.

After they'd exhausted every relevant bit of conversation, Laura saw an expectant look on the other woman's face. Clearly, Mrs. Phillips was ready to get back to work. Only then did Laura reluctantly head back to the work area.

She couldn't tell by Mitch's expression if he'd accomplished his mission. And when he lingered for another fifteen minutes, she became truly concerned. Then it hit her—the journals must not have held anything worthwhile. Disappointment followed the realization, but she tried to keep a smile on her face as they signed out, thanked the records manager and left.

Once the door shut behind them, Mitch increased his pace. ''Good job, Laura.''

''Sure, but if you didn't find anything—''

A frown pulled his brows together. ''O ye of little faith.''

"But I thought from the way you were acting—"

"If I'd been dancing on the table, the manager might have suspected something," he replied dryly.

She blinked, then stopped, turning to him. "What did you find?"

"Handwritten records from the month you were born." He grinned. "Apparently, there was at least one dinosaur working here who didn't trust the keypunch department."

"Bless him or her," Laura breathed, scarcely able to believe their luck and completely unable to hide her anxiety. "Were you able to copy everything?"

"I'm afraid not."

Shock and disappointment whooshed through her. "Then why—"

He put a finger to her lips and pulled out a green leather journal from his portfolio. "Desperate causes merit desperate measures."

"You took the entire journal?"

"Yes. Unfortunately, they didn't have it divided with a separate volume for just your birthday. We'll copy the entire book, make sure we have everything we need, then I'll drop by the hospital to pick up the jacket I 'forgot.' I'll return the journal at that time. I don't think anyone will notice it's gone. I spread the remaining books so that they fill the same amount of space."

"Pretty tricky, aren't you?"

His charming lopsided grin emerged. "I like to think so." He ruffled Alex's baby-fine hair. "Now, here's the real champ. I saw you turn those killer eyes on the manager."

Alex chortled in reply.

Mitch plucked him from the stroller. "We make a pretty good team, don't we, bud?"

Watching Mitch carry her son, Laura swallowed an unexpected lump in her throat, wondering why the sight moved her so.

THE REMAINDERS OF Mrs. Plummer's dinner were tucked into the refrigerator, the dishwasher hummed and the lights were turned down a bit. Not enough to darken the house, just to soften the edges of a long, difficult day.

But a rewarding one, Mitch admitted. He had intended to return to the office with the journal to study it. It had been difficult to refuse Laura's dinner invitation, though, and even more so to dampen her good spirits.

He had been playing with Alex since dinner. Now the child was tiring. Mitch picked him up and secured him in his lap. Alex didn't protest, relaxing against Mitch's chest.

Mitch pulled the journal from his portfolio, then opened it.

Since the entries were in chronological order, he was able to scan them and narrow down the pages he needed to read. As Mitch read the journal aloud, he made up nonsensical stories for Alex's benefit. But soon, tired little eyes drooped.

Mitch supposed he could take Alex to the nursery, but he didn't mind the trusting weight, the protective feelings the child evoked.

"Looks like he conked out on you," Laura said quietly, entering the den. "I can put him to bed."

''There's no need. Unless you think he's not comfortable.''

''Actually, he seems very content.'' Her gaze fell on the journal. ''Have you had a chance to read much of it yet?''

''Because of the medical terminology, it's like deciphering Chinese, but I'm getting through it. There are some interesting notations—things you wouldn't normally find on computer-generated reports.''

''Such as?''

''Names of nurses who were on duty, as well as the physicians. If there're similar notations next to your birth date...'' He paused, flipping ahead.

Unable to contain her impatience, Laura leaned forward. ''Can I read along with you?''

He held out the book and she scooted next to him on the couch. Together they read the pages. Absentmindedly, Mitch stroked Alex's leg when the child stirred.

But the excitement in Laura's voice distracted him. ''Look, Mitch! There is a list of nurses! Doctors, too! And a notation about the babies who were born!''

Mitch followed her gaze, letting the information sink in. They could be onto something here, but it wasn't conclusive. ''Laura, don't get your hopes up.''

''Why not?''

Hearing the frustration in her voice, he took her hand. ''This is good information, and I'll photocopy the entire book tonight. But, we can't be certain we have the right hospital.''

''We eliminated all the hospitals built since I was

born and that did away with a considerable number,'' she pointed out. ''And we eliminated several
that didn't have births on that day, along with the
ones that didn't have any births of females.''

''Right, and this may be a good lead, but again,
don't get your hopes up too high, Laura. There's no
guarantee this is the hospital.''

Her face sank. ''I suppose you're right.''

Mitch hated to steal her excitement, but he
doubted she could survive the roller coaster of highs
and lows an investigation could entail if she counted
too much on each discovery.

''This was one of the reasons I wanted to work
alone. I know how hard it is when you're personally
involved to keep a clear head, to not jump at every
glimmer of information. And unfortunately, a lot of
leads *are* dead ends.''

''But you'll keep digging, won't you?''

He could discern traces of the vulnerability she
usually kept so well hidden. And he was very aware
of her soft presence beside him. While entranced
with the journal, she hadn't seemed to notice their
proximity.

Any onlooker would see a man, a woman and a
beautiful child. The picture of the ideal family. And
the irony wasn't lost on Mitch. He knew absolutely
nothing about the ideal family. It wasn't in his experience. It wasn't in his plans.

Alex turned to bury his face against Mitch's chest,
and Mitch wondered about the emptiness of those
plans. Catching the expectation on Laura's face, he

resisted the desire she stirred. Instead, he squeezed her hand a little tighter.

"You bet I will. And I won't stop digging till we hit pay dirt."

CHAPTER NINE

AFTER ENTERING through the rear gate of the cemetery, Laura walked through the flat rows of grass populated with markers. Some were small, nearly obscure gray stones. Others were grandiose marble-and-granite statues that looked as though they were grasping for heaven—an observation Laura didn't find much humor in.

Reaching her parents' graves didn't take long. Together in death as they had been in life, they shared a monument. In many ways it had been a blessing that they had died together in the car accident. Neither would have found any happiness without the other. She had always thought they were the perfect couple, so dedicated to each other. In many ways they were a complete unit unto themselves. Laura had occasionally wondered if she had been an afterthought. Now it seemed a certainty.

Tracing their names on the marker, she felt a small measure of comfort. Yet at the same time, she sensed the distance. And again, the stark feeling of no longer being connected to anyone else in the universe.

What would her parents think of the situation she now faced? Certainly if they were alive, she wouldn't be searching as she was. They could provide so many answers. Maybe they were watching out for her now, nudging the investigation along. If only she could ask them, if they could tell her what she so desperately needed to know.

"Laura?"

Startled despite the softness of the voice, she whirled around. "Rhoda!" She put one hand over the runaway beating of her heart. "I wasn't expecting to find anyone here."

"Me, either."

Laura saw the strain in her aunt's face and pushed her own concerns aside. "Is something wrong?"

"No, I just needed to visit your mother. You know, before she and your father married, she and I were as close as two sisters can be. We confided everything in each other. I miss that."

"You said before she got married. Didn't you still feel close to her afterward?"

Rhoda tilted her head, her gaze straying back to the headstone. "Not as much. Your mother and father were such a perfect match. They really didn't need anyone else."

So Laura wasn't the only one who had felt it. "I understand what you mean."

Rhoda grasped Laura's hands. "I didn't mean you, dear. You were needed, wanted and very much loved."

Laura couldn't speak. There were so many unanswered questions, so much more she was now curious about.

"Laura, don't doubt that. I realize this investigation is creating a lot of strain, but it shouldn't mean the end of your belief in your parents and how they felt about you.''

"I wish they could tell me what I need to know so I could locate my birth parents.''

"But, darling, don't you think the national donor bank will come up with a suitable candidate soon? That's what I was discussing with your detective the other day.''

Surprised, Laura forgot the substance of her aunt's question. "You met with Mitch recently?''

"We had tea,'' Rhoda explained.

Laura tried to keep her voice even. "When was this?''

"A few days ago. Why? Weren't you aware of his visit?''

Laura cleared her throat. "Of course.'' She glanced around, suddenly wanting to talk to Mitch, to learn why he hadn't told her about the visit. "Aunt Rhoda, I was about to leave. Why don't I give you some time alone with Mom.''

"Are you sure, Laura? I didn't mean to intrude.''

"You're not. In fact, I have a rather urgent errand.'' She bent forward and hugged her aunt.

Not looking back, Laura practically loped out of the cemetery. If Mitch hadn't told her about the visit, what else had he concealed?

"I HAVEN'T BEEN hiding anything from you!'' Exasperated, Mitch spun on his heel.

"Then why didn't you tell me you saw Rhoda?''

He hesitated. "Because I had the sense she was holding back something from me.''

"That's ridiculous. She wants to help. She's said so in exactly those words."

"I don't doubt she wants Alex to get the operation he needs, but I think she'd be happier if the donor was anonymous."

Laura was shaking her head. "That doesn't make any sense. My parents are gone now. Finding my birth mother can't hurt them."

Mitch shrugged. "I don't have anything solid—just a feeling. And that's why I didn't tell you about the visit. You're worrying enough already."

"Why don't you let me decide that for myself?"

"What?"

She pushed her dark hair back. "It's not that I don't appreciate your concern, but I'm used to watching out for myself. I don't need anyone to protect me."

"Not even just a little bit, Laura?"

He could see the apprehension in her expression, her visible withdrawal. "Not now, not ever. I'm responsible for my son's life. And for a mother, there's no time off from the work." She drew herself up like a warrior, fierce and proud.

But he doubted she was as invincible as she made herself out to be. "Fine." He tossed her a new printout. "Then start scanning this."

She caught the hefty document. "What am I looking for?"

"Paper trails." Quickly he outlined the details.

Settling into one of the chairs, she began to search the pages.

He picked up his jacket, knowing he had to be on

his own for the next job, wishing she hadn't chosen today to decide he was concealing things.

She glanced up in surprise. "Where are you going?"

He made his answer purposely vague. "We'll make better time if we divide up tasks. I'll be back in a few hours or so."

Seeing that she planned to question him, he left quickly. Despite what she thought, there were some places even the fiercest mother bear couldn't tread.

ALTHOUGH MITCH HAD BEEN a private detective for several years, he had never completely left his police roots behind. Because of that he examined all possibilities. And he couldn't repress a niggling hunch that they were running into too many dead ends in the search for Laura's biological mother.

In his experience blind alleys were created to cover up something. And that made him wonder if Laura's adoption had been illegal. If so, a doctor had probably been involved. Now he needed to learn if there were any doctors who could be counted on to "locate" babies without a lot of questions.

Luckily, Mitch hadn't lost touch with his contacts. Street contacts. Those snitches, along with his bureaucratic contacts, were the difference between someone like Laura searching for her birth mother and himself.

Which brought him to Eddie. He possessed the eyes of a poet and the fists of a killer. The qualities merged into a psychotic philosopher of sorts. Having served time for manslaughter, Eddie currently ran a newsstand, which shut down periodically when

Eddie's fists got out of control and he was serving time. Along with the standard news fare, Eddie carried wildly artistic literature. His only regulars, however, were either equally offbeat, or hardened downtown dwellers who paid no mind to edgy Eddie.

Mitch didn't fall into either category. And that gave him an edge of his own. But today Eddie wasn't a font of information.

"I'm telling you, Tucker, I don't know anything."

"You don't know or you're not telling?"

Eddie's hands curled.

Mitch glanced at the telling sign of Eddie's agitation. "You have any children's books, Eddie?"

"What?"

"Books for kids."

Eddie's eyes narrowed. He wasn't easily distracted. "What for?"

"A kid."

"This have something to do with your questions?"

"You're a smart man, Eddie. You tell me."

"You're looking for a doctor involved with black market adoptions thirty years ago. So what's the dirty doctor got to do with the kid?"

"I don't find him, the kid might not live."

"I'm not a humanitarian, Tucker. But you offer enough bait, I'll put out the trawlers."

"Deal."

Eddie stared at him suspiciously. "Just like that? No negotiating?"

"The boy's life isn't negotiable. Just make sure

you trawl deep and far.'' Mitch pressed some tightly folded bills into Eddie's hand.

The money disappeared quickly. And just as quickly Eddie turned to a customer, ignoring Mitch.

But that didn't bother Mitch. He had other snitches to get in touch with.

LAURA DUG THROUGH the boxes, unearthing more memories than she felt capable of handling. When her parents died, she had been unable to deal with the store of treasures they had collected. Instead, she had hauled home the boxes containing papers and pictures. They had been resting in the attic ever since.

It seemed her mother had saved every scrap of paper from Laura's school days. And each picture, as well.

Hearing footsteps coming up the ladder to the attic, she sighed. While she appreciated Mrs. Plummer's good intentions, Laura didn't want an intrusive presence as she sorted through her parents' things.

''Mrs. Plummer told me you were in the tree house.''

''Mitch!'' Startled, she met his gaze, and was surprised to find a kind, sympathetic note there.

''You can kick me out if you want,'' he offered. ''But I thought you might need a hand, or a friendly face.''

To her amazement, he didn't feel intrusive. In fact, she welcomed his support. ''It's kind of hard,'' she admitted. ''I haven't gone through my parents' papers and pictures. I've been putting it off—I'm not sure what for. But I guess now's the time.''

He knelt beside her. ''Good thinking. There may be something here we wouldn't find anywhere else.''

She relaxed at his words. ''That's what I thought.''

Together they sifted through the piles. Occasionally, Mitch would pick up a paper or picture and utter kind words that either comforted or made her laugh. The process was easier, less heart-wrenching, this way. Still, she couldn't stem a few errant tears.

She came across a Mother's Day card that she had made in elementary school, decorated with loopy flowers and childish lettering. Her mother had carefully placed the construction-paper card in plastic, as if it were a prized treasure. ''I guess she really did love me,'' Laura murmured.

Mitch tipped up her chin. ''I don't think that's ever been in question. And if she'd known withholding the truth would have caused you so much pain, I'm sure she would have told you about being adopted. Your parents could never have guessed there would be a serious medical problem with Alex. Their actions may have been shortsighted, but that's not a measure of their love.''

Laura felt more tears building. ''I keep wondering what they would do if they were alive.''

''They would be helping you find your birth mother.''

''You really think so?''

''Of course. It's not fair to think otherwise. They're not here to tell you so, but you know what kind of people they were. Would they want you to lose Alex?''

''Of course not.'' Lifting her eyes, she met the concern in Mitch's. She was curious about this caring side of him. Cavalier, charming, handsome—that was the Tucker she knew.

Who was this impossibly kind man who allowed her to cry, yet kept her from wallowing in the pain? In the same instant, she remembered the incredible feeling of his touch, the taste that had made her hunger for more.

The angled walls and cramped space in the attic created a sense of isolation, as though they were the only two people on the planet. And they were only a hand's span apart.

So close that she could lean just a bit closer. As if he read her thoughts, Mitch locked his gaze with hers.

''Laura!'' Mrs. Plummer's voice broke the silence and shattered the moment.

Jerking backward, Laura cleared her clogged throat and managed to reply, her voice sounding rusty and unused. ''What is it?''

''Alex has a fever.''

Shaken, Laura scrambled to her feet. ''I'm coming!''

In moments she was down the ladder, sprinting to the nursery.

''Don't panic, Laura. It's a mild fever, but I thought we should monitor him.'' Mrs. Plummer trailed Laura, her gait slower but steady.

''Maybe his room is too hot,'' Laura suggested, hearing the desperate hope in her own voice.

"I don't think so," Mrs. Plummer disagreed.

Laura smoothed her hand over Alex's forehead, feeling the elevated heat of his soft skin. Trying not to panic, she picked him up, loosening the top buttons of his sleeper. "How's my boy?"

"He's great, aren't you, champ?"

She hadn't heard Mitch following, but now he stood beside her, calm, offering support. He didn't seem at all fazed. Perhaps it was his solitary male presence, but his steadiness was reassuring.

"He *is* warm," Laura replied.

"What's his temperature?" Mitch asked.

"It's up only a few degrees," Mrs. Plummer answered. It was clear from her stance that the woman disapproved of Mitch's presence.

"Is it within reasonable parameters, Laura?" Mitch asked.

She glanced up, her head clearing a bit. "The doctor said he would be prone to mild fevers."

"So no cause for alarm?" Mitch queried.

"Not yet, no," Laura agreed, feeling her breath coming a little easier.

"We need to watch him," Mrs. Plummer insisted, showing her resentment at his interference.

"Of course," Mitch confirmed, his voice still easy. "But it doesn't sound like there's reason to panic."

"I wasn't panicking," Mrs. Plummer told him stiffly.

"Of course not. You were doing your job. I'm the novice here."

Mrs. Plummer thawed somewhat. "It *is* important that Alex is watched closely."

''I doubt there's a baby anywhere who gets better care.''

Mrs. Plummer went into meltdown. ''Well.'' She sounded flustered. ''Well. I think I'll get him some juice.''

''You handled her like an expert,'' Laura said after the older woman had left. She didn't even try to hide the wryness in her voice.

Mitch lifted one brow. ''I didn't grow up in a house full of women for nothing.''

Laura wanted to ask more about his family, but her attention was too focused on Alex. ''It's times like now when I wonder how this can be, how an innocent baby could be struck down by...''

''It's not a punishment, Laura. It's a medical condition. A *treatable* medical condition.''

She was amazed at the comfort she felt just from his being there. It was an unexpected calm in the storm her life had become. Yet he couldn't completely still the fear. Looking into the trusting face of her young son, Laura doubted anyone could.

''I suppose you plan to stay up with him all night,'' Mitch mused.

''I don't plan to keep him up,'' Laura countered.

''But you don't plan to get any sleep.''

She shrugged. ''I'll do what it takes.''

''Why don't I sack out on the couch and spell you. You take a shift, then I will.''

''But—''

''I'm not a doctor.'' His gaze lingered. ''Or a mother. But I *can* call you if there's any change.''

She hesitated. No doubt Mrs. Plummer would stay and help, but frankly, she welcomed Mitch's presence more. Mrs. Plummer fanned her agitation, while Mitch made it disappear. Yet it seemed too much to expect. "I can't ask you to do that."

"You didn't ask. I offered."

Grateful, she glanced down at her son, seeing his eyelids droop. Then a thought occurred to her. "You've been working since early this morning. You can't stay up half the night, as well."

"As I recall, you were combing through records all day, too."

"But I'm his mother!" Laura protested.

"And I'm his mother's friend," he replied quietly. "Stop being so strong for a moment. No one else needs to know you accepted some help."

"I'm not worried about other people," she told him honestly.

He met her gaze. "Which makes accepting help that much harder for you."

Her breath caught; she was stunned by his words. "It does?"

Mitch's eyes seemed incredibly wise. "I'm afraid so, Laura. And that's a pity."

CHAPTER TEN

"HEY, CHAMP!" Mitch greeted the toddler, relieved that he appeared back to normal. He turned to Laura. "He's looking good."

Laura, too, was relieved. "He does, doesn't he?"

Mitch picked up two coffee mugs, hiding a yawn behind the back of one hand.

"But you look exhausted," Laura informed him. Then her tone softened. "I can't thank you enough for staying. To be honest, Mrs. Plummer would have driven me bats, and I was already slightly crazed."

"For good reason," he remarked, thinking how lovely she appeared despite the long, trying night.

She traced her fingers over the handle of the mug, fiddling unnecessarily with the thick stoneware. "I had a lot of time to think last night."

Mitch placed his own mug on the desk. "About?"

"What you said, about my not caring about other people. It's not completely true. That's why I want you to know that I do appreciate your help."

"I didn't doubt it for a moment." He chucked Alex beneath his chin. "Did you, champ?"

The toddler banged plastic keys against the stroller tray.

"He agrees," Mitch told her.

"I can't argue with both of you." Laura hesitated. "Where are we headed this morning?"

He noticed she didn't use her more assertive, in-charge tone. It was a start. "I copied the journal, so I need to drop it by the hospital before anyone notices it's missing. And then I want to locate the nurses and doctors listed on the entry."

Laura nodded.

Mitch glanced at her, guessing she still wasn't sure he would welcome her assistance today. "If we're going, I think we'd better get started."

Her gaze brightened.

Once Alex and his gear were in the car, they headed toward the hospital. Mitch knew the back streets of Houston as well as the color of his own eyes. The knowledge allowed him to evade the snarling traffic that choked the city's freeways.

"I always thought *I* knew the city," Laura commented in a rueful tone. "But these back streets are a whole new world. I feel as if I've been out of touch in some way."

"Most people are more comfortable with the known. Taking a new route makes them uneasy."

He could see her swallow, then glance out the window before finally meeting his gaze. "Is that what you think of me?"

But he couldn't add to the enormous worry already nearly crushing her. "I think you're too hard on yourself."

Although she was still quiet, her expression softened.

Within minutes, they pulled into the hospital parking lot.

Mitch opened Laura's door, then the back door, retrieving Alex and his stroller. "You and Alex will be a great cover when I return the journal."

Laura nodded. "The records manager did seem rather taken with him, didn't she?"

"I'm counting on it."

Once inside, they walked down the winding corridors of the hospital to the records department. Mitch signed them both in as he had the first time.

The receptionist accepted his explanation that he was there to collect a forgotten jacket. In the records room, Mitch slipped the journal back into place and pulled his jacket from behind the box where he had stuffed it.

Pleased at the clean maneuver, he grinned as he ambled back to the reception area. Just then, he spotted Mrs. Phillips, the manager.

But Laura spotted the woman, too. She pushed the stroller forward, snagging the manager's attention. The woman was again charmed by Alex. When Mitch approached, Mrs. Phillips included him in her smile.

He held up the jacket. "I was glad to see this was still here."

The manager nodded.

"Well, dear, we'd better be going," Mitch told Laura.

"Say bye-bye," Laura instructed Alex, picking up Mitch's cue.

Mrs. Phillips waved goodbye, as well.

"A clean escape," Mitch murmured as they headed back to the car. "Nice work, team."

THE SMILE FADED from Mrs. Phillips's eyes. She
hadn't remembered seeing the jacket in the work or
storage areas. And even though this man, woman
and child looked like an average family, she had
been in the records business long enough to know
that people often did outrageous things to get into
confidential files. Lawsuits were lost or won on the
evidence contained in them.

Scanning the desks, Mrs. Phillips saw nothing out
of place. But she wasn't satisfied. She glanced
through the closest storage areas, then remembered
that the young man had persuaded her to allow him
into even the remote file room.

Quickly she strode there and looked over the rows
of shelving. Initially, nothing seemed out of place.
Then her gaze landed on the overhead shelf. Yesterday she had noticed that one of the handwritten
journals was missing. She'd had all the clerks
searching for it.

Now it was back on the shelf.

Why hadn't anyone informed her it had been located?

"Susan!"

The clerk turned and hurried at the summons.
"Yes, Mrs. Phillips?"

"Do you know anything about the journal?"

"Only that it's missing." Susan's gaze traveled
toward the shelf, then her mouth opened in an O of
surprise. "It's been found."

"But not by you?"

"No." Susan shook her head. "I thought it was
still missing." Her face grew puzzled. "In fact,

everyone is still searching for it. How do you suppose it got back on the shelf?''

The journals remained in the records area only because their absence on the inventory would raise questions, a red flag to the administration. There had been virtually no risk in keeping them. No one had looked at them in years. Mrs. Phillips had felt their presence was completely nonthreatening. Until now.

But she didn't want to stir any more curiosity. ''The books must have been out of order and I missed seeing it.''

''But—''

''I said they were out of order, Susan. Now, why don't you get back to the project you were working on.''

Although the clerk didn't appear convinced, she left.

Mrs. Phillips kept a calm expression on her face as she returned to her own office and shut the door. Once inside, she quickly picked up the phone and dialed a number forever imprinted in her memory.

''It's me.'' She swallowed. ''I think we have trouble.''

MITCH GLANCED over at Laura. ''Can you read the next name on the list?''

''You were right, some of this really is chicken scratch.'' She angled the paper, a photocopy from the handwritten journal. ''I think it's Edward—oh, it must be Edwards. I. Edwards.''

Mitch scanned his physicians' directory but couldn't find the name. He punched in a familiar number on his cell phone. It was one he used often.

Nursing professor Mary Jo Westien knew the names of all the physicians in the area, active and retired. She also knew how to contact them. And when she said there was no Dr. I. Edwards, past or present, he knew she wasn't wrong. Puzzled, he clicked off the phone.

"Well?" Laura questioned.

He could hear the expectancy in her voice, but he couldn't lead her on. "It's a dead end."

"But the name's here in the journal," she protested.

"Which makes me question the other entries," he admitted.

She blinked. "You mean, they may have been altered?"

"Possibly," he admitted. "Of course, this could be just a bad entry."

Laura scratched her head. "Do you suppose we could check another similar entry?"

"You're reading my mind."

From the back seat Alex banged his cup.

Laura smiled at him, opening a bag of cereal.

"Is he okay?" Mitch asked. While he was coming to enjoy having both Laura and Alex accompany him, he worried that it might not be good for the child.

"You're turning into a giant worrywart!" But she tempered the words with a smile. "I keep telling you he's getting the proper nutrition and naps. He drops off almost every time the car's in motion. The only one who's hurting from this is Mrs. Plummer."

"She still bent out of shape?"

Laura pantomimed Mrs. Plummer's stern face.

"She acts as though I'm kidnapping him every morning."

"Doesn't she have any family of her own?" It seemed to Mitch that the woman was a little too territorial about Laura and Alex.

"She had a daughter."

"Had?"

"She's dead. She would have been about my age, I understand."

"Really?"

Laura faced him. "There was a funny tone in your voice just now. Why?"

"It's nothing." But wheels were clicking in his head. So Mrs. Plummer's daughter would have been Laura's age? It probably wasn't connected, but he'd been a cop too long to ignore a warning flag. "Now, about that next entry."

"Oh, yes, here it is."

For the next few hours, they traced the doctors on two other birth entries. Although both were retired, the facts checked out. So did the names of the newborns.

"So what does this mean?" Laura questioned. "That some of the entries are valid and others aren't?"

"Possibly."

"Now what?"

"I head back to the office to check on mail and phone calls. I'm hoping we might have some responses from the newspaper ads I placed."

She looked at him in surprise. "I didn't know you did that."

"I've been telling you all along that this investigation is a lot broader and a lot more detailed than you know.''

"So you have.'' Laura hesitated. "What does the ad say? Come claim your thirty-one-year-old newborn?''

Mitch angled his head. "Discretion is a big factor. I use the usual hooks—considerable inheritance, searching for relatives, that sort of thing. And I put ads in all the big Texas papers.''

"Not just Houston and Galveston?''

"Nope. Even though your aunt Rhoda said she's sure you were born here, your birth mother could have moved. But she likely has relatives.''

"Who read newspapers,'' Laura concluded. She was quiet for a moment. "I hope she has a huge family tree.''

In her voice he could hear the need for hope. "It's probably an entire forest.''

Unexpectedly, she laughed. "With lots of branches?''

"A regular lumber factory.''

ALTHOUGH THE VOICE on the phone was quiet, it carried power and more. "I want you to investigate everyone on that sign-in sheet.''

A second male voice replied. "I thought you had an idea which one it might be.''

"That's not the point. Phillips could be wrong about the connection. What we are sure is that the journal disappeared and then it was replaced. I want to know everything there is to know about everyone who walked into that department. Do I make myself clear?''

"Crystal." There was a slight hesitation. "What if Phillips is right?"

There was no hesitation on the other end of the line. "We eliminate the problem."

"Eliminate?"

The voice rocked with finality. "Eliminate."

CHAPTER ELEVEN

THERE HAD BEEN no responses so far to Mitch's multiple newspaper ads, but he was narrowing down the number of female births on the same day as Laura's. By tracing each woman, he was able to exclude those who were not Laura and those who were deceased. That tightened the numbers.

But it wasn't the only option Mitch was pursuing. He had ordered copies of all death certificates on infant girls for the month after Laura's birth. Once again he was following a hunch. He still had a gut feeling that Laura's adoption may not have been legal. He remembered that glimpse of fear in Rhoda's eyes, her reluctance to discuss the adoption. Neither was conclusive, but he couldn't ignore the instincts he had developed over the years.

He also knew that if Laura had been a black market baby the chances of finding her birth parents decreased dramatically. In his career as a detective, he had investigated only two other black market adoptions. But in each case, the transaction had occurred out of state, so he knew the same people couldn't be involved.

But in those cases the adoptive parents had been alive and had provided enough information to locate the birth mother. So Mitch realized he had to be more inventive. He had to think of the angles a black market racketeer would. And he was damned glad he'd put out all those feelers with his street contacts.

LAURA WASN'T SURE why she was fussing so. It was only dinner. And only Tucker.

But a nice table was a nice table.

And baloney was baloney.

Laura stopped short of adding candlelight. But then, high chairs and candlelight really didn't mix.

Strange. When Mitch was around, she never thought of him and Alex not mixing. They'd taken to each other from day one. Which was rather remarkable, considering that Tucker was not in any way a family man. She wondered why he didn't value permanence. He had been candid in expressing how much he enjoyed his lifestyle, his lack of commitment.

It wasn't only her bad experience with her ex-husband that made her long for permanence. It was this new unsettled feeling since she'd learned about being adopted, the sense that she no longer had a connection with anyone.

Alex toddled past her just then, and she amended her thoughts. She was definitely connected with her precious son.

Hearing a quiet knock, she scooped up Alex and headed to the door.

"Hey, champ!" Mitch greeted them. "I was afraid he might be asleep."

"Nah. He's roaring to go."

Alex reached out chubby arms to Mitch.

Refusing to ponder the rightness of her action, Laura handed her son over.

But then she wondered about the sheepish grin on Mitch's face.

"What is it?"

"Actually, I brought something along."

She glanced back toward the dining room. "I thought you knew I was going to cook."

His grin broadened. "This isn't to eat. She's waiting in the car."

Laura struggled to keep her smile in place. He had brought another woman to dinner? Of course Laura and Mitch weren't dating. Theirs was strictly a business relationship. Still...

"That will be fine." Resolutely, she took Alex back from Mitch and set him on the floor by her feet.

As soon as she did, Mitch headed back outside. Laura glanced again at the table. After she met the woman, she would have to set another place.

Smile fixed, she waited with Alex. But when Mitch returned, he didn't have a woman by his side.

Shrieking with delight, Alex struggled to reach what Mitch did have in his arms. "Pal!" he was hollering. "Pal!"

A puppy?

Laura released Alex's hand, her eyes flying to Tucker.

All sorts of protests were on her tongue, but they died there. Ecstatic, Alex and the puppy were bounding toward each other. It was hard to tell which was more excited—the furry bundle of licks and doggy kisses or her son.

With a rueful half grin, Tucker met her gaze. "Pal. Sounds like a great name."

She felt her lips twitch. "So, this is your ferocious guard dog?"

His grin increased. "First impressions can be deceptive."

Laura watched Alex cuddling the puppy. "I can see that."

Mitch shrugged, a charming gesture that she guessed would delight most women. "She *could* grow up to be ferocious."

"Have you fed her?" Laura asked.

"No, but the shelter gave me a small bag of dog food."

"Not even a sad tale about how you found her rummaging for food, or how she followed you home?"

"I could point out that all the dogs at the shelter need homes or they'll be—"

"Stop!" She put out her hands in defense. "Let's dwell on the fact that this one has been saved from that fate."

His grin broadened. "You old softy. Who'd have thought?"

Taken aback, Laura was at a loss for words. She didn't want people to see her weaknesses. It made her too vulnerable.

But Mitch was concentrating on Alex and the puppy. "So, champ, what should we name the puppy?"

"How about Killer?" Laura suggested, watching as the dog rolled on her back when Mitch rubbed her tummy.

"Pessimist," Mitch retorted. "Besides, I think I like Alex's original suggestion. Pal. She can be Alex's pal."

"Is she old enough to eat regular dog food?"

"She's three to four months old. Someone abandoned her. Probably brought her home when she was six weeks old, figured out dogs require care and then dumped her."

Laura was touched in spite of herself. "So there is a sad tale."

"Not so sad." Mitch glanced up. "Look at how she and Alex are getting along."

Laura groaned. "I knew it. 'A boy needs a dog.' Don't think you've fooled me. You planned this all along."

"Hey, it's love at first sight."

Startled, Laura stared at him, wondering if she'd heard him correctly. "What?"

"Alex and the puppy. It looks like a lifetime match."

"So it does." Feeling incredibly foolish, Laura turned toward the dining room.

"Laura?"

Composing her features, she turned back. "Yes?"

"You aren't really angry, are you?"

"No. As you said a boy needs a dog."

He peered over her shoulder at the table. "You've gone to a lot of trouble. Seems I didn't pick a very good time to bring the puppy."

"It's just dinner," she said dismissively, further embarrassed that he'd noticed the pains she had taken with the table.

"Why don't I put the puppy in the garage," Mitch suggested. "At least until after dinner."

"And separate those two?" Laura shook her head. "Uh-uh. We'll put her in the kitchen. I have an old blanket and I can probably find a heating pad. That should keep her happy while we eat."

"Let me do that," he insisted. "I didn't grow up in a house full of women not to understand what unappreciated effort is." He gestured toward the table. "It's nice, Laura. Real nice. Now, where's the puppy gear?"

She started to protest, then realized she *would* like his assistance. "The blanket's in the laundry room. The heating pad should be in there, too."

He sniffed. "Smells delicious."

"Just soup and something on the grill."

"Can I help?"

"Yes. Keep Alex and the puppy entertained until the food's ready."

"You got it."

A short time later, Mitch had the dog's quarters organized and Alex was installed in his high chair. Laura had placed the skewers on the grill. The shrimp and vegetables cooked quickly. And she had already ladled out the soup.

Mitch was inhaling deeply, a look of pure pleasure on his face. "Lobster bisque?"

"Yes, a light version."

"How in the world did you whip this up so quickly?"

"I cheated," she explained. "I keep homemade stock in the freezer. The rest is a breeze."

"It's fantastic," he proclaimed.

Seeing the genuine enthusiasm in his expression, she relaxed a bit, wishing she didn't feel so awkward around men. Around this man. "I'm glad you like it."

"And Alex seems to be enjoying his—" he hesitated "—stuff."

She finally laughed aloud, a cleansing hoot of relief. "That was tactful. I make his baby food. Nothing exotic, but it has less salt and sugar and more vitamins."

He frowned. "I thought I saw you feeding him stuff out of jars."

"You did. I'm not an extremist. Bottled baby food keeps until the jar's opened. Homemade doesn't travel as well, especially in the heat."

"Whatever you do with it, he likes it." He reached out to tag Alex's kicking feet and gave them a fond shake. "Almost as much as I like mine."

When Mitch dug into the shrimp, he was equally complimentary, but she waved away the words. "Really. All I did was wrap some peppered bacon around the shrimp and stick it on a skewer. Nothing Julia Child-ish about it."

"Maybe it's how you wrap it," he observed. "Maybe you've just got the touch."

Her eyes skittered to meet his.

And she could nearly feel his touch. She could certainly remember it.

Alex banged his spoon against his dish. "More!"

"Sure, sweetie." She turned away from Mitch, concentrating on the baby, giving his food more time and attention than was necessary.

The rest of the dinner was unremarkable. Probably because Laura avoided Mitch's gaze. When they finished eating, he started to clear the table.

"No, please leave it. I'll clear if you'll take Alex in the other room."

She wondered if he sensed that she was trying to get rid of him, but he didn't mention it. Instead he plunked Alex on his shoulders, making her son shriek with delight as they bounced into the den.

Laura dawdled over the dishes as long as she could. Even then she glanced around the kitchen, searching for something else to clean, anything to delay interacting with Mitch.

"You could wax the floor," Mitch suggested. "Or perhaps repaper the walls."

Startled, Laura whirled around. "I didn't hear you come in."

"Relax. I haven't seen you this hyper since you flew into my office and demanded that I get into gear."

Laura wondered if she had been completely obnoxious. "Was I that bad?"

"Worse," he admitted candidly.

Her nerves suddenly disappeared. "That was blunt."

He laughed. "And look where it's led us."

Hope didn't flourish, but it was making a slow recovery. "Where's that?"

"On the right track. If you hadn't insisted on coming along and then insisted on bringing Alex, I probably couldn't have gotten away with that journal."

Laura felt a deep wave of both relief and gratitude. She had badly needed to know she was helping, even if only in some small way. "Thanks."

"For what?"

She shrugged. "For making me feel a little less useless."

Mitch cupped her chin. "You may be many things, Laura Kelly, but useless isn't one of them. Give yourself some credit. How many mothers would have flung themselves out on the front line the way you have? Most would have sat back, waiting for someone else to make the results happen. Not you. When Alex gets his donor, there will be one person to thank, and that's you."

Laura knew it was ridiculous, but she felt her throat clog with emotion. "Not just one person."

His eyes locked on hers and she knew that she could take one step closer, fit into his arms and explore what they had begun that day.

But the sanctuary would be temporary at best. Mitch didn't want permanence. And she couldn't live with temporary.

So instead of moving forward, she stepped back. "I should check on Alex."

His expression told her he knew she was fleeing, yet he smiled that lopsided, devilish grin of his. "Wait until you see him."

Together they returned to the den. Alex and the puppy were sound asleep, side by side.

"They're really something," Mitch murmured.

"A boy and his dog," she replied dryly.

"Yep."

"I don't suppose you even had a good story ready for why you were leaving the puppy with Alex."

"Nope."

"I'll get you for this," she retorted in a whisper.

"You want some help putting Alex to bed?"

She almost accepted, but she was becoming too accustomed to his presence. When they did find her mother, he would vanish. To get too used to him, to count on him always being there, wasn't smart. Slowly she shook her head. "We'll be fine."

Again his eyes sought hers. "That you will. And don't forget it, Laura."

CHAPTER TWELVE

MITCH DUG THROUGH the stacks on his desk. Bills. Those could be ignored. Responses to the ad. He put those in a separate stack, to be sorted. They might contain something. Last was the courier packet containing the death certificates he had ordered.

Playing his hunch, Mitch opened the last envelope. He flipped through the certificates inside until one caught his eye.

A baby girl who was born and died on March 22, 1970—Laura's birth date. He read further. Female infant Gateley had been born in LaSordia Hospital, where he had recovered the handwritten journal. And he had already eliminated all the other births for that day. If he were in Vegas, all three cherries in the slot machine would have slammed into a single row.

The certificate listed Barbara Gateley as the mother. He turned to his computer and pulled up a few screens. The woman still lived in Houston. Pay dirt.

Glad that he had come into the office so early, Mitch grabbed the certificate and loped toward his car. He had needed a few hours to work alone, get his papers and Laura's profile in order. Now there was plenty of time to reach Laura's house before she left.

He tried to decide how to tell her so as not to build up her hopes. He considered, but rejected, a dozen different approaches. In the end she simply looked at his face when she opened the door—and somehow she knew.

"Tucker?" she questioned weakly.

He nodded.

"Are you sure?"

"No. It's just a lead. But a really strong one." Quickly he explained how he had come to his conclusions. "You have to understand, I could be wrong. However, often in cases like this, a death certificate is faked so that the child can be adopted for a price."

"Isn't that illegal?"

"Yep. But usually all it takes is a doctor, lawyer and young mother who desperately needs the money."

Laura swallowed. "You mean she sold me?"

"We don't know that. There may have been a good reason for what she did. And Laura, this may not be your mother."

"Did you eliminate all the other females born on the same day?"

He nodded.

"Then it must be her!"

"There's a good chance," he admitted. But he knew better than to voice his strong feeling that they had found the right person. This wasn't horseshoes. Close didn't count.

"Does she live here in town?" Laura inquired, her voice ripe with hope.

"Yes. I have an address on her."

Since Laura looked ready to bolt out the door, he laid a restraining hand on her arm. "Laura, you have to prepare yourself. Not all birth parents are eager to meet their children."

"She doesn't have to be eager to meet me," Laura protested. "But once she hears about Alex—"

"Laura, you don't know that she'll help you."

"I realize that. But I don't want to want to waste another second."

"But showing up unannounced—"

"If we warn her, she may not speak to me," Laura interrupted.

"I don't think you're considering all the consequences of this visit. You might want to prepare yourself. It could be very painful."

Laura gripped the edge of the hall table. "That doesn't matter. I'm not looking for an emotional mother-daughter reunion. I want to save my son's life. And surely this woman will understand that."

Mitch resisted the urge to pull her close. "I hope you're right."

LAURA'S HANDS were knotted helplessly together. All of her and Mitch's searching had come down to this moment. In a few minutes she would know if she had been successful in finding the help her son so desperately needed.

And she would also be meeting her mother for the first time.

The house was remarkably unremarkable. A weathered Old English Tudor was set far back from the road. Ivy climbed over the aged brick, winding toward the oversize windows. Old oak trees shaded the walkway and house. It looked like a house that had history, a place for a family who had put down deep roots.

But Laura knew some of those roots had been severed forever. Again she wondered why. Why had her mother chosen to give her away? But she hid the conflicting emotions as she walked beside Mitch to the front door. Grateful for his calm presence, she felt his hand at the small of her back, a gentle reminder that he was with her.

Meeting his eyes, she pushed the doorbell. It took a few minutes, but then the door opened.

A woman of about Laura's age stood there, an expectant expression on her face. "Yes?"

Laura glanced at Mitch.

Taking her cue, he spoke. "We're trying to find Barbara Gateley."

The woman's expression turned sympathetic. "I'm afraid she's dead."

Dead! The word reverberated through Laura's mind. All her expectations for Alex, even for herself, were shattered in that single instant. Stupefied, she could only stare.

Through a fog, she heard Mitch ask the woman if she was a relative or if she knew how to locate any of Barbara Gateley's family. But because of the terms of the house sale—the house had been in probate—the woman only knew that the former owner was dead. She seemed genuinely sorry that she couldn't be more help.

Mitch thanked her.

Still numb, Laura allowed him to guide her back to the car, to help her inside.

Dead? How could that be? And now what was she going to do?

"IT'S A SETBACK," Mitch was telling her.

He had placed a cup of bracing coffee between her hands. Somehow they had arrived at his office. He knew she wouldn't want her son to see her so upset, nor was she ready to face strangers in a public place.

She didn't reply, flinching when the bird squawked suddenly.

"Knock it off, Morgan," he ordered the nervous parrot. Mitch could hear the sound of ruffled feathers as he knelt next to Laura, gentling his voice. "Drink."

Although she obviously didn't want to, she obeyed. He watched as the lightly bourbon-laced coffee traveled down her throat. She didn't sputter at the unexpected taste. Instead, she lifted her head.

"I can't believe it. How could we have worked so hard, just to hit this wall?"

He took her hand. "Laura, we didn't completely hit the wall. I'm sure she has relatives. Remember, this is what I do. I find people. I'll locate her family."

"But how long will that take?"

"You'll be amazed at how fast I can find them."

"I'm not sure I can take any more amazement."

"Laura, your disappointment isn't simply in not finding Alex's donor today. You thought you were going to meet your birth mother. You just learned she's dead. It's okay to be upset about that."

"I told you I wasn't expecting a tearful reunion," she protested.

But he could see the traces of vulnerability, the pain that still lingered in the depths of her impossibly blue eyes. Her face mirrored disappointment and renewed fear. "Maybe not. Maybe it's only me, but if I thought I was going to meet a parent I'd never known, I'd be pretty shook." The irony wasn't lost on him. He could merely imagine his reaction if faced with the same situation and an opportunity to meet his erstwhile father.

She sagged back against the couch. "Right now, I have to think about Alex, not feel sorry for myself."

"I figured you might feel that way. That's why we came here. I plan to find your mother's relatives today." He swung around to his desk and logged on to the computer.

"Today?" Her voice, still thick with disappointment, now echoed with hopeful disbelief.

"Today." He flipped through the screens. "If it means I'm still at it after midnight."

BUT IT WAS ONLY nine-thirty that night when Mitch stopped looking. Armed with a list of Gateleys and their addresses, which he'd culled from his computer, he had conducted the rest of his search in person.

And it looked as though he had a lead. Barbara

Gateley's sister, Ellen. He'd located a new address for her from one of her former neighbors. She had recently moved from the address indicated in the computer.

That she had, was in itself strange. She had lived at her other address for over thirty-five years, yet had relocated in the six months since her sister's death. He wondered if the incidents were connected.

But he was damn tired. Everything seemed to be connected.

Now he hoped she, too, wasn't forever out of their reach.

THE MORNING SUNSHINE was almost painfully bright. So bright that it burned away the smog, revealing endless miles of green broken only by the rows of nondescript houses. It was one of those new urban neighborhoods that apparently prided itself on sameness. Architecturally, aesthetically, all-consuming sameness. It was the sort of place that you could get lost in, much like a maze, without any differentiating landmarks.

So this was the place her mother's sister had chosen to live. Familiar with the neighborhood she had moved from, Laura could only wonder why. The former was filled with charm and individuality.

Laura decided she must be going crazy. Why did she care where the woman chose to live? Perhaps it had been the endless night without sleep. A night wondering about the mother she would never meet and, worse, wondering if she could save her son.

Mitch slowed the car to a stop. "This is it." He turned off the key. "Are you ready?"

She met his eyes, seeing the reassurance there, once again tempted to draw on his strength. But she still couldn't. Instead, she nodded.

"Okay. But remember, initially let me do the talking."

Again she nodded, her throat choked with a wellspring of emotion.

On the front steps, he gave her hand a reassuring squeeze before dropping it to ring the bell.

A blond, middle-aged woman opened the door, a cautious look on her face. "Yes?"

"Are you Ellen Gateley?"

The caution deepened; her eyes immediately became suspicious. "Yes. Who are you?"

"My name is Mitch Tucker, of Tucker Investigations. This is Laura Kelly."

Still cautious, the woman nodded.

"We're here to talk to you about a very private matter. May we come in?"

"What sort of private matter?" the woman countered.

"It concerns your sister, Barbara," Mitch replied.

"She's dead," the woman said immediately, starting to close the door.

But Laura shot forward, fear and desperation propelling her. "Please don't shut us out. I must talk to you. It's a matter of life and death!"

The woman hesitated, her gaze traveling between Mitch and Laura. It seemed she was going to refuse. Then her gaze returned to Laura's desperate face and she reluctantly opened the door.

Although she offered Laura and Mitch seats in the living room, the woman perched stiffly on the edge of the chair nearest the front door, as though she might bolt at any moment.

Mitch leaned forward. "We apologize for intruding without calling first."

The woman listened without responding.

He continued. "But because of the sensitive nature of our request, we didn't want to approach you by phone."

If anything, the woman grew even more uncomfortable.

"We have been trying to locate Miss Kelly's birth mother."

Ellen Gateley's eyes flew toward Laura.

Mitch's voice was even, professional. "She was born on March 22, 1970. I believe your sister had a baby on that same day."

Stiffly Miss Gateley nodded. "I'm sure there were many babies born that day in a city this size."

"You're right. But only three females in LaSordia Hospital."

The woman's eyes shifted, but she didn't reply.

Laura twisted her hands, barely able to conceal her anxiety.

Mitch's voice was soothing; his face, concerned. "Miss Gateley, it's vital that we locate Miss Kelly's birth parents."

"I'm afraid I can't help you."

"But you must know something!" Laura blurted.

The woman visibly drew back, then stood, indicating the interview was over.

Laura saw the look on Mitch's face. Apparently, he thought she had handled herself badly.

Still, he tried to repair the damage. "Miss Gateley, perhaps after you've had time to think, you might recollect something that could help us." He withdrew a business card. "This has my office and mobile numbers. Please call me any time of the day or night if you remember anything."

Although she accepted the card, Laura could see that she didn't intend to call. Not ever.

Laura took one step across the threshold, before turning back for a moment. "My son's life depends on this." She couldn't stop the tears that welled, the fear that gripped her. "If I don't locate my birth mother, I won't be able to find a bone marrow donor for him. He's only eighteen months old. He's just a baby. Please."

The woman's face softened for a moment, but still she didn't speak.

Mitch reached for Laura's arm. "We should be leaving." Then he glanced back at the woman. "I'll be in touch."

But Laura couldn't see anymore. The flood of tears blinded her. Shoulders shaking with sobs, she allowed Mitch to lead her away. Away from possibly the only person who could tell her the truth.

CHAPTER THIRTEEN

MITCH PUSHED through the stacks of papers, his gaze beginning to blur. Eyes, red-rimmed from hours in front of the computer screen, screamed for rest. But he couldn't rest.

He intended to press Ellen Gateley for answers; still, he couldn't guarantee that she would talk. And he had to be prepared in the event that she refused to cooperate.

He had examined and reexamined each scrap of relevant information. He had come to one inescapable conclusion: he had eliminated all other female infants born the same day as Laura; if Barbara Gateley wasn't Laura's mother, he had hit a wall.

Grimly he realized Ellen Gateley could be the only link to helping Alex. Because if Laura's adoption had been the black market variety, he might never find her birth parents. Records were falsified, "misplaced" or even destroyed. With enough money to grease willing hands, almost anything could be covered up.

Mitch couldn't stop thinking about Ellen Gateley's face. If he was right, he had seen fear in her eyes. Why? True, a woman living alone was wise not to invite strangers into her home. But that did not seem to be what was bothering her. She had become even more uncomfortable after she had heard the purpose of their mission.

If Barbara Gateley's baby had died a natural death, what was there to be afraid of?

However, another face intruded on his thoughts. He couldn't get past the image of Laura's haunted eyes. And he realized that for the first time in his career, he had abandoned all his professional distance.

When Ellen Gateley had shut them out, he had felt Laura's pain, her despair. And his own anxiety about Alex was heightened. The case was a heartbreaker; still, it wasn't the first one of its kind that he had tackled. He had stood beside other clients as they had been rejected by their birth parents. While he'd always been sympathetic, none had reached in and squeezed his heart.

When he had felt Laura's hope drain away, she had taken some of his with her.

He'd never before had a client dog his steps and work beside him. But it was more than that. Far more.

Even now, despite his fatigue, all he could think about was going to her house and checking on her. Just to assure himself that she was all right. It sounded good, he told himself. Yes, just to check on her.

THE HOUSE looked hushed. Almost too hushed to disturb. Mitch nearly turned away at the door. But at the last moment he knocked, a quiet sound in the quiet night.

Laura pulled open the door, her frame silhouetted against the low lamplight. "Mitch."

He noticed that she didn't call him Tucker and wondered why.

"I came by to check on you." He needed to voice the excuse, to make it appear credible.

She shrugged, a gesture he had come to recognize she used when uncertain. "I'm all right." But she closed the door behind him, leading him into the silent den.

Automatically, he searched for Alex.

"He's asleep and I finally got Mrs. Plummer to leave."

He could hear the weariness in her voice and realized she was wearing a long, voluminous nightgown. The demure garment was no more revealing than a terry robe. "I won't keep you up, then."

But as he turned to leave, she snagged his arm. "Don't go."

Reaching out, he smoothed the dark hair over her shoulders. She seemed so fragile somehow. It wasn't a quality he'd ever seen in her. Before she always seemed so strong, not wanting anyone to glimpse any vulnerability.

She lifted her eyes, the blue deepening to near violet. The depth of emotion in them beckoned. He eased the back of his fingers over the soft curve of her cheek, his voice an equally soft caress. "Laura."

For several long moments she stood in his loose embrace. Not wanting to press any advantage, he started to draw away.

But her voice was a whispered plea. "Just hold me…please."

Knowing she needed comfort, he offered only his strength. His embrace was still casual, still only as one friend holding another.

Then she leaned into him, her breasts indenting his chest.

Mitch sucked in his breath, seared by the intimate contact.

As he had since they had kissed, he longed for her taste, her touch. He had dreamed of it, remembering, torturing himself with the need to experience it once again.

As though she read his mind, she trailed her lips across his jaw.

He dipped his head, covering her mouth, each movement a greedy sampling that made him hunger for more. But even as she clung to him, Mitch knew he had to do the honorable thing.

Wishing for an ice-cold thunderstorm, he broke away. "Laura, I can't do this. You're hurting…vulnerable. I may not be your white knight, but I'm not this kind of jerk."

But there were no tears in her eyes. Instead, her moist lips opened in a breathy sigh. "I don't want a white knight. I want you."

He tried anew. "That's what you think now, but—"

She placed two fingers against his lips. "It's what I know."

He made one final, valiant effort. "If you still feel this way tomorrow—"

"We'll have wasted tonight," she replied. "I know you're trying to be a good guy, but I don't want to be alone tonight. Can you understand that?

I have to feel connected to someone. It's as though everyone in my life has been ripped away. And maybe even Alex will be taken from me. I need to be part of someone.'' Again she lifted her incredible eyes. ''Will you be that someone?''

He couldn't withstand her plea any more than he could ignore her allure. With a sureness that surprised even himself, he lifted her into his arms, then found her bedroom as though he had traveled there a thousand times before.

He knew she needed understanding, comfort and reassurance. But he hadn't counted on the passion that poured from her lips, her clever hands or her hungering body.

Carried on the whirlwind of her desire, Mitch unfastened the buttons of her long, prim gown. When it fell to the floor, he realized it was her singular garment. Sucking in his breath, he took in the breadth of her beauty.

But she seemed impatient to rid him of his clothing, too. Shrugging off his shirt, he was pleased by her tenuous touch at his waistband. But then impatience gripped him, also, and the remainder of his clothing disappeared in his urgency.

Naked flesh sought naked flesh and their mutual gasp collided amid tangled limbs and silken hair.

Her skin sang beneath his fingertips, her softness bewitching him. Nevertheless, he had to be certain she knew what she was doing…and with whom.

Gripping her face between open palms, he locked his gaze on hers. ''Laura.''

Her voice was a thick whisper. ''Yes, Mitch?''

He could see the recognition in her eyes. More,

he saw her decision. What he didn't see was regret or uncertainty.

And so again he claimed her lips.

Laura knew that he wanted to be sure. But all she could be certain of was her overwhelming need. She had told him the absolute truth, bared her soul utterly: she needed this connection, this sense of belonging to someone other than herself. And something deep inside echoed that she needed him.

Although she refused to listen to that last insistent thought, her heart yearned for renewal. And her soul longed for it even more. But she spoke with her body, insisting that her heart remain mute.

Yet she couldn't deny that while Mitch's hands inflamed, they were incredibly, unbelievably, gentle. She could feel his strength in each caress, his giving in every touch. And it was the giving that stunned her.

And as he took them over the edge, she was suddenly and dreadfully afraid that he had taken her heart along, as well.

LAURA LEFT THE DRAPES in the bedroom drawn. She didn't want the probing morning rays to waken Mitch. She doubted he would approve of what she intended to do.

The bedroom seemed uncommonly cozy. Mitch's muscled frame was sprawled across the bed, his sleep deep and uninterrupted. She felt a vague pang of guilt at using him so shamelessly. She knew he hadn't intended for the previous night to occur. But it wasn't a well thought out plan on her part, either.

She picked up his jeans and folded them over the

chair. Then she reached for his shirt and drew it close. It carried his scent, one she now knew intimately.

But she didn't have time to linger. Still, her gaze drifted again toward Mitch. He seemed younger, less driven in his sleep. She was tempted to drop a soft kiss on his forehead, but she didn't dare waken him. Besides, she had asked for a night, no more.

With one last look at him, she slipped out of the room and into the nursery. She had already phoned Mrs. Plummer, asking her to wait until that afternoon to come in. She knew Mitch wouldn't appreciate the woman's inquisitive presence. Especially when he awoke alone in Laura's bedroom.

Having already fed Alex, she quickly dressed him. Picking up his diaper bag and her purse, she escaped.

Retracing the route to Ellen Gateley's house wasn't difficult. Each moment of the previous day was imprinted in her memory.

Laura had noticed the woman's rose garden, as well. It was meticulously cared for and Laura suspected that like many Houstonians, Ellen Gateley might work in her garden before the hottest time of the day.

Laura also suspected that the woman wouldn't open her door to either Mitch or Laura again.

She parked at the end of the street, unwilling to have Miss Gateley spot the car. Mammoth drops of dew still clung to the grass as Laura walked quietly across the lawn. Hope flared when she spotted Ellen Gateley working quietly in her rose garden.

Hitching Alex up a bit on her hip, she approached. "Miss Gateley?"

Startled, the woman spun around, dropping her basket of clippings.

"I didn't mean to disturb you," Laura apologized, bending to retrieve the basket.

Warily, Miss Gateley accepted the basket. "I don't mean to be rude, but what are you doing here?"

Laura kept her voice firm but soft. "The same as yesterday. I thought maybe if you met my son..." Laura fought to keep a smile in place, not to give in to tears again. "This is Alex."

The woman wavered. "He's quite beautiful."

Laura bit her lips, wanting to ask so much, yet horribly afraid to offend the woman into silence. "Does he resemble his grandmother?"

Ellen Gateley looked from Laura to Alex and then back again. Laura wondered if it was her own fear she saw mirrored in the other woman's eyes. "I couldn't say."

Desperate, Laura placed her hand on the other woman's arm. "Please. I'm begging you." Unable to stop the tears, Laura allowed them to run unchecked down her cheeks. "My son is all I have and he means more to me than my own life. I have to find out if there is anyone I'm related to who can be a bone marrow donor...." She struggled to force the words past her sobs. "If I don't, he will die!"

Alex put his chubby arms around Laura's neck, agitated by her crying. "Mama," he whimpered.

Ellen Gateley dropped her gardening basket. Grasping Laura's elbow, she guided Laura and Alex inside, gently pushing Laura into a kitchen chair. She fetched a box of tissue and pressed it on Laura. "Please don't cry, dear."

"I'm sorry. I'm not usually this emotional." Sniffling, she tried to get a grip on her weeping. "But with Alex…"

"Of course, because you love him."

Slowly the sounds of Laura's weeping died away.

And in the silence she heard Ellen Gateley sigh. Glancing up, she met her gaze and saw that the other woman had come to a decision.

"I don't know if this will help you…."

Hope flared so wildly that Laura could feel its pain beating against her chest.

"But my sister's baby was stillborn."

Hope, so new, extinguished itself in an even more painful burst.

"Are you certain?" Laura knew she was grasping at the impossible, but she couldn't believe her only chance was being so cruelly snatched away.

Ellen hesitated. Finally she met Laura's eyes again. "My sister never believed so."

Laura gripped the side of the table, her other hand smoothing Alex's legs in a comforting manner. "What do you mean?"

"Barbara said she heard her baby cry. Of course it could have been because of the medication they'd given her. When it happened, she was heartsick and confused. But as the years passed, she became more and more certain that her baby wasn't stillborn."

"The baby that could be me?" Laura whispered.

Ellen Gateley bent her head, her own voice hushed. "I suppose so."

Trembling with relief, Laura put her cheek to Alex's. "Thank you, God," she murmured.

But Ellen Gateley was shaking her head. "We don't know anything for certain."

"There must be a way to find out." Blankly Laura stared ahead. She should have brought Mitch. He would know how to find out. "This is going to sound crazy, but can I use your phone? I want to call Mitch, the man here with me yesterday. Would it be all right if he came by? He's a detective. He'll know what questions to ask."

This time Ellen Gateley didn't hesitate. "If I'm in for the inch, I'm in for the mile." She held out her arms. "May I hold the baby?"

Impossibly, Laura found herself smiling. "Of course."

IT DIDN'T TAKE LONG for Mitch to reach Ellen Gateley's house didn't take long. He had been up, dressed and anxiously roaming Laura's home. Not knowing where she was, he hadn't wanted to leave. And he had needed to make certain she wasn't cursing him for the previous evening.

But her call had rocked them both.

Now, seated in Ellen Gateley's kitchen, he listened to the two women recount what they had learned. But he sensed there were still details not yet uncovered.

"Miss Gateley, did your sister ever tell you what she suspected had happened?"

Ellen Gateley paused, her eyes seeming to weigh him. "She thought that her baby had been switched with another, stillborn, infant."

Mitch absorbed this. "There were two stillborn deaths recorded at LaSordia Hospital that day. The other baby was a male."

"Which she wouldn't know if they wrapped him in a pink blanket," Laura speculated.

"She didn't see the baby when it was born," Ellen confirmed. "Barbara said she heard her cry, but then they whisked her away. The first time she saw her was when they brought in the body."

"She wouldn't have unwrapped him," Laura stated, guessing. Her voice thickened. "She probably kissed that tiny head, the small fingers...."

"And then they could have switched the babies," Ellen agreed, sounding tormented.

Mitch stood, putting one hand on Laura's shoulder. "It's one scenario."

"But why?" Laura questioned. "Why would someone do that?" She raised anguished eyes to Mitch. He was pretty sure he knew, but he didn't think she could bear learning the truth just now.

"What's more important is you've probably found your relatives."

Realizing this, Laura jerked her head back toward Ellen. They shared wobbly smiles.

"It would be best if we could make DNA comparisons," Mitch continued. He addressed Ellen. "Would you consent to one from your late sister?"

Ellen blinked, lost in thought for a moment. "Yes. I think you need to know the truth. We all do. But how can we get samples?"

Mitch tried to choose his words with care. "That depends. How did she die?"

"It was a hit-and-run accident."

Laura winced, but Mitch knew he had to press on. "Because her death was so recent, the coroner should be able to provide tissue samples." He hesitated. "If not, her body may have to be exhumed."

Ellen nodded, but Mitch could see that it pained her to talk of her sister. "I'll sign what's necessary."

"There's one more thing," Mitch continued.

Both Laura and Ellen turned to stare at him.

"At some point we may have to consider comparing the DNA of the baby Barbara buried."

Ellen met his gaze. "Exhume her, you mean?"

"It's the only way to know positively."

Ellen nodded. "It's what Barbara would have wanted, I'm sure." She laid one hand over Laura's. "She never stopped thinking about you. Not for a day, not for an hour. And she never got over losing you. This last year she had become obsessed with finding you." Ellen's face was stricken. "But then she died."

Mitch watched as a few quiet tears rolled down Laura's cheeks. Feeling his own heart constrict, he wanted to save her the pain, but knew she needed to hear the truth, and to accept it in order to heal.

Laura lifted her chin. "And in many ways I've never gotten over losing her, either. There's been this missing piece..."

One she'd tried to fill with him, Mitch realized suddenly. No wonder she had crept away before he had awakened.

Ellen nodded, her voice vague with wonder. "I noticed the resemblance yesterday, but I couldn't believe it was actually true."

"We've asked for so much already," Laura began.

And Mitch saw where the question was headed. Mentally and emotionally, he crossed every finger.

Laura's gaze didn't leave Ellen's face. "Would you consider being tested yourself to see if you're a donor match? It's not a kidney or anything that major," Laura added in a rush. "Alex needs bone marrow."

"Of course." Ellen smiled down at Alex. "Is today soon enough?"

Laura clasped the other woman's hand. "I certainly hope it turns out that we're related." She dropped a kiss on her son's head. "For all kinds of reasons."

Ellen's smile was tinged with sadness. "I wish Barbara could have lived to see him. To see you."

Mitch didn't want to disturb the warm currents in the room, but his suspicions were alerted. He intended to get a look at Barbara Gateley's death certificate. If they were dealing with a black market baby racketeer, all bets were off.

CHAPTER FOURTEEN

HOPE WAS a curious beast. Without it, despair flourished. And with it, Laura could pretend that everything was going to turn out all right.

More than a week had passed and she was waiting on the results of Ellen Gateley's testing, to learn first if she could be a match.

Mitch had contacted an attorney and all the necessary paperwork for the exhumation of Barbara Gateley's baby had begun. Now they had to wait for word on whether their request would be approved. Fortunately, having contacts in the police department helped.

If all went well, soon Laura would know if she had a donor for Alex and if she had been born to a mother who had truly wanted her.

What she didn't know was what was between her and Mitch.

He had been working tirelessly to push through and circumvent the red tape. He had contacted every bureaucratic official required to perform the exhumation and the subsequent DNA testing, in the hope of hurrying the process.

And during that time Laura had acted as though nothing had happened between them. He had tried to broach the subject, but she had shut him out, letting him know their lovemaking was something she wanted only to forget.

It was the coward's way out, she knew, but she didn't intend to allow her already fragile heart to be further damaged. The emotions he'd unlocked had stunned her. So much that she had tenuously allowed herself to imagine a life with him. But he wasn't a family man. And she valued stability as much as he didn't.

She couldn't have chosen anyone more mismatched. That thought stopped her. She had already chosen poorly. And once burned, she should know better.

Still, she had been terribly fearful that he might be ready to close her case now that they had located Ellen Gateley. And she wanted his expertise until they were certain about the testing. She didn't want to believe it was because she had become accustomed to depending on him…or because it would be the end of their time together.

Gazing out the window, she didn't see the neatly manicured borders of her lawn. Instead, she envisioned how empty her life would be. And yet there was no other outcome. At least, not for them.

MITCH STARED at the envelope. It contained the latest paperwork on the exhumation. It was a small bit of news he could pass on to Laura.

However, bringing the envelope was an excuse. And he knew it. An excuse he needed, because she had made it clear she wanted to pretend nothing had happened between them.

But he couldn't pretend.

Not when his every thought was of Laura, of his need to simply hold her close, to take her hand in his. And it was only because of the circumstances that he hadn't pressed.

Yet.

He could have couriered over the papers. And he should be concentrating on building a new client base since Laura's case was winding to a close. Instead, he was standing on her doorstep like a love-sick teenager.

When Laura opened the door, she took his breath away.

"Mitch!" For a moment her eyes softened, and he could hear the pleasure in her voice. But then wariness settled over her features. He wondered at the cause. Did she think he had brought bad news? Or was it simply her reaction at seeing him?

She opened the door wider. "Come in. Alex and I were just about to have some ice cream."

"How's our little guy?"

She froze for a moment, then pushed a smile into place. But Mitch could see the effort in it. "He's great."

They entered the kitchen, and Alex whooped when he saw Mitch. At the same time, the puppy jumped up at his knees, her tail wagging madly.

"Hey, champ!" Mitch greeted Alex, pleased that at least the small duo seemed glad to see him. He reached down, patting the dog, receiving a moist welcome.

"Tuck!" Alex rocked a bit in the high chair, banging on the tray.

"Is it okay if I take him out for a minute?" Mitch asked, seeing that Alex wanted to come to him.

"Sure." Laura was facing the counter, but she turned to glance at him. "I'll be putting our sundaes together."

Mitch unlatched the tray and lifted out Alex. "Come on, big guy. You're ready to rock and roll, aren't you?"

Laura laughed. "He's ready for something. All day he's been bounding with energy. Even the dog couldn't wear him out—and they were at it for hours!"

Mitch placed Alex on his shoulders. "Maybe he's ready to roughhouse!"

Alex shrieked with delight. "House! House!"

Laura rolled her eyes. "Fine habits you're teaching him, Mitch Tucker."

"Tuck," Alex agreed.

"Us guys have to stick together, don't we, champ?" Mitch carried him over to the wind chimes, and gleefully Alex rattled the long pewter tubes.

Laura watched them, her gaze long and searching before she turned back to the ice cream.

Mitch gently disengaged Alex's curious fingers. "Let's get in the high chair again, big guy. Your mom's got ice cream."

Like Laura's other culinary creations, even the ice cream sundaes were decorated artistically. The fruit was cut in triangular, diamond and heart shapes. And she had shaved long curls of dark chocolate, which rested in swirls of whipped cream.

"Alex has a tamed-down version," she explained,

putting a dish of plain vanilla topped with only a dollop of whipped cream on his tray.

Mitch winked at Alex. "Still looks good, doesn't it?"

Laura glanced between them again and then at her ice cream.

Mitch wanted to place a comforting hand on hers, but nothing about her invited the gesture. Instead, he dug into his own dish of ice cream. He noticed that Laura only picked at hers. But then, she was feeding Alex, as well.

"Why don't you let me do that," he offered. "All your ice cream is going to melt."

"I'm used to it."

"You don't have to be," he countered. The tension thrummed between them, an almost visible thing.

Something in her finally relented and she handed him the spoon.

As Mitch fed Alex, he noticed that Laura still wasn't eating, instead pushing the ice cream around in her dish. As he watched, her gaze went to the envelope he had brought in and then laid casually on the table.

"It's not bad news," he told her quietly.

Her gaze jerked from the envelope up toward him. "Oh." She made a vague stab at her ice cream, then her eyes slid again to the envelope. "Is it good news?"

Even though revealing the contents meant his reason to stay any longer was evaporating, Mitch took pity on her. "It's a copy of the last motion filed for the exhumation." It was from the attorney he had trusted to prepare the court documents, the same attorney he used to prepare the court orders he routinely filed requesting original birth certificates. The man was good and he had taken a sincere interest in the outcome for Alex.

"And?"

"And it's going well. The attorney thinks we should hear something soon."

Her expression brightened. "I hope so."

Just then the phone rang and she made a small face. "That's probably Mrs. Plummer, calling to make sure I remembered to feed Alex."

Mitch chuckled, but the sound died away as he watched Laura's face.

She continued to listen, then finally mumbled out a numb-sounding thank-you before hanging up the phone.

Laura met his questioning gaze. "I'm glad *you* had good news." She took a deep breath. "That was Dr. Fletcher. Ellen Gateley isn't a match." Her eyes closed and Mitch could see the shadows beneath them, the worry etched in the tightness around her lips. "They won't have the results of the other tests for more than a week, so we don't know yet if she's my mother's sister." Grimly, she met his eyes. "But as for finding a donor, we're back to square one."

THEY WEREN'T EXACTLY back to square one, but damn close. Mitch had silently cursed every available source; it hadn't helped much.

Which was why they were at Ellen Gateley's house again.

When she opened the door, she glanced hopefully

between them. "Does this mean we have good news?"

Laura firmed her chin, but her eyes were filled with despair. "No. Actually, that's why we're here."

Ellen ushered them inside. "Do you mean I'm not a match?"

Laura nodded. "I just heard from the doctor."

Ellen grasped her hands. "I'm so sorry. I was hoping so much that it would work."

"Me, too."

Mitch cleared his throat. "Miss Gateley—"

"Ellen," she corrected him. "Of course we don't know yet, but we may be family. There's no need to stand on ceremony."

Laura's gaze flew to meet Mitch's.

But he ignored the undercurrent. "Ellen, we have another favor to ask."

"Let's hear it."

"Do you have a copy of the birth certificate?"

Puzzled, Ellen shook her head. "I wouldn't think so."

"I thought you might have kept some of your sister's papers or personal effects," Mitch suggested.

Ellen drew her brows together. "Actually, I may have it. Barbara had a box. She called it her treasure chest. I couldn't bear to go through it, so I put it in with some other boxes when I moved here. It's in the storage closet."

After she left the room, Laura leaned forward. "Do you really think this will help?"

"It could. We're going to try to find every blood

relative you have. And that includes your father. His name should be on the certificate.''

Slowly Laura nodded. ''I feel as though the very fabric of my being is being turned inside out for inspection. I imagine Ellen thinks I'm doing that to her sister, as well.''

''Her sister's fate has already been determined. Alex's hasn't.''

He could see that Laura was considering his words. Then she stood as though unable to sit for another second and strolled to the window. ''Every direction you look in this neighborhood it's the same. Sure, it's all new and fresh, but beyond that I can't imagine why she chose to leave the university area to move here.''

But Mitch was thinking about Ellen's words from the other day. About how her sister had died in a hit-and-run accident. At face value, it wasn't implausible. But he had learned to take little at face value.

''Can you?'' Laura was asking him.

He shook his head. ''I'm sorry. My mind was wandering.''

''It wasn't important. Just trying to guess why Ellen would choose to leave her charming neighborhood for this one.''

''Mmm.'' Then what she said penetrated. It did seem strange that Ellen had left a home she'd lived in for the better part of her life. He remembered it had struck him as odd when he'd first learned she had moved.

''Maybe she made a lot of money on her house,'' Laura mused. ''That area is real pricey now.''

"Mmm." It seemed the more he learned on this case, the more questions it presented.

"I found it!" Ellen carried a wooden box as she hurried into the room.

Mitch watched Laura's expression change as she focused on the container, a finely carved mahogany box that resembled a miniature Bombay chest. It was the first tangible link she had to the woman who might prove to be her mother. Despite the tension between Laura and him since the night they had spent together, he took her hand.

She glanced up, her eyes filled with both gratitude and trepidation. He realized she was afraid. He gave her hand a gentle squeeze.

Ellen took a deep breath and grasped the lid of the box. Mitch could see a slight tremor in her touch. "Here goes." First, she set aside some small pieces of jewelry, then sifted through several folded sheets of paper.

Mitch continued to hold Laura's hand as they waited expectantly. Since they had yet to get a ruling on securing an original copy of Laura's birth certificate, this could speed up the process immensely. Provided Laura was Barbara Gateley's child.

Ellen unfolded yet another sheet of paper. But this time her hand began to shake in earnest. "I think this is it."

Laura leaned forward, her voice hoarse. "May I see it?"

Silently Ellen relinquished the yellowed paper.

Although Mitch dropped Laura's hand so that she

could hold the birth certificate, he put his arm around her shoulders, adding his strength.

Her voice still hoarse, Laura read aloud the pertinent information: "'Mother, Barbara Gateley. Father, James Smith.'"

Mitch felt his hopes sink. The father might as well be called John Doe. Such a common name as James Smith sent up a flag, as well. But before he could consider the implications, he had to attempt to locate the man.

Meeting Laura's eyes, he tried not to signal the breadth of such a search. He could see from her expression, however, that she had grasped the significance, and he could feel it in the trembling of her body.

CHAPTER FIFTEEN

LAURA PACED THE lengths of Mitch's office. Lengths she now had memorized. Mitch was still on the computer. And the phone. As he had been most of the previous two weeks.

The search to find James Smith wasn't proving to be easy. But she could see the determination in Mitch's eyes. Which was why she was there, helping in any way she could. So far she had organized almost every stack of loose papers in the office.

But it didn't seem like enough.

She turned, having now traveled the same path more than a dozen times.

Mitch put a hand over the phone receiver, muffling his voice to the caller. "The mail, Laura. Check for responses to the ads."

Relieved, she carried the wire basket over to the couch. She sorted through the envelopes, noticing a hefty percentage contained bills. Good thing her parents had left her a comfortable inheritance. She imagined her bill for this investigation would total the stack of bills she was sorting.

She glanced over at Mitch. Funny. He hadn't mentioned the mounting costs, or even a bill, and the amount must be considerable. Never having used an investigator, she wondered if this was customary.

Then an uncomfortable thought crawled through her brain. She hoped he wasn't stalling about the bill because of what they had shared.

Laura began to ask, but when she glanced up again, she saw that he was deep in conversation with someone on the phone.

So she opened the responses to ads. Reading them took a while. Most couldn't simply be scanned. Handwritten, they weren't all easily decipherable and many rambled on before coming to the point. Plus Mitch had advertised in regard to several different aspects of the case. She knew, however, that he wanted to concentrate on responses related to locating any Gateley relatives and finding James Smith.

She was drawn most to the letters that were in reply to the search for Gateley relatives. Laura acknowledged she couldn't yet be positive that Barbara Gateley *was* her mother. But logic couldn't still her gut feeling that she had found her. Every instinct Laura possessed told her she was right.

And so each letter was like an introduction to possible family members. She wondered if any of them might really belong to the right Gateleys. The name wasn't common, however, and she was disappointed to find so few letters had come in.

But there were dozens regarding James Smith.

Laura noticed that Mitch had hung up the phone.

"Mitch, didn't you say you specified in the ad that we were looking for a James Smith born in 1945?"

He didn't take his eyes from the computer screen. "Yep."

"Well, we have responses related to men twenty years older, twenty years younger and everything in between."

He shrugged. "Welcome to the wonderful world of private investigation."

"Mitch, there must be hundreds of James Smiths!"

"Thousands," he replied without hesitation.

She knew there would be an abundance of James Smiths, but she hadn't guessed this many. Slowly she sank back against the couch, murmuring disbelievingly, "Thousands?"

"But I'm narrowing the search," he continued.

"Still…finding the right one seems nearly impossible!"

"You keep forgetting. It's what I do." He glanced up from the computer and met her gaze. Then he sighed. "Laura, we're going to find a relative who will be a donor match."

Nevertheless, she was stunned, overcome with the staggering weight of the search.

Mitch rose from his chair and walked around the desk to stop in front of her. "How about responses from Gateleys?"

She indicated the pitifully small pile.

"It's a starting point. And so is the family tree Ellen Gateley is doing for us." He pointed to the computer. "And I'm working up a list of addresses and phone numbers for the names she's already given us."

Laura glanced down at her hands. "I know you've been putting in killer hours on this. In fact, I should probably be giving you a payment on what

I owe you. I'm sure the retainer has run out by now.''

He frowned. ''I don't remember handing you a bill.''

''No, but...'' Her words trailed off as her gaze rested on his stack of bills.

His lips tightened. ''I'll let you know if I'm about to file for bankruptcy.''

Realizing she had just jabbed his male pride, she was immediately remorseful. She stood, snagging his arm as he turned away. ''Mitch, I know I've bungled what I'm trying to say.''

He turned back slowly, his eyes meeting hers.

She hesitated, wondering why the words were so hard to utter. ''Thank you, Mitch.'' She glanced down. ''That's what I've been trying to tell you.''

''Laura Kelly, you're a trial, you know that?''

Surprised, she blinked, then raised her face. ''What?''

But he was smiling, that incredibly endearing grin of his. ''How can one woman be so infuriating and captivating at the same time?''

Somehow the reference to infuriating rolled over her. Captivating? A warm blush started somewhere near her throat and traveled up over her face. But she couldn't speak.

She bit her lips, then made a useless movement with her hands.

Mitch gave her a tiny shake. ''And you're entirely too distracting. Now, I need to carry on with the search.'' Yet his hand smoothed the hair back over her shoulders. ''You okay?''

She nodded.

"Then let's get back to work."

Heartened, she continued to sort through the mail. As the hours passed, she grew more and more impressed with the amount of work he accomplished. The mail alone was a full-time job. How did he keep up with it, the phone calls, the computer searches and the legwork? And at the same time hold her hand to keep her from falling apart?

She'd noticed today, even though she had brought in some lunch, that he subsisted largely on endless cups of coffee.

Retrieving her own mug of coffee, she picked up yet another envelope and slit it open. But this one was far different from the others.

It was a neatly typed missive: "Drop the search while you can."

Laura's throat closed.

Reading and rereading the brief message, she couldn't stop the sudden quaking of her limbs, the gasp of disbelief.

"Laura?" Mitch questioned.

Vaguely she heard the sound of his chair as it scraped back, the thud of his boots on the wooden floor. Then he was taking the paper from her hands.

His face was grim as he met her fearful gaze. "Laura, putting an ad in the paper brings out all kinds of kooks. Some people get a charge out of mindless intimidation."

"What if it's real?"

"We'll face that if we have to, but chances are it's just from some nut."

She wasn't convinced. "Mitch, what have we gotten into?"

His face was closed and she couldn't read beyond the determination in his darkening eyes. "Nothing we can't handle."

MITCH LEANED AGAINST the battered doorway of the precinct office, watching his old partner. Randy had been one of the best things about being a cop. They had worked together before either had been promoted to detective. Theirs had been a partnership of both trust and friendship.

But Mitch had tired of the bureaucracy, the feeling that despite his best efforts, he wasn't making any real difference. And although some might view it as a sellout, he felt more personal satisfaction as a P.I. He could see cases to their conclusion, assured his clients hadn't been short shrifted due to budget cuts or arbitrary orders of his superiors. And then there was his independence...

At that moment Randy sensed his presence, and his face lit up. "Well, don't just stand there. Get in here."

Mitch grinned. Randy wasn't hard to read; an endlessly kind and open man, he didn't seem like the sort to be a cop. But he was the best.

"What're you doing here?" Randy was asking, shaking Mitch's hand in a hearty welcome.

"Can't find a decent cup of coffee anywhere else."

"You came to the wrong place," Randy cautioned him, the perpetual twinkle in his eyes betraying him. "But we have some damn good doughnuts."

Mitch laughed for the first time in days. "You old faker."

"So, you tired of that cat-and-mouse game of yours? Ready to handle a real job again?"

Mitch lifted one brow. "What's wrong? Enlistment at the academy down?"

"Nah, just miss having the best partner on the force."

Mitch acknowledged the words with a silent nod.

"But I'm guessing you're not here to discuss your career options," Randy stated.

Randy's ability to cut to the heart of the matter was one of the things Mitch had always admired most about him. His instincts were the best, both as a cop and as a friend.

"I need a favor."

"I'm listening."

Mitch leaned forward. "I have to see the police report on a hit-and-run."

Randy frowned. "Sounds a little far afield for your current gig."

Mitch quickly outlined Laura's search and its reason.

In typical fashion, Randy's mind clicked quickly. "So you think maybe her mother's death wasn't an accident?"

"That's premature, but yes, I'm suspicious."

"Then we'd better have a look at the report."

Randy didn't waste time, locating the case number, then retrieving the file from records storage.

Once he had the file, he didn't even open it, instead handing it to Mitch.

"I'll get some fresh coffee," Randy told him, leaving Mitch in the office to read the report.

And he didn't return until he had allowed Mitch enough time to sort through the file.

Mitch glanced up when Randy put the coffee on the desk. "Thanks."

"So?"

"Isolated location, almost unbelievable vehicle speed, no witnesses."

"What about the car?"

Mitch met his gaze. "Disappeared. No line on it."

"And you're thinking?"

"The same thing you are."

Randy's eyes narrowed in concentration. "The accident has the marks of a professional hit."

"Or a simple hit-and-run."

"But you don't believe that," Randy wisely concluded.

"On the surface, that's an acceptable explanation. But it's just too damn neat."

"And it doesn't raise the suspicions that a stray bullet would. Even if the perp had disappeared as completely as the car."

Mitch nodded. Then he met his old partner's gaze. "There's a lot riding on the outcome of this investigation."

"The child?" Randy said.

"Yep. But maybe it's even more for someone else."

"Shady adoption?"

"I've wondered. Still, is that worth murder to cover up?"

"Someone could have thought so." Randy's eyes were grim. "Mitch, I know I don't have to tell you this, but watch your back."

CHAPTER SIXTEEN

"LAURA, we have to face it. No James Smith born on that day is living in Texas. According to computer records nationwide, there are only two. One died when he was twelve. The other was in Vietnam when you were conceived."

"But you said there were thousands of James Smiths!" She realized her protest was futile, but she was unable to believe they had been stopped yet again.

"We only need one," he reminded her. "A very specific one. One who doesn't exist."

"But that doesn't make sense! He has to exist." She paused. "Doesn't he?"

"Unless Barbara Gateley falsified the father's name on the birth certificate."

Laura didn't understand. "Why would she do that?"

"She was unmarried," Mitch reminded her. "Times were different. While she wouldn't have been stoned, being an unwed mother wasn't as acceptable as it is now."

"So she just made up a name?" Laura asked, trying to grasp this new obstacle.

"She could have."

"But what about the real father?"

Mitch couldn't entirely conceal a grimace. "He may have been married. She could have been doing the noble thing."

"Very noble. Now Alex's life is at stake!"

"Something she couldn't have foreseen."

Laura passed a hand over her forehead. "Of course not. And for years she thought her baby was dead."

"Laura…"

She heard a note in his voice she didn't like. "Yes?"

"You have to be prepared in the event that the DNA tests come back negative. We aren't certain Barbara Gateley was your mother."

"But you eliminated all the other possibilities!"

"I know that," he replied calmly. "But if the adoption wasn't legal, the records could have been altered, or you could have been born in another state and brought here."

Even though dread swamped her, Laura met his gaze evenly. "I refuse to accept that alternative. If I do, it means Alex dies. I won't ever accept that."

A half smile lifted his lips. "Good. Now, just keep that resolve, because we have another difficult task ahead of us."

Laura steeled her strength. For her son she would do anything. "What is it?"

"We have to confront Ellen Gateley."

Laura raised her brows. "Ellen?"

"She may know more than she's told us."

ONCE AGAIN Mitch noted the sameness of Ellen Gateley's neighborhood. It was almost as though she wanted to blend into the camouflaging landscape. Again he wondered if there was a reason.

But she was cordial as she greeted them, and insisted on preparing tea.

"I've been working on the family tree," she told them, bringing a filled tray into the living room. She poured a cup for each of them, offering fresh cookies, as well.

"I had an impulse to bake this morning," Ellen rambled on. "I don't really know why—I live alone. But the urge just struck. So I'm glad you stopped by."

For a moment they sipped the tea, tasted the fragrant oatmeal cookies.

"These are delicious," Laura commented politely, even though she had taken only a tiny bite of her cookie.

Ellen smiled. Suddenly, she looked as if she had just remembered something. "Oh, you probably want to see what I've done on the family tree." She started to rise.

"Actually," Mitch said, "we're here about something else."

She sank back into her chair, glancing between them. "Oh?"

"It's about Laura's birth certificate."

Wariness entered her eyes, although she tried to maintain a composed expression. "Yes?"

"It lists James Smith as my father," Laura stated.

"Yes," she replied in a small voice.

"And that particular James Smith doesn't exist," Mitch told her.

Ellen stared between them, obviously stricken.

"Is there anything you can tell us about Laura's father?" Mitch asked gently.

Ellen swallowed, lifting her eyes to the ceiling for a moment, then peering at the floor. "Yes." She paused for so long that Mitch wondered if she would continue. But as he and Laura silently waited, Ellen raised her face again. "James Smith was a fictitious name."

"Why?" Laura asked.

Ellen hesitated. "My sister wanted to do the right thing and she didn't want anyone hurt."

"Was the man married?" Mitch questioned.

Ellen nodded. "And Barbara was in a dilemma." She turned to Laura, her expression anxious. "Despite how this sounds, she was a very honorable person."

"Then I think she would want *you* to do the right thing," Laura replied. "She would want you to help Alex."

Ellen looked down again. "I want to honor her wishes...."

"Then tell us his name," Mitch urged gently.

"Couldn't we wait until we learn the DNA results?" Ellen asked hopefully.

"Each day we wait puts Alex more at risk," Laura pointed out.

"Oh," Ellen responded in a small voice.

Laura glanced over at Mitch, her eyes imploring. Then she directed her words to Ellen. "I just heard from the doctor this morning. Alex's tests weren't good. I don't know how much time we have left."

Mitch felt as though he'd been sucker-punched. Why hadn't she shared this vital information with him? Didn't she think he cared about Alex's condition and deserved to know about it?

But he dragged himself back to the present question, turning to Ellen. "His name?"

Ellen closed her eyes briefly, as though uttering a prayer. "James Farley."

In a lesser way, her words took the wind out of him, as well. "*The* James Farley?"

Miserably, Ellen nodded. "He was very charismatic. Barbara never had a chance. It would have been easier to resist a Kansas tornado. By the time she found out he was married, she was already pregnant."

"Was he aware she didn't list him as the father?"

Ellen drew herself up. "Oh, yes. It was his idea. He didn't want it known that he had fathered a child outside of his marriage. Barbara couldn't resist listing his first name, though. James."

Laura gasped. Mitch took her hand, realizing she'd received another blow. If these were in fact her parents, she had just learned that she had been cut out of her father's life with deliberate precision.

"I'm sorry, child." The concern on Ellen's face deepened. "I understand this isn't what you wanted to hear."

"I need to know the truth," Laura replied, looking pale.

Mitch squeezed her hand. "Yes. Thank you, Ellen."

She nodded, looking drained herself.

But Mitch had to ask one more question. "Has he tried to contact you?"

"Farley?" Ellen appeared shocked, almost frightened. "Why would he do that?"

"Sometimes a birth parent has second thoughts, wants to contact his child. You would be a natural connection."

"Not James Farley," Ellen responded with chilling finality. "That man never cared for anyone except himself."

Again Laura flinched, but she reached out to take Ellen's hands. "Thank you."

"I can't see what will come of you knowing." Ellen looked sorrowful. "But if it can help..."

Laura hugged her gently. "It has to."

Ellen stood at her front door, watching as they got into the car. She was still watching as they drove away.

"Why didn't you tell me about Alex's prognosis?" Mitch asked.

She glanced out the window. "I'm handling it."

His jaw tightened. So she was still shutting him out, still being the strong one. She hadn't learned to lean, and apparently didn't want to begin.

Then she glanced back at him. "James Farley?"

"Yep."

"The industrialist?"

"Yep. The one who owns a good chunk of the city."

Her brows drew together. "He's not going to be happy about this, is he?"

"Ellen didn't seem to think so."

"But that's not going to stop us, is it?"

He hesitated. He had the gut feeling that they

were opening a can of worms, one that someone had gone to a great deal of trouble to keep hidden.

The mystery was thirty years old. To have kept it hidden had taken a lot of determination. Possibly even murder.

"Mitch?" she questioned. "It's not going to stop us, is it?"

He shook his head. "No. But you need to consider what we're unraveling here."

Her brows lifted. "We're talking about Alex's life. As far as I'm concerned there is no other consideration."

In his heart, Mitch agreed. But logically, he knew proceeding wouldn't be easy. James Farley was no doubt blanketed with security, armed with top-notch attorneys and, for the most part, protected behind a wall only great wealth could provide. And that was a hell of a wall to scale for one very small child.

THE HOUSE SEEMED unusually quiet. The dinner dishes were done. Alex was asleep after a bad day with another fever. Even the puppy was quietly sleeping in the kitchen.

And Laura was exhausted.

She had been putting on a brave face first for Mitch and then Alex, but inside she was nearly numb.

She couldn't get the afternoon out of her mind. It wasn't simply a case of a father not certain he wanted his child. James Farley wanted his name eradicated from any association with her. Mitch had been very understanding, but she needed to be alone, to give in to emotions she couldn't let him see.

"Has Mrs. Plummer left?" Mitch asked.

"Finally. She's been hovering far more than usual."

Mitch frowned. "Is there some reason she's so overprotective?"

"It might have something to do with the way her daughter died."

His gaze sharpened. "And how did she die?"

Laura hesitated. "I don't know, but I sense it's something really sad. She's never really said. She's just mentioned how much she wanted grandchildren, but that her daughter was dead and there would be no grandchildren in her future."

"Did you ever ask her what happened?"

"Sort of. But I got vague answers and she clearly didn't to talk about it."

"Mmm."

Seeing his inquisitive investigator-cop look, she grew exasperated. "That's perfectly normal. It must be painful to discuss."

"Of course," he agreed.

But she had a feeling he was agreeing only to mollify her. "There's not a dark shadow skulking under every bush."

"I think that's a mixed metaphor," he replied mildly.

Exhausted, she sank onto the couch. "Probably."

"But I'm glad you brought up the subject."

"What subject?"

"Of skulking shadows."

A pit formed in her stomach and she closed her eyes. "I don't think I'm glad."

"Laura, we need to talk."

Opening her eyes, she searched his face. And the pit in her stomach grew. But she knew she had to listen. "What is it?"

"I think there's more to the falsification of your birth certificate than appears on the surface."

She swallowed her misgivings, wishing she didn't have to hear this. "Like what?"

"Farley may have been involved in more than simply keeping his extramarital affairs quiet."

Somewhere deep in her mind she heard a screaming voice cautioning her to stop listening before it was too late. But too much was at stake for her to heed the advice. "Such as?"

"I don't think your adoption was legal. If Barbara Gateley didn't agree to an adoption, there must have been a cover-up. And Farley had a lot at stake if he was involved."

"You think he covered up my adoption?"

Mitch's golden-green eyes darkened to near jade. "It's a possibility. But there's something else you have to know."

She tried to steel herself, but her reserve of strength was rapidly dissipating. Again she swallowed. "What is it?"

"The police report on Barbara Gateley's accident leaves a lot of questions."

"What kind of questions?"

"The manner of the hit. No witnesses. The car completely disappearing."

Shock was setting in. "You think she was murdered?"

Mitch's voice was carefully controlled. "I'm not saying that. But it looks very suspicious."

To her horror, Laura could see where he was heading. At the same time, she remembered Ellen Gateley's words. "Ellen said that her sister had been obsessed with learning the truth."

"Which may have been very dangerous for her."

Laura sucked in her breath.

But Mitch didn't relent. "And could be just as dangerous for us…if we continue the investigation."

"If?" Laura shook her head. "There's no if for me."

"We can keep working on the Gateley side," Mitch suggested, watching her.

But she was climbing out of her fatigue, fueled by a new desperation. "It's not enough."

He met her gaze. "It would be for most people."

"I'm not most people."

Once more, he searched her eyes. "I've noticed."

She glanced away. "I want the truth from him, from Farley."

"That might not be the best approach."

But she wasn't backing down. "I deserve the truth and I intend to ask for it."

"That's not only foolhardy it's dangerous."

She was afraid. She could feel it in her pores, in the chilled hair on her neck, but she couldn't give up now. "I can understand if you don't want to get involved any deeper." It cost her, but she kept her chin in place. "I can continue alone. There's no need for you to put yourself in danger."

"I *am* rather fond of my neck," he replied. "But you really don't think I'm going to let you continue alone, do you?"

Relief was trickling past the fear, diluting it. "I'm letting you off the hook," she said, trying again, though even to her own ears her resolve sounded weak.

Somehow his arms were around her, pulling her near. "I've always been a sucker for a damsel in distress."

"Damsel? I'm no—"

But his lips were cutting off her indignation. And suddenly her protest didn't seem at all important. Not nearly as important as the warmth of his arms holding her tight and the sanctuary she was finding there.

Closing her mind, she also closed off the warning bells that had been ringing for so long. Just for the night, she told herself. Just for the night.

CHAPTER SEVENTEEN

MITCH WAS HAVING a hell of a time breaking through the carefully constructed barriers surrounding James Farley. Despite the effectiveness of his usual methods, they weren't working this time.

He had run through all the public sites on the computer, then a few places he had to hack into. Although the standard statistics were available on Farley's corporation, very little could be found on the man himself. Nothing about his personal life or origins. Each available newspaper or magazine article focused on the corporation or other boards Farley sat on, his humanitarian efforts. There were a few notices in the social columns, but nothing about the man prior to his success. It was as though Farley and his corporation were born simultaneously.

By gathering information on Farley, Mitch was simply hedging his bets. He was hoping a contact would come through the Gateley line so that they wouldn't have to confront Farley. But he had to lay the groundwork in the event that they couldn't find a donor through the Gateleys.

And so he took to the streets again, putting the word out to his contacts. He had greased many palms very well. If there was anything dirty on Farley, he would hear. Which was why he was back to Eddie.

Finished with a customer, the snitch turned to him. "You're playing with fire, Tucker."

Although Mitch's eyes narrowed, he shrugged in an offhand manner. "Meaning?"

"You're a smart guy." He paused, his expression slightly mocking. "For a cop. You figure it out."

"Just keep your ears to the ground."

Eddie's gaze remained sharp. "This have anything to do with the dirty doctor?"

"I'm not paying for an analysis, just information."

"It's your funeral, Tucker."

Despite the fact that Eddie was at least three-quarters unbalanced, Mitch felt an unwelcome chill at his words.

LAURA WOUND HER WAY into the backyard she knew so well. The old magnolia tree still dominated the lush space, its glossy leaves and cream-colored flowers an elegant centerpiece to the towering oaks and pines.

Amid the box hedges and rosebushes, banana trees flung their fronds upward, demanding equal attention. This diversity of plants flourished in the humid days and warm nights. Traditional English flowers thrived next to tropical greenery.

But Laura couldn't really appreciate the beauty. Her mind was too full. Too confused.

She spotted Rhoda sitting at the round glass table beneath a fluttering umbrella. For a moment she imagined her aunt dressed in a long flowing gown, a wide-brimmed hat hiding her face from the sun, as she waited for that special beau who never arrived.

But in an instant the image was gone. Her aunt had never been married, but that didn't make her a long-suffering Southern belle.

Laura wasn't really sure why she was here, except that she needed to speak to her remaining link to the past. Her father, an only child, had been the sole member left in his family. His parents had been long dead by the time Laura was born. And her mother's family had been nearly as small, with Rhoda the only relative.

As Laura approached, Rhoda glanced up, her face easing into a smile. "You're just in time to join me for a glass of lemonade."

Laura returned her smile. "Not mint juleps on the veranda?"

Rhoda idly fanned herself with a straw fan that Laura recognized from her childhood. "And no bourbon balls beneath the pecan tree, either." She patted the chair beside her, a deep-cushioned rattan rocker.

Laura accepted the invitation. Easing the chair into a rocking motion, she recalled the days when, as a child, she and her mother had come to visit. A bittersweet wash of memories assailed her. Briefly she closed her eyes, remembering those carefree times.

"What is it, child?"

Laura shrugged, unable to voice her mountain of concerns.

"Is it Alex?" Rhoda persisted.

"Yes."

Rhoda leaned forward. "How is he?"

"He's lost weight," Laura admitted, knowing each ounce represented a foothold gone.

"Oh, Laura, I really thought the donor bank would have found a match by now."

Laura drew her fingers through the beaded condensation on her glass. "No, but we found something else."

Rhoda waited expectantly.

"I think we may have located my birth mother."

Rhoda set her glass down so abruptly the lemonade sloshed onto the table. "What?"

"We're not positive yet, but my instincts tell me it's her."

Rhoda cleared her throat. "What does Mitch think?"

"He says I shouldn't get my hopes up prematurely."

"Maybe he's right."

Laura stared at her aunt. "It sounds as though you don't want me to find her."

"That's not it, dear." Rhoda fiddled with the lemonade pitcher, before finally pushing it to the other side of the table. "I just don't want you to get hurt."

"Not finding a donor for Alex is what will hurt."

Rhoda glanced up. "Of course." She was quiet for a while, as her eyes took on a faraway gaze. "It seems like just yesterday that you were his age. Always into something, always laughing. It was such a happy time."

Laura placed one hand over Rhoda's. "It will be

a happy time again. As soon as we locate Alex's blood relatives.''

Rhoda's smile was wobbly. ''Then we'll have to pray that happens soon.'' She squeezed Laura's hand. ''Thank goodness you have Mitch to lean on through this. I told you he was a keeper. What would you have done without him?''

Laura wondered that, as well. Worse, she wondered what she would do when she eventually bade him farewell.

MITCH HELD THE court order in his hands. At last they had the approval to unseal Laura's birth records.

Laura was so anxious she could barely speak. She had been in much the same state during the three-hour drive to Austin, the state capital, where the vital records were maintained.

And so he had spoken to the clerk, who had thoroughly examined the document and then copied it before leaving to locate the birth certificate.

Now they were waiting, the time seeming to barely pass.

Laura stood suddenly. ''How long can it take?'' She started to walk toward the counter.

Mitch snagged her hand and pulled her back, not wanting her to agitate the bureaucrats. ''The clerk said it could be a while. If we bug them, they could make us wait all day.'' He stood, as well. ''Why don't we get some coffee.''

''I don't need any coffee,'' she snapped at him. Then her eyelids closed briefly as she drew in a deep breath. ''I'm sorry. I didn't mean to be so short with you. I feel as though I'm about to explode. And instead of being able to help myself, my fate…Alex's fate…rests in everyone else's hands."

He reached for one of her hands and gave it a gentle squeeze. "It's not always a bad thing to accept help from others."

He saw her swallow, saw the sheen of moisture in her eyes that she rapidly blinked away. Then she managed a half smile. "Maybe not."

"I spotted a coffee machine down the hall," he said, leading her that direction.

"You're awfully patient," she remarked. "I want everything to happen right this instant."

"That would be my preference," he agreed. "But I've been dealing with government agencies too long to hope things will work that way. Besides, this is information worth waiting for."

She met his gaze, another tremulous smile emerging. "You're right."

He dug in his pocket and located the change for the vending machine. Knowing how she took her coffee, he punched in the right combinations, then handed her the first cup.

When he had his coffee, she held up her cup, gently touching his. "To success."

Admiring her spirit, he nudged her cup in return.

Although they lingered over the coffee, when they returned to the document room, the clerk still hadn't emerged with the certificate.

Even though Mitch had recommended patience, his own was stretched to the limit as the hours passed. While statistical bureaus weren't known for their speed, he had never waited this long for an unsealed birth certificate.

Glancing at Laura, he could see the strain painted across her face.

"Something's wrong," she said, catching his gaze on her.

"You don't know that," he protested, but was having the same thought. Earlier, he had checked to make certain they hadn't been forgotten. The clerk had stared at Mitch uneasily before reassuring him that they were still searching for the document.

"You sense it, too," she responded.

Still looking into her eyes, he realized she had uncannily read his thoughts. "It normally doesn't take this long," he admitted.

She swallowed. "We've come so close."

He reached for her hand. "Don't waffle on me."

Although she didn't reply, she burrowed her hand more deeply into his.

And the wait continued.

Another hour passed and Mitch felt his own optimism dim. Laura was right. Something must be terribly wrong.

Just then the clerk who was helping them reappeared. Seeing the serious set to the man's face, Mitch felt his stomach sink, knowing their worst suspicions were about to be confirmed.

In unison, he and Laura stood and crossed to the counter.

The clerk glanced between them, his manner somber, his voice even more so. "We have searched extensively for your records."

Mitch and Laura waited.

"However, we haven't had any success," the man stated. "I have called on all our support staff and I have checked with my superiors."

Which was what had taken so long, Mitch realized. "And?"

"We have come to the conclusion that there is no original birth certificate to unseal."

"But I *was* born!" Laura blurted.

"No one's disputing that, ma'am." He held out a copy of her birth certificate that listed her adoptive parents. "But this is the only birth certificate relating to you that we have."

"But there should be an adoption file," Mitch protested.

"In adoptions, yes." The man's expression was grim. "However, we have no record of an adoption."

Laura's eyes grew wide. "No record?" she whispered.

The clerk shook his head. "No. Consequently, we have no other records pertaining to your birth."

It was what Mitch had suspected. An illegal adoption, the records altered, leaving absolutely no trail to follow.

He felt Laura sag against him. Putting his arm around her shoulders, he held her close. With his other hand he pulled out a card and handed it to the clerk. "If you find anything else. *Anything*," he stressed. "I can be reached twenty-four hours a day. We have a vital medical need for her records."

The clerk looked at Laura, his expression turning to one of sympathy. No doubt the man had figured out what Mitch had. In an illegal adoption, records were nearly impossible to uncover.

Mitch led Laura outside, hoping a rush of fresh air might put some color in her cheeks. But once outside, she turned to him, burying her face against his shoulder.

"Oh, Mitch!" she sobbed. "Why?"

Holding her quaking body, he wondered that, as well. As he had every time he had worked on uncovering an illegal adoption. But Mitch knew he had to move past the wondering. Because the next step they were being forced to take would be even worse.

CHAPTER EIGHTEEN

ELLEN GATELEY received the news without flinching. The exhumation had been approved by the appropriate government agencies. She had been grateful for Laura's invitation to drive with Mitch to the cemetery. It wasn't a good day to be alone.

It had come to this. If there was a baby in that grave who matched Barbara Gateley's DNA, Laura knew she had to accept the inevitable. She also would have no need to continue thinking about James Farley and their possible connection to each other.

The day was exceptionally sunny. It should be gloomy, overcast, Laura thought. There should be nothing bright and sunny about disturbing a grave, unearthing three decades of what had caused Barbara Gateley so much anguish.

Ellen Gateley stood to one side, silent tears sliding down her face as she watched them bring up the impossibly tiny coffin.

Mitch stood at Laura's side, his arm anchored around her, shoring her up as he had since they had learned the truth about her birth certificate.

Representatives from the district attorney's office and the police and sheriff's departments maintained a quiet, respectful presence. Looking around at the small group, Laura couldn't help wondering how many mourners had been here on that long-ago day. Had Barbara Gateley been surrounded by caring friends? Or had the small coffin been lowered in an equally lonely fashion?

As she watched, the lid was opened by one of the officials. His gasp was audible. Unable to wait a second longer, Laura broke Mitch's grasp and rushed forward.

This was it—the end of the wondering. Was the wrong baby buried here? Or was this Barbara Gateley's true child? Had Barbara just imagined the cries? Was this all just a horrible, incredibly painful wild-goose chase?

Nearing the casket, Laura felt her feet lag, then she stumbled. What if she and Mitch were wrong?

Could she bear to see and know the truth?

The man who had opened the coffin stepped back as she approached.

Heart pounding, scarcely breathing, she forced herself onward. Mitch and Ellen closed ranks beside her. The three of them took the last steps, a united if fearful front.

What Laura saw stopped her.

The pink, satin-lined coffin was empty!

Ellen Gateley swayed and Mitch reached out to steady her. Slowly Ellen lowered hands that had flown to her mouth to cover a gasp. "It's what Barbara believed all along! Her baby didn't die!"

The police photographer took more photos. Before and after shots, Laura realized numbly.

Mitch moved forward, once again placing an arm around her.

"How could this have happened?" Laura whispered, feeling as though they had disturbed far more than just the grave.

"Much as we initially guessed."

"But you said there were two stillborn babies," Laura told him.

"I said two stillborn deaths were recorded. Obviously, one was falsified."

Laura briefly closed her eyes, thinking of another mother's anguish. "And so you think I might have been right? That she was shown the other stillborn baby?"

"Probably. Distraught, she wouldn't have known it was a male baby since he was no doubt wrapped up, as you suggested," Mitch reminded her. "And remember, she had never seen her own baby. She only heard her cry."

Laura couldn't force her gaze away from the empty coffin. "But what about the family of the truly stillborn baby?"

"I highly doubt they knew anything about the deception. After the charade was played out, the perpetrators probably returned the baby to the morgue."

"And the rightful family never knew what deception was playing out." Laura completed the possible scenario, thinking how horribly reprehensible and sad the entire deed had been.

"It was an act without conscience," Mitch agreed grimly.

As they watched, Ellen Gateley knelt beside the grave, picking up a handful of loose dirt. Her head was bowed, and it appeared she was uttering a silent prayer.

Then she turned to them. "My sister suffered all her life because of this...this..." Apparently, she could find no word vile enough to describe the deception. "But she will rest easier knowing you have been found, Laura, that in some small way she can help you." Ellen straightened her shoulders, her resolve visible. "We will both help, no matter what the consequences."

MITCH FOUND HIMSELF again at the police station. He needed to bounce off a few ideas, and there was no one he trusted more than his ex-partner.

Randy extended his usual welcome, then listened as Mitch updated him on the situation.

"Whew!" was his initial comment.

"My thoughts exactly," Mitch agreed glumly.

"Sounds like you're digging into a pile of lit dynamite. You have a sudden penchant for putting your neck in a noose?"

"Not especially, but I'm not going to let that stop me."

Randy's eyes narrowed. "Is there something you aren't telling me about this client?"

"Such as?" Mitch replied, making certain his tone was casual.

"Such as why she has you tied in knots."

"I didn't say that!"

"You didn't have to," Randy informed him. He shoved a box of pistachios in Mitch's direction after taking a handful for himself. "I'd give both thumbs for a cigarette,'' he said mournfully as he pried the shell away from one nut.

''Women already think we're a little too closely related to apes,'' Mitch reminded him.

''Is that what she thinks?''

''She?'' Mitch asked, feigning ignorance.

Randy tilted back his chair. ''Just give me a name. I feel like I'm on some half-witted game show trying to guess.''

''Laura,'' Mitch admitted, knowing he couldn't keep this to himself, uncertain he wanted to. Perhaps he'd needed to discuss more than the case with Randy.

''So what's her story?''

Mitch lifted his brow.

''Right, you just told me her story. But how serious has it gotten between you?''

''I didn't say it was serious.''

''You didn't say you were the best cop ever to work in this precinct, but that's a fact, too.''

Mitch grinned sheepishly. ''You're just saying that because you got stuck with ailing Al Cookson.''

''You haven't lived till you've spent the day with a guy who stuffs meatball sandwiches in his face like they're sticks of gum. Jeez, I keep waiting for him to explode.'' Randy pulled his chair upright, planting his feet on the floor. ''But no changing the subject. Is this Laura the one?''

''I'm not sure there is a 'one.' ''

''Still the darling of all the ladies?''

Mitch waved away the description. ''I like women. I never made any secret of the fact.''

"And they like you," Randy commented. "So how does Laura feel about that?"

"She's got some scars from an unfaithful husband."

"Once burned, twice shy?"

"Something like that. The truth is she doesn't think she needs anyone."

"And what do you think?"

"You're a cop. You know there aren't too many happily-ever-afters. She's looking for a white knight, an instant family man."

Randy watched him in speculation. "And you don't think that's you?"

"What do I know about being a family man?"

"Just because your father bailed, it doesn't mean you can't be a good father."

Mitch shifted uncomfortably. "It also doesn't mean I'm what Laura wants."

"Don't you think you should let her decide that for herself?" Randy asked sagely.

Mitch took the advice into consideration but realized it was time to tuck away his personal concerns. Besides, Randy didn't know Laura. He couldn't see that Mitch was the total opposite of what she wanted in a man. "I need more than your advice on my love life."

Randy took the hint with rueful good humor. "Starting with?"

"James Farley."

Randy whistled. "You going to take on the big guns?"

Mitch couldn't halt a small flinch. "You think it'll be that bad?"

"If he's part of what you're trying to uncover, it would be wiser to play with that dynamite."

Mitch met his friend's gaze. "Then maybe you could hand me a stick. I'd like to review that hit-and-run accident again."

Randy's brows lifted. "In regard to James Farley? You realize his connections only begin with the commissioner. From there it's a very short leap to the governor, senators, you name it."

"I won't let your name get mixed into my inquiries."

Randy casually waved a hand in dismissal. "And when did I ever worry about my sterling reputation?"

"You're up for lieutenant, pal. I don't want to blow that."

"Neither do I. So you'd better do one hell of an investigation. You nail any big boys and maybe they'll hand me the commendation."

Mitch laughed. His friend didn't care about awards. He was one of the last of the truly good guys. A cop who wanted to change the world for the better. "You planning to help me, then?"

Randy's eyes were somber. "Count on it."

Sobered, Mitch met his gaze. If Randy thought he needed help to watch his back on this one, he really was tackling the forbidden. Yet at the same time Mitch knew he couldn't retreat. Laura and Alex were counting on him.

Realizing what he'd just thought hit him with stunning force. When had they become more important to him than his own safety? Insidiously, they had crept under his skin and into his heart. And what the hell was he going to do about it?

CHAPTER NINETEEN

LAURA FUSSED OVER ALEX, even more concerned about him than usual.

But Mitch was composed, by comparison positively tranquil. "Laura, he's just a little pale. Don't come unglued."

"He's had a fever," she said, fretting.

"I know what he needs," Mitch announced.

She looked at him uncertainly. "What?"

"A few hours at the zoo."

"The zoo?"

"You know, animals in cages. Sort of the same principle as Noah's ark, but no boat and lots less water."

"I'm not sure...."

"What do you say, champ?" Mitch picked up the toddler. "You want to go see the animals? Lions, tigers..."

"Tijers!" Alex agreed heartily.

"Shouldn't we be doing something—" she glanced at Alex "—about the investigation?"

"I've put out the word with my contacts, every Gateley we have found, and in case you haven't noticed, it's Sunday. Even I can't open certain doors on Sunday."

Still, she was reluctant, not wanting to waste a

precious moment. But it would be at least a few more days until they learned if Barbara Gateley was her mother. "I wish we had the DNA results back."

"An even better reason to go to the zoo. It will take your mind off those things we can't control. And what better excuse to escape Mrs. Plummer?"

She glanced again at Alex. He seemed so at ease in Mitch's arms. And she had to admit he did look a little better since the zoo had been mentioned. She wavered. "I guess it couldn't hurt to take a small break."

"Try to contain your enthusiasm," Mitch replied dryly.

Realizing how ungracious she sounded, Laura amended her words. "It's actually a lovely idea. Shall we take along a picnic lunch?"

"And miss out on hot dogs and cotton candy?"

He appeared so horrified at the idea that she found herself laughing.

Mitch tapped her on the nose. "That's better. You were looking positively grim." He tickled Alex's tummy. "And we don't take grumps to the zoo, do we, bud?"

Alex chortled.

Watching them, Laura marveled again at what Mitch brought out in both her and her son. The three of them were a picture of the perfect little family. To think that they might never be was heartbreaking.

Ridiculously, she felt her throat thicken with emotion. Shaking her head to clear her thoughts, she held up her hands in surrender. "Fine, I'm outnumbered. But I do have one demand."

Mitch's expression grew serious. "And what's that?"

"We ride the little train around the park." She paused for effect. "Or you get dunked in the lake with the ducks."

Surprise took him aback for a moment. Then he shouted with laughter, Alex joining in even though he didn't know the joke.

MITCH DECIDED that at least a hundred years had gone by since he'd visited a zoo. But the wait had been worth it.

Seeing Laura's face crinkle in disgust at the snake house, her reaction to the two-toed sloth, her fascination with the beautiful cats in the tiger and leopard house and her faint embarrassment at the monkey house. He loved that slightly prim side of her, especially since he knew how passionate she was. He hadn't known such a woman still existed. She was as rare as she was lovely.

And Alex was a hoot a minute. Everything was a new experience for him.

"Haven't you ever taken him to the zoo?" Mitch questioned.

"Yes, but it was before he was sick. And babies don't have real long memories."

"Ah. So we're making new memories."

Laura's eyes brimmed with questions at those words.

But he didn't have any answers. Especially when he knew she wasn't in the market for a man like him to share her life.

Alex saw the elephants and his little legs pumped

in an effort to stand up in the stroller. "L'lfants!" he hollered.

Laura squatted beside Alex's stroller. "Yes, sweetie. Elephants."

Mitch spotted the sign for the petting zoo. "Shall we head that way?"

She agreed and soon they were amid knee-high goats and small, timid deer. Alex was particularly fascinated with the abbreviated horns on the goats, nearly climbing out of the stroller in his excitement. Laura was fighting a losing battle to keep his fingers detached from the animals' horns.

Mitch bent over and picked up Alex from the stroller. "Gotta be nice to the animals, champ. Just like your puppy. Can't pull her tail, can we?"

Alex shook his head, but he was still looking longingly at the goats, his body stretching in their direction.

"It takes a few times for him to get it," Laura commented. Then she smiled, her eyes soft, a beguiling blue. "But that's the way he learns."

Unable to resist, Mitch leaned forward and kissed her gently.

Laura's eyes widened in surprise, but she didn't draw back. Instead, her expression grew even softer, her eyes seeming to fill with dark secrets and womanly mystery.

"Goat!" Alex shouted as a small group scampered away. His outcry coincided with the moment Mitch deepened the kiss.

Mitch grinned. "I'll try not to take that personally. Why don't we just say he's protective of his mother?"

Laura grinned, as well, looking younger and more carefree than she had in weeks. "Don't you want to know if I share his opinion?"

His gaze didn't waver. "I think I'll take my chances."

She moistened her lips, then eased them into an incredibly gentle smile. "Wise move."

"Can I buy you some lunch?"

Her smile curved in a way that did something wicked to his insides. "What did you have in mind?"

Mitch had to resist the reply that jumped to the forefront of his thoughts. The zoo was hardly the place to tell her that she was driving him wild with desire. Instead he resorted to a safe suggestion. "Hot dogs?"

Her voice was suddenly stern. "You mean disgustingly greasy hot dogs overflowing with chili and cheese and sauerkraut?"

He nodded cautiously, wishing she didn't always have to be in maternal mode.

She grinned. "Sounds wonderful."

Loving this side of her, he matched her grin. "I haven't met a woman since my sisters who appreciated a real hot dog."

Still smiling, she slanted a questioning gaze at him. "Your sisters? As in multiple sisters?"

"Five."

She stopped short. "Five? You have *five* sisters?"

"Yep."

"And how many boys in your family?"

"Just me."

She laughed. "Well, you and your father."

His smile faded. "No. Just me."

Concern replaced the amusement in her eyes. "I'm sorry. I didn't know."

"He didn't die, Laura. He cut out on us."

"That must have been very hard for you," she replied gently. "You must have missed him terribly."

"I never knew him, Laura. Wasn't much to miss."

This time she took his hand, leaning her head against his shoulder as they walked toward the hot dog stand.

And for the first time when discussing his father, Mitch didn't feel quite as bereft.

THE DAY AT THE ZOO lengthened, and by the time they returned to Laura's house, Alex had fallen asleep in his car seat. There was a shared sense of comfort among them as they entered the house through the back door in the kitchen.

But that sense of comfort was shattered when Laura flicked the lights on.

The table, chairs and breakfront were upended. The cabinet doors were flung open, their contents scattered over the counters and onto the floor. Drawers had been emptied and tossed on the floor, as well.

"Wh-what?" Laura stuttered, shock and disbelief seizing her.

Mitch turned and pulled her from the house.

"But—" she began to protest.

Mitch didn't heed her protests, instead guiding her to the car. After yanking open the back door, he placed Alex and his car seat in the rear. Then he shoved his cell phone into Laura's hands. "Call 911."

"But I—"

"Now, Laura!" he ordered.

Hands shaking, she began to dial.

Mitch ran quickly and silently back through the yard. Reaching into the gun belt at the rear of his waist, he pulled out his gun and checked the safety.

His years of experience on the police force kicked in.

Keeping to the exterior walls, he skirted the corner and approached the back door. It hung open as they'd left it. Carefully he entered, but nothing inside the kitchen had changed.

Using caution, he made a systematic search of the house. What he saw sickened him. Even Alex's room had been ravaged.

Going back into the kitchen, he heard a faint whimper in the pantry. Pistol aimed, he kicked open the door.

Pal wagged her tail in pathetic welcome. Mitch exhaled. Thank God the goons hadn't decided to kill the pup.

"Hey, Pal. Alex is going to be glad to see you." He scooped up the dog, accepting the grateful licks.

Just then, he heard the shrill sound of police sirens approaching the house.

Rejoining Laura, he saw how frightened she was.

The police cautioned them to stay back as they went inside, but Mitch knew they wouldn't find anything.

"I've never had my house burglarized," she told him, clutching Alex close.

Mitch weighed the alternatives and knew he had to tell her the truth. "This wasn't a simple burglary."

Fear vaulted into panic. "It wasn't?"

"No. Whoever did this was looking for something specific. Not television sets or stereo equipment. You don't rip open furniture cushions if all you want is something to pawn."

"What *were* they looking for? I don't have anything valuable hidden."

"That depends on your definition of *valuable*." He gripped her arms. "Laura, we're digging up secrets people went to a hell of a lot of trouble to bury. And we've obviously hit a nerve. Tonight, they were probably looking for any documentation we found, or…"

She gulped. "Or what?"

"Or this was a warning to back off."

Her hold on Alex grew even more protective. "But I can't! We can't!"

"Laura, these people mean business."

"So do I!" she shot back. "I won't be intimidated. They can tear up my house all they want. I'm not going to stop searching until Alex is well!"

He sighed, thinking of the consequences, knowing he had no more choice than she did. "As soon as the police come out, go pack a bag. One for you, one for Alex. And don't you have a portable crib thing? The one Mrs. Plummer uses."

"Yes." Confusion clouded her features. "Where are we going?"

"Home with me," he replied decisively.

"I can't—"

"Yes, Laura you can. And you will. Whoever did this will probably come back. I can stay here, but with all the entrances, the first-floor windows, your house is more vulnerable than my apartment."

She still looked undecided.

"If you really want to save Alex, you'll do as I ask."

The police were heading toward them.

She glanced searchingly at Mitch one more time and then headed inside, leaving him to deal with the police.

After the report was completed, Mitch put Alex in the car seat and helped Laura into the car, as well. After stowing their bags, he drove away quickly, keeping Laura's hand tight in his.

He regretted that his apartment was so neglected, but at least it was safe. For now. Since he had always had his mail sent to his office address, he doubted anyone tracing him would realize that he had moved from his condominium. It wasn't a long-term guarantee, but it gave him time to decide where Laura and Alex could be protected.

Once at his building, he made Laura stay in the lobby while he checked out his place. He was pretty certain it was safe, but he remained cautious.

The doorman eyed him uncertainly when he returned. "I was telling your girlfriend—no visitors here today or in a week for that matter."

"Thanks," Mitch replied curtly. "Could you get the bags?"

The man nodded without a great deal of enthusiasm. "Sure."

Since Laura was clinging to Alex, Mitch picked up the portable crib and the puppy, then put his hand under Laura's elbow and guided her to the elevator.

Once inside, Mitch put the puppy down, then tipped the doorman generously, asking him to keep an eye out for any strangers asking to see him or requesting access to the apartment. Then he set the dead bolts.

When he turned around, Laura met his gaze, her own shaken. "I just can't believe this is happening."

He hugged her, Alex between them, sleepy but contented. Then he ruffled the child's hair. "But the danger's worth the risk, isn't it?"

She nodded but didn't speak.

"I'll set up the crib thing," he said, filling the void. "Why don't you relax."

Laura still looked shaken, and worse, uncertain.

Mitch took the crib into the low-lit alcove between the dining room and his bedroom. It was a quiet place where Alex wouldn't be disturbed, yet it was close enough to the bedroom that Laura would feel reassured.

On impulse, Mitch detoured into the bathroom, where he filled the tub with steaming, hot water. Scrounging through some unpacked boxes in the closet he managed to find one candle, a fat pillar, which he lit.

"The apartment is really scruffy," he apologized, returning to the living room.

She peered around as though noticing at it for the first time. "It's fine."

Mitch knew it wasn't. But he also knew she needed to unwind. Luckily, Alex's little head drooped against her shoulder.

Mitch knelt beside Laura. "I think it's time to put him to bed."

Glancing down at her son, she seemed surprised to see that he had fallen asleep. Still, she was reluctant to release him. "Yes, I suppose."

"I have the crib set up," he told her, reaching for Alex.

As she relinquished him, again she was reluctant.

"Why don't you come with me," he suggested, leading the way.

In a few minutes, Alex was tucked into the crib, his baby sighs signaling sleep. Pal curled up beside the crib. It was hard to tell if the dog was in the role of protector, or the one seeking protection.

"Now it's your turn," Mitch told her.

"I can't sleep yet," she protested.

"I didn't think so." Taking her elbow, he guided her into the bathroom.

Although he didn't have any sort of scented bath salts to toss in the water, the candle lent a subtle tang of almonds and amaretto.

She turned in surprise.

"For you," he replied to her unspoken question.

"But—"

"No arguments." He pointed to the thick terry robe that hung on a hook. "The robe's for you. But I do have a few house rules."

She tilted her face upward.

Mitch couldn't resist cupping her cheek, tracing its soft lines. "Rule number one, you have to soak until you're absolutely pruny."

She didn't smile, but he could see a fraction of her despair fading.

"Rule number two, no worrying about Alex while you're soaking. Leave that to me. I won't be more than a room from him while you're in the tub."

Slowly she nodded.

"And most important, rule number three, no rubber duckies. If you have the urge to play, I'm only a shout away."

Her lip curled in ever so faint a motion.

Knowing it was the most he could hope for, Mitch dropped a kiss on the top of her head. "Now, I'm outta here." Closing the door behind him, he waited until he heard the rustle of clothing.

He checked on Alex and saw that his quiet sighs had escalated into tiny baby snores. The day had been exhausting and Mitch guessed the child wouldn't wake until morning.

Carrying Laura's bags into the bedroom, he tried to look at the room through fresh eyes. And those eyes were disapproving. Quickly, he stripped the bed and put fresh linen in place. Then he picked up some discarded clothing and stuffed it out of sight in a hamper. The quick freshening wasn't a complete facelift, but it was an improvement.

While Laura bathed, Mitch searched his kitchen. He unearthed two wineglasses and a fairly respectable bottle of Merlot. After filling one glass, he carried it to the bathroom, and knocked gently on the door.

A moment passed and she answered softly. "Come in."

The sight of her in his tub nearly made him spill the wine. But he knew it wasn't the time for romance. She needed comfort, not seduction. So he knelt beside the tub. "Good. Almost pruny."

Her voice was dry. "I'm happy you approve."

He offered her the glass. "Oh, I definitely approve."

She cast her eyes downward. "I'm glad."

Remembering his resolve to remain a gentleman, he focused on keeping his tone light. "House rule number four, all baths must be accompanied by wine."

She lifted her face. "You have an awful lot of rules."

He smiled. A fraction of the real Laura was struggling to return. "I forgot you're such a rebel."

She sipped the wine. "I didn't think it was possible, but I am relaxing."

"You forget. I'm the master."

A shadow eclipsed the beginnings of calm in her eyes. Then she glanced away from him. "Of course. Silly of me not to remember."

He wasn't certain why she had closed up again. So he stood and turned to the door. Before he left, he looked back at her, guessing she would soon be ready to get out of the tub. "I'll bring in some towels in a few minutes."

She nodded, but he had the sense that he had somehow disturbed her relaxation.

Once in the kitchen, he pulled open the shuttered doors that concealed his washer and dryer. He located two large bath sheets, then put them in the dryer on high heat.

When they were warmed thoroughly, he retrieved the towels and returned to the bathroom. ''Cabana boy,'' he announced, entering the room.

She was just stepping out of the tub, and eyed him in surprise.

His throat dried, his blood warmed, and for a moment all he could do was stand and gape. Reminding himself of his resolve, he edged forward and draped one of the warm bath sheets around her.

''Thank you,'' she replied in a shaky voice.

But he didn't speak; instead, he moved the towel over her shoulders, blotting her soft skin.

She turned around and he focused on the spot where the towel dipped between her shoulder blades. Mitch followed that dip, slowly caressing her skin, with only the towel between his hands and his fantasies.

The towel inched down her back, over her hips, then teased the length of her legs. Mitch turned her to face him. He slid the towel over her fragile collarbone, aware of the leaping of her pulse beneath his fingers. The curve of her breasts tempted him, but Mitch knew he couldn't continue. If he did, he would lift her into his arms, carry her to the fresh bed and rumple it beyond repair.

Remembering his resolve to remain a gentleman, he stepped back. But he couldn't control the hoarseness in his voice. ''I'll leave the rest to you.''

She blinked as though startled, but made no move to stop him.

However, there was no relief in his escape. Back

in the kitchen, he downed the wine in his glass in a rapid gulp. But he couldn't stand still.

He stalked into the living room and punched the buttons on his stereo, making certain the volume wouldn't waken Alex, and soon the sound of Celtic music filled the room. It suited his mood. The notes of lost but noble causes.

Laura appeared in the doorway of the bedroom. Damp curls dangled enticingly on each side of her face, curls that had escaped from the topknot she had secured. As he studied her, she fiddled with the overly long sleeves of the robe. "I want to go to bed now."

"Sure," he replied, wondering if he could feel more awkward. His gaze traveled to the couch. Hers followed.

She crossed the room, her hand extended toward him.

He moved forward, as well, until he could clasp her hand.

She moistened her lips. "I don't want to be alone tonight, Mitch."

Mitch felt his resolve disintegrate. They were only a few steps from his bed. And even less distance to unlocking his heart forever.

LAURA TOLD HERSELF that her eyes were wide-open. She knew what she was getting into and she could handle it. So Mitch wasn't into forevers. She still had today. And she desperately needed today.

How was it that his hands were simultaneously strong yet gentle? And how did he know to hold her in such a way that her breath caught, threatening to push the very air from her lungs?

Questions whirled, but Laura wasn't looking for answers. She needed his strength, the comfort he offered. And more.

It was the latter that made her open the robe and push it from her shoulders, to pool at her feet. It also fueled her desire to remove his clothes, to fit her heated flesh against his.

She recognized the questions in his eyes, but she acknowledged it wasn't a time of promises. Instead, she longed for him to obliterate those questions.

Where he would be gentle, she was impatient. Still damp from her warm bath, her skin glided against his. Again it was like the stunning intensity of their first encounter. His hands ignited a passion she hadn't known she possessed.

But the sensation wasn't caused by slick sophistication or any sort of practiced technique. Instead, his incredible tenderness, coupled with an assurance that made him capable of endless giving.

And that made her want to return the fountain of feeling. She stroked her hands over his broad chest, admiring his tight abs and trim waist. Then her fingers danced down his hips and over muscled thighs. When she reached the tender skin of his inner thighs, she heard him suck in a deep breath.

A purely feminine instinct basked in the power to make him react so.

Then his arms reached down to pull her up, and cradle her over him, hipbones to hipbones, flesh seeking flesh.

For a moment her head was thrown back, then

she lowered it to meet his kiss, one that rendered a tender promise of its own.

Closing her eyes, she wished he believed in family, in forevers. And just as desperately she told herself it didn't matter...for the moment.

CHAPTER TWENTY

MITCH REPLACED the phone receiver, frustration unsettling him. The lab still didn't have the results on Barbara Gateley's DNA testing, and he hadn't received any worthwhile responses in his effort to locate any Gateleys related to her.

Unfortunately, Barbara Gateley was from a very small branch of a very small family. In ways, it was too bad James Smith wasn't Laura's father. Mitch could find Smiths without even trying.

He glanced around his trashed office. Whoever had broken into Laura's house had done a number on his office the same day. Ironic that just twenty-four hours ago Laura had straightened up all the piles. Now the place looked like a garbage heap.

But whoever had done this didn't know he carried the most vital case papers in the glove compartment of his car. So Laura's original birth certificate was still safe. Mitch was certain that was what they had been after.

He crossed to the window and looked down the grassy slope to the minuscule pond. Laura and Alex were waiting there. He hadn't wanted her further upset by seeing the condition of his office.

Mitch suspected she would soon question the safety of his apartment. He still believed his recent move hadn't yet been detected. He hadn't filed a change of address. The utilities were included in the rent. Even his phone bill came to his office address. Of course, he was no fool. He knew that in time a determined investigator could find him.

But at this point, he guessed someone was looking for papers rather than Laura or Alex.

And he had an inkling that he knew the only person who might have other important papers in her possession.

Ellen Gateley.

Stepping outside, Alex locked the door behind him. Not that it would do any good, he acknowledged. For the professionals who had already broken in, he could have just as easily left a sign saying Come On In.

It didn't take long to collect Laura and Alex. She was quiet, as she had been all morning.

No doubt she was regretting the previous evening spent in his arms. But he couldn't bring himself to regret the same.

Once at Ellen Gateley's house, he detained Laura as she was about to get out of the car. "Are you all right?"

She met his gaze, then slipped her hand up to trace his jaw. "Don't worry so. It will spoil your carefree image."

"Image isn't all it's cracked up to be," he replied soberly.

She searched his eyes, before finally standing on tiptoe to kiss his cheek.

Mitch picked up Alex, and with his free hand he

sought Laura's. Together they approached the house.

Again Ellen Gateley was cordial, but Mitch could see the anxiety she barely kept hidden.

After pleasantries were exchanged, she looked at them expectantly. "I would like to think you're here simply to visit, but I'm afraid that isn't the case."

Mitch met her eyes, knowing the woman deserved a direct answer. "Actually, we're here to see if your sister left any other papers or diaries."

Barbara sighed. "Yes, but I thought we could wait for the results of the DNA testing before I passed them on."

"Something has happened that makes that difficult." Briefly, Mitch described the break-ins.

Ellen looked truly horrified. More telling, she looked frightened herself. "But what does that have to do with Barbara's papers?"

"We don't believe whoever did this was hunting for easily pawned objects. They wanted something specific."

"Like my mother's papers," Laura stated softly.

Ellen bit her lip. "I'm just not sure...."

Mitch hated what he was about to say but knew it was necessary. "The papers may be safer with us."

The fear in Ellen's eyes escalated. "Safer?"

He gentled his voice. "Can you tell us why you moved here, Ellen?"

She stood abruptly, her composure dissolving. Then she walked to the window. "You may have noticed that this is a rather bland neighborhood."

"One a person could melt into and practically disappear," Mitch commented.

She dropped her head. "Yes. At least, I thought so when I chose it. My thinking was that if I could become like a chameleon, I might escape notice."

"Does this have something to do with Barbara's death?"

Ellen looked at him, then her gaze lingered on Laura. "My sister was haunted for thirty years by that cry. And as each year passed, she became more and more certain that she hadn't imagined it, that her baby had been born alive. Perhaps if she had been told that the child had died after birth, she would have believed the story, but as it was..." Ellen turned again to look out the window. "About six months before she died, Barbara became very vocal. She was demanding answers. From the doctors, the hospital, anyone who would listen. Someone contacted her, told her they had information for her." Ellen slowly faced them, her lips quivering. "Barbara drove out to meet the person. The meeting place was far outside of town, an isolated spot. I told her she shouldn't go. Or at least she shouldn't go alone. But she said the person wouldn't talk unless she came by herself. And she wouldn't listen to reason."

"And?" Mitch prompted, though he knew the outcome of the story.

"The next thing I knew the police were calling, saying there had been an accident."

"But you didn't believe it was an accident," Laura offered in a quiet, horrified voice.

"No. I tried to tell the police, but they thought I

was simply overwrought.'' She glanced down at her hands. "After the funeral I went to her house. But someone else had been there first.'' She raised her eyes to meet Laura's. "It was the same sort of break-in you described. It wasn't a burglary. Someone had ripped apart everything in the house, searching.''

"So you haven't any of her papers?'' Laura asked in a heartbroken tone.

"The only wise thing she did was to give me all her papers before she went to the rendezvous. For safekeeping, she said.'' Ellen's lips quivered again. "Maybe in some way she knew she was stepping into danger. But nothing would dissuade her.''

"So you do have her papers?'' Mitch asked.

Ellen nodded. "And her diaries.'' She turned back toward the window. "I know you'll think me a terrible coward, but after I saw what had happened to her house, to Barbara herself, I was afraid.''

"So afraid that you moved here,'' Mitch concluded.

Again she nodded. "It's foolish I know. Anyone could find me. You did.''

"Which is why the papers might be safer in our possession,'' Mitch told her.

When Ellen looked at them her face signaled that she had come to a decision. "You're right, of course.''

As they sat in tight silence, she left the room. Several minutes later she returned with a large box of detergent soap. She managed a rueful smile. "I'm no Mata Hari, but I figured the box might be a good disguise. I keep it out in plain sight in the laundry room.''

"People often overlook the obvious," Laura agreed.

"My thoughts exactly," Ellen replied. "That's why I covered the books with powdered detergent. You'll have a time shaking all the granules out of the diaries."

Laura smiled. "That's very clever."

"But I'll feel better knowing the diaries are in safer hands."

"Speaking of safety," Mitch began. "Anyone you can stay with? Someone not easily traced?"

Ellen's face sagged. "Do you really think I must?"

"I don't know, but I wouldn't feel right leaving you alone," Mitch countered. "And I couldn't be certain you'd be safe at my apartment, either. We will be gone while I'm conducting the investigation. I don't think it would be wise for you to be there by yourself."

"As you're aware, we have pitifully few relatives," Ellen replied.

"Friends?" Laura queried.

A completely new expression crossed her face. "Well…" She met their gazes, slightly embarrassed. "I had a neighbor before, someone I think I can trust."

"Then it might be a good idea to see if she's agreeable," Mitch suggested.

"It's a 'he,'" Ellen corrected, even more embarrassed. "He's a former neighbor, a widower who lost his wife a few years back."

"Can he be trusted to keep your presence confidential?" Mitch questioned.

"Yes, I believe so. He will probably wonder about the secrecy, but he wouldn't violate it."

"You can tell him as much as you feel comfortable," Mitch said. "It may make the situation easier."

Ellen nodded.

"And having someone you can trust and depend on makes a world of difference," Laura offered.

Mitch pivoted to meet her gaze, wondering if even a fraction of her words were directed at him.

"You're right, of course. I'll ask him," Ellen decided.

Mitch tore his gaze from Laura. "Would you mind calling him while we're here, Ellen? I'd rather not leave until we know you've made arrangements. Also, you won't want to take your car there, and we can drive you."

"I hadn't thought of that!" she exclaimed.

"Parking your car at his house would be equivalent to posting a sign in his yard announcing your presence."

"Good point," she agreed. Then, looking more than a bit hesitant, she retreated to make the phone call.

While she was gone, Mitch exerted all his self-control and didn't ask Laura if she had been referring to him. Could she possibly be letting down her guard, even allowing herself to lean a tad?

A short time later Ellen returned, her face suffused with softness and gentle color. "He's perfectly agreeable," she announced. "In fact, he was rather horrified by what I confided and said that if I didn't come there, he would come here.''

Laura and Mitch exchanged smiles. The man sounded a tad smitten.

"Do you need some help packing?" Laura asked.

"That would be nice," Ellen replied, and together the women retreated.

It didn't take long for Ellen to pack or for them to drop her at her friend's home. For just a former neighbor, the man was very solicitous, assuring them that Ellen would never be out of his sight.

"We probably just helped him as much as her," Mitch commented as they drove away from the charming neighborhood.

"Do men really need an edge?" she questioned idly.

"Sometimes they need an entire bloody advantage," Mitch replied, thinking he certainly did. At least with her. It wasn't something he'd required with other women. But she wasn't like the previous women in his life.

"Mmm," she murmured.

"Laura, I want to take you and Alex somewhere safe while I go to my office."

"We'll be safe with you," she protested.

He sighed. "I can't be sure of that. And I also have to check with my street contacts, which isn't a baby-friendly activity."

"Oh," she replied in a small voice.

He laid a hand over hers. "Perhaps Mrs. Plummer might be ready to see the little guy again."

She blinked. "I haven't even thought about her since that call to tell her not to come in. I suppose we could see if it would be all right to visit with her while you're doing the macho thing.''

"It's not macho. It's necessary," he corrected, as she activated her cell phone. Even more now than before. Because before they had been the pursuers, rather than the pursued.

MITCH KNEW the instant he entered his office that he wasn't alone. It wasn't simply the scent in the air or the way the hair on the back of his neck stood at attention or the subtle changes in the papers strewn across his desk.

It was all those things—and more. It was a gut instinct that couldn't be taught, only sensed.

Automatically, he reached for the revolver at his waist.

"That won't be necessary." Although the voice was that of a cultured person, probably even Harvard educated, an unmistakable nuance of Texas remained. The sign of a native.

So a cultured native had broken into his office. It wasn't particularly comforting.

"You have me at an advantage," Mitch said, his eyes scanning for and then resting on the man. "You know who I am."

"My name is David Farley."

The reply shouldn't have surprised him. Yet it did.

The dark-haired man was in his late thirties, impeccably dressed and expensively put together, from his precision-cut hair to the thousand-dollar loafers he wore with ease. "I suspect you know why I'm here."

"Why don't you tell me," Mitch countered.

"As I see it, you have a client who's gotten you into deep water—dangerously deep water. Your inquiries haven't gone unnoticed. In fact, they're causing quite a bit of trouble for you. I understand an examination of your private investigator's license is imminent. However, if you switch clients, you could find yourself not only out of trouble but also financially rewarded."

"Switch clients?" Mitch questioned. This was an angle he hadn't expected.

"I want Laura Kelly to back off," David Farley announced. "And I'm willing to pay you enough to make certain she does."

"Doing your father's dirty work for him?"

But David didn't react—not even a flicker of distaste. "I am set to inherit my father's entire fortune, Mr. Tucker. I don't intend to let anything stand in the way of that. I'm prepared to offer you $100,000 to make certain that Laura Kelly remains out of the picture."

"You realize she may be your sister?" Mitch asked, wondering what made this stuffy, self-proclaimed aristocrat tick.

Farley shrugged one elegant shoulder. "I have no need for more relatives, Mr. Tucker."

And he didn't sound too fond of the ones he did have, Mitch noted. Except for their ability to leave him wealthy. "But she may need you."

David Farley didn't miss a beat. "No doubt. The Farley fortune seems to bring out need in a great many."

"Not all need is monetary," Mitch shot back.

"You don't look like a fool, Mr. Tucker. I'm offering you more money than this two-bit operation can earn you in years."

Mitch felt a moment's temptation. Not to sell out Laura, but to take the bribe to mislead David Farley. But he sensed that rather than protecting Laura, he would be putting her in more danger. "This may surprise you, but the Farley money can't buy everything."

David Farley possessed remarkable control. But the set of his jaw and the slight accompanying tic betrayed him. "Then you are a fool. Make no mistake, though. You haven't heard the last of me." He crossed the room, then paused at the door. "And if Laura Kelly pursues any claim to the Farley family, she will regret it."

A chill lingered in the room after he left. Farley's threats had not been idle. It was also painfully clear that the man would not consider a child's fate any of his concern.

With a sinking heart, Mitch pondered how he would pass this news on to Laura.

CHAPTER TWENTY-ONE

MITCH HAD LOCATED the Gateley second cousins. Only two remained in Texas, but Mitch had worked tirelessly until he'd found the others, who were strung out across the country. The family was small, but it was spread out. With Ellen's assistance, each one agreed to be tested as a possible donor.

Laura tried to be patient while waiting for the results. But the anxiety stirred, until she thought she might explode. It didn't help that she'd had to practically abandon her own home.

Convincing Mitch to accompany her to her house today had taken all of her persistence. And then he had insisted on her leaving Alex with Mrs. Plummer.

"This isn't a good idea," he muttered for at least the dozenth time.

"I told you I need some more things."

His eyes continued to scan the exterior, shifting uneasily. "I still don't like it." He started toward the house. When she began to follow, he stopped. "Wait until I check it out."

"It's the middle of the day," she protested.

"This may surprise you, but crooks don't operate only in the dark."

"But it looks perfectly fine."

He rolled his eyes. "Humor me, okay?"

In a few minutes, he returned.

"Well?" she asked.

"No one's in there right now," he admitted.

She tried not to sound smug. "I told you it looked all right."

But he was frowning. "It's difficult to determine, but things seem to have been shifted. I think someone has been back since the initial break-in. Probably to see if anything had been overlooked the first time."

She eyed the house uneasily. "Maybe it just appears that way because of all the mess."

"Let's get in, get what you need and get out." As Mitch spoke, he scanned the street.

"What are you looking for?"

"Anyone who's looking for us."

Chilled, she hurried beside him as they entered the house. The sight of all her possessions practically destroyed was sickening. Taking a deep breath, she headed toward her bedroom.

At the same time, Mitch veered toward the nursery. She could hear noises from the room, and was curious what he was doing. But she concentrated on quickly pulling clothes from her closet and drawers.

Glancing around the destroyed room, she wondered again at the kind of people who could do this sort of thing. Frightened, she snapped her bag shut.

Mitch was emerging from the nursery just as she crossed the threshold of her bedroom. "Are you ready to go?"

She gestured to the room behind him. "No. I have to get a few items for Alex."

He held up an overstuffed bag. "I packed for him."

"Clothes?" she asked.

"Yep."

She started toward him. "He'll need toys, as well."

"Got 'em," Mitch replied.

"And his books."

He nodded.

"And that little bear he sleeps with."

"Ditto," Mitch said.

Suddenly, she was overwhelmed by this man, who had stepped into their lives and taken the time and care to know her son's needs so well. Ridiculously, she felt her eyes tear up.

Mitch edged forward. "Are you okay?"

She made certain her smile was bright. "Sure. It's just difficult to see my home looking like this."

He seemed to accept the excuse. "Right. So, let's get out of here."

"Okay. Will you grab Alex's high chair?"

He did, his hands now filled with Alex's belongings.

They were on their way to the front door, when she suddenly remembered something. "Wait, Mitch. I left my sunglasses in my car. It'll only take a minute to grab them."

He sighed, that sound only males could make when humoring a woman. If they hadn't been surrounded by the savaged remains of her home, she would have smiled.

Laura walked into the garage from the connecting

door in the rear hallway. She reached for the car door handle—

The connecting door flung open at the same instant, slamming against the wall.

Startled, she dropped her hand and spun around.

Mitch flung himself through the doorway.

Immediately frightened, she shrank back. "What is it?"

"Don't open the car," he warned.

Laura wondered if he had gone over the edge. She put her hand back on the door handle. "I just want my sunglasses."

"And you might get a lot more."

"What are you talking about?"

Instead of answering, he gently pried her fingers from the handle. "Stand over there," he instructed, pointing to the connecting door.

The grimness on his face told her not to argue. When she stepped away, he examined the door handle, then slid beneath the car.

"What is it?" she whispered, not certain why she was keeping her voice down, nonetheless scared.

"The car's been wired," he replied shortly as he got to his feet.

"Wired?"

"Someone wanted to make sure you weren't going to drive away. Ever."

She could feel her eyes widen, first in disbelief, then horror. "You don't mean…"

He met her eyes. "If I'm right, it was set to blow when you opened the door."

"But I could have been holding Alex!" she cried.

This went beyond belief, beyond fear. And suddenly she couldn't breathe.

Mitch was next to her in seconds. "You're hyperventilating, Laura." Not wanting to lift the large, rolling garage door in case it, too, was wired, he pulled her back into the house and then outside into the fresh air. She was still gasping. He tugged off his sweater and fashioned a sort of tent that held the air in.

Even though Laura was gulping in huge drafts of air, she couldn't breathe.

Mitch yanked the sweater over her head. She nearly panicked, but he held her hands, his quiet voice assuring her she would be all right.

In a few moments her strangled breathing eased, finally returning to near normal. Mitch's gentle hands smoothed her hair back in place.

Still stricken, she stared at him in horror. "What do we do now? Call the police?"

"We call my ex-partner, Randy. It might be best not to let whoever did this know you're shook."

"How would they know?" she questioned, still shuddering, still unable to believe what had almost happened.

"The Farleys have powerful connections."

"*They* did this?" She didn't believe it was possible to be more horrified, yet she was.

Mitch took her hands, warming the cold skin. "I don't know."

Meeting his eyes, she saw that he was answering honestly. "I hate to think I might be related to people who could act without conscience," Laura cried. "It's worse than having no relatives at all."

Mitch's expression remained grim. "What if they're your only hope?"

That very hope was dissipating. She met Mitch's gaze, not hiding her uncertainty and indecision. "What are we going to do? What should I do?"

MITCH GRAPPLED with his choices. He could be Laura's white knight.

Or he could accept the bundle of cash that had just come by messenger.

Apparently, David Farley thought everyone had his price. He had tossed in another $50,000 to sweeten the bribe. God knows, Mitch could use the money. He could redeem his business, even his car. Yet the gleaming pile of green seemed almost obscene.

An image of Laura's face instantly came to mind—her eyes that were just beginning to show trust; the way she had placed herself in his hands, believing he could protect them. Laura's image was followed swiftly by one of Alex—his toothy grin, his chubby arms held out to Mitch in welcome.

"Hell," he swore to no one in particular.

"Hell," the parrot repeated, swinging from side to side.

"You said it, Morgan." He slid the money back into the envelope, then stuffed it inside his jacket. It was time to pay Farley a visit.

About to leave the office, he had another thought. He picked up Morgan's cage, threw the cover over it and carried the bird to the car. He suspected his office would be hit again, probably more severely than on the last visit. Morgan might not be so lucky this time.

None of them might be.

DAVID FARLEY'S secretary told Mitch that he was expected. The bastard no doubt thought he was there to grovel.

Instead, he threw the stuffed envelope in the middle of the elegant, brazenly expensive desk. That wasn't quite as satisfying as pummeling the man's smug face, which Mitch was tempted to risk his P.I. license to do, but Alex was more important than his own desire to beat the hell out of the man.

Farley glanced with disdain at the money. "Not enough, Tucker?"

"You haven't got enough money to buy me off."

Farley sneered. "I know your type, Tucker. Barely enough money to cover your rent. Not two cents put away in investments, certainly nothing for the future."

Mitch took a deep breath, resisting the urge in his fists. "I didn't come here to exchange insults. I want you to know why Laura is searching for her family. She has an eighteen-month-old son, Alex. If he doesn't receive a bone marrow transplant, he'll die."

David shrugged negligently. "What does this have to do with us?"

"Laura only recently learned she was adopted. That's why she has to find her real parents. Her son's life depends on it."

Farley, however, was not moved. "I've heard all sorts of angles. I have to admit this one's unique, but I'm not buying it. She's no different from the dozens of other fortune hunters who want Farley dollars. I'll repeat my earlier advice. Do yourself and her a favor. Take the money and make sure she forgets about the Farleys.''

''I may not have a blue-chip portfolio,'' Mitch replied, disgust and anger roiling within him, ''but I know the value of my own integrity. Pity you don't.''

LAURA WAS RELIEVED that Mitch was home. Although she felt fairly safe in the tall towers, protected by a doorman, she had been on edge since he had left.

Alex and Pal were playing happily with the blocks and toys Mitch had collected from the nursery. Normally, she would have kept the dog and baby toys separated. Somehow that didn't seem quite as important today.

Mitch was eyeing the living room, now dusted and vacuumed. ''Hey, this looks great.'' He picked up a pair of bookends and turned them over. Then he glanced at the Oriental figurines displayed on the sofa table.

''I hope you don't mind,'' Laura replied. ''I unpacked the carton in the closet. I just had so much time on my hands today and I couldn't sit still.''

''Mind? No. It's great. When I got out of the hospital I didn't really see any point in unpacking. I didn't plan on staying that long.''

Laura studied him. ''Why?''

''I lost a lot when I was hurt—my home, my car, almost my business. But I plan to get it all back. So why bother with a temporary apartment?'' His gaze narrowed. ''You know what I mean. Otherwise, why wouldn't you have put your stamp on your house?''

She shrugged, realizing he'd trapped her. ''Well, Counselor, you have me dead to rights. I didn't particularly want to be there. It was simply a place I escaped to. And someday, I'll put my stamp on it.''

Mitch stopped moving around the room and turned to face her. ''Laura, I spoke to David Farley today.''

''*David* Farley?''

''James Farley's son.''

And possibly her brother, Laura realized. But from the look on Mitch's face, she realized he didn't have good news. ''I'm guessing he doesn't want to be tested as a donor.''

''He wants you to stay away from the Farley family. He made that very clear.''

The wheels in her mind clicked as the knot in her stomach deepened. ''Do you think he had something to do with the break-in at my house?''

Mitch nodded.

Despite the agony it caused she had to know. ''And the wiring of the car?''

The sympathy on his face told her the answer. ''I can't be certain, but it's a fair guess.''

So her brother wanted her dead rather than in his family. Hardly the warm fuzzy reunion she might have hoped for. ''But that doesn't mean he speaks for his father, does it?''

Slowly Mitch shook his head. ''We can't be certain. But it's likely that he's the family spokesman.''

She met his gaze, refusing to flinch. "Then there's only one way to be certain."

Mitch watched her, trepidation painted across his face.

Laura tried to sound more confident than she felt. "We visit James Farley."

She saw the potential arguments flash in Mitch's eyes. Then his gaze cut across the room to rest on Alex. His sigh was deep, resonant. "I guess you're right. We'd better be certain."

CHAPTER TWENTY-TWO

IT WAS HARD to say who was more surprised. Laura, because she had been able to make an appointment with the formidable James Farley. Or Mitch, because she had accomplished it with just one phone call.

The house was what she had expected. Ornate, extravagant, impressive. Cold marble floors. Brooding oil paintings. Dark, heavy furniture. Grimly she realized it reminded her of a high-class mortuary.

Then they were ushered into James Farley's private study. The inner sanctum, she mused, not failing to grasp the irony.

He was an impressive man, with a shock of thick gray hair and eyes the blue of freezing ocean waters. He didn't stand, so she couldn't tell if he was tall. Despite the circumstances, she eagerly gathered the details, wondering if this stiff authoritarian could be her father.

Farley motioned for them to sit. Mitch made certain she was seated before seating himself. The massive leather chairs dwarfed them and absurdly she felt like a child called to the principal's office.

"I understand you wish to see me, Miss Kelly," Farley began, making it clear who was in charge of this interview.

"Yes." She took a deep breath and explained her mission, Alex's need for a bone marrow donor, her subsequent discovery of her adoption. Finally her tale wound to an end, and she studied the man across the desk.

He had steepled his fingers; he tapped them before speaking. "Certainly an interesting story, Miss Kelly. But I don't see how it relates to me."

Laura leaned forward earnestly, aware she had to convince him somehow. It didn't matter if she had to humiliate herself. She would do anything to save Alex. "As I explained, Barbara Gateley is my mother."

Farley glanced between them. "I see you two have done your homework. It's true. I had a brief affair with Barbara Gateley." All traces of the benevolent grandfather disappeared as his eyes hardened. "But you would do well to heed the warnings to leave the past alone."

"I can't!" she cried, knowing she couldn't be cowed. "My son's life is at stake."

"That's where you're wrong. Your son cannot be related to me. Apparently, you didn't do your research as well as you thought. The baby Barbara Gateley bore was stillborn."

Farley paused, clearly waiting for their reaction, just as clearly expecting them to be stunned.

Mitch met the man's gaze with no sign of intimidation. "I'm afraid that's where *you're* wrong. Although great pains were taken to make it seem that way. Barbara Gateley's child was born alive and then switched with a stillborn child."

Laura expected denial, but she didn't expect the

sudden gray pallor beneath his expensively acquired tan.

"Who told you these lies?" Farley demanded.

"There's an empty grave with Baby Gateley's name on it," Mitch responded flatly. "And it tells no lies."

Farley stood, his voice and manner pure ice. "You've been warned, Miss Kelly, not to interfere in affairs that do not concern you. I suggest you heed that advice."

"But you don't understand," she pleaded. "My son will die without your help!"

"I understand that I want you out of here." His nostrils flared and for a moment his composure slipped. "And I don't ever want to see you again!"

Numbly she stood, allowing Mitch to guide her to the doorway of the study. Entering the vast expanse of the entry hall, she caught sight of a man in his late thirties descending the stairs. Instinctively she knew he was David Farley.

As she watched, he exchanged a significant glance with Mitch. A glance that told her more had passed between them than conversation. And with a sickening pit in her stomach she wondered what it had been. She eyed Mitch. And if he would tell her the truth.

MITCH SUFFERED through several minutes of silence, wondering when Laura would question him. He had seen the surprise on her face in the Farley mansion when they had encountered David Farley. Questions had ricocheted across her face like wayward bullets.

When she finally spoke it was a relief. "That was David Farley, wasn't it?"

He nodded.

"He looked at you, Mitch. Like there was something between you."

Mitch considered lying. She would never know the difference. But he would. "He offered me a lot of money to keep you away from the family."

She swallowed. "A bribe?"

"Enough to regain my home and put the business back on its feet."

The old snakes of distrust slithered through her thoughts, clouding reason, reopening pain. "That must have been very tempting."

He was quiet for just a moment. A fraction of a second longer than he should have been. She bent her head, not wanting to believe the worst but remembering how she'd felt like a fool when she'd refused to acknowledge the truth about her ex-husband. If there hadn't been anything to hide, why hadn't Mitch told her about the bribe?

"Laura, the man's garbage. And he expects everyone else to be, too. But there's one thing I'm certain of. That wasn't an idle threat. Randy says your car was definitely wired."

She nodded, taking in this other disturbing news. But she wasn't sure which was worse. Knowing the truth about her relatives. Or not being certain about Mitch.

AGAINST HIS BETTER judgment, Mitch allowed Laura to accompany him to the office. There was still mail to be sorted and Gateleys to be located.

Despite the distinct chill between Laura and him, he hadn't lost any of his resolve to see the case through to its bitter end.

But because there could be trouble he had insisted on leaving Alex with Mrs. Plummer. She wasn't quite as interfering, since her hands were now full with an energetic toddler, an untrained puppy and a noisy parrot.

He was busy himself, installing the new computer he had purchased.

"Is that going to work?" Laura asked from across the room.

"Fortunately, the moron who smashed the old one didn't realize I had everything backed up on the zip drive, and that I have matching programs on my computer at the apartment. It'll take a little while to reboot and reinstall, but my files aren't damaged."

"Good," she replied, looking at the piles of papers scattered around the floor.

Noticing that the sight of the intrusion disturbed her, he pulled out a key. "The mailbox is on the post at the corner of the parking lot. Do you want to check and see if we have any good leads?"

"Like Gateleys from heaven?" she suggested.

"Or Farleys," he added.

But Laura didn't even crack a smile. She accepted the key, then exited quickly, as though she couldn't wait to get away from him. "Didn't take much to make her disappear," he muttered.

But without Morgan to add an answering wisecrack, his words echoed hollowly in the room.

Suddenly, he heard an unholy screech. Not even hesitating, Mitch shot out of his chair and through the doorway. A silver Mercedes barreled through the sparsely occupied parking lot.

"Laura!" he hollered above the noise, running toward the post in the far corner of the lot. As he ran, he pulled out his gun.

Laura spotted the car at that precise instant. And her hesitation was only momentary. Darting in front of a parked vehicle, she dodged the oncoming Mercedes. The car braked, fishtailing as the driver pointed it once more in Laura's direction.

She bolted again. Before the car could turn to follow, Mitch fired. The bullet creased the fender. A second shattered the rear window. Then the car roared away, before Mitch could get the license plate number.

In moments, he held Laura in his arms. Shock and fear set in. Quaking uncontrollably, she collapsed in his embrace. Tenderly, he smoothed her hair, rubbing her back in a comforting motion as she sobbed.

Feeling all her control crumbling, he lifted her into his arms and carried her into the office, then locked the door behind them. Inside, he laid her on the couch, stroking her cheek and murmuring comforting words.

"It was just like my mother's death!" she finally managed to cry between great, hiccuping sobs. "She must have been so terrified. All alone. No one to help her." Again she broke down, the sobs obliterating any words.

"But you're not alone," Mitch reassured her, knowing he never wanted her to be alone, to be vulnerable, to be without him.

Drawing her into the circle of his arms, he held

her until the sobs faded, until the tears finally ceased and until his heart constricted with the love he could no longer deny.

MITCH CONSIDERED simply killing the man. It was no less than David Farley deserved. Regrettably, Mitch knew he possessed morals and a conscience. At the moment he wished for neither.

Stalking past Farley's startled secretary, Mitch pushed open the heavy oak door of his office.

An equally startled Farley stood at the intrusion.

The worried-looking secretary darted in behind Mitch. "Mr. Farley, I'm terribly sorry, but this man just burst in. Do you want me to call security?"

Farley studied Mitch's face, apparently deciding that wouldn't be wise. "No, I'll deal with this. Close the door, Juanita."

"Yes, sir."

The door had barely shut when Mitch advanced. "You filthy piece of slime. I ought to kill you."

"I doubt you've come here simply to insult me. What's your latest angle?"

"Angle? Is that what you call attempted murder?"

Wary caution tempered by surprise entered the other man's eyes. "Do you enjoy being melodramatic, Tucker?"

"No. And I don't enjoy seeing the woman I love nearly being run down and killed. Any more than I enjoyed seeing her come close to being blown up by the wire bomb you set in her car."

Farley blanched. "If this is some sick attempt to extort even more money—"

Mitch slammed his palm against the desk. "I told you I don't want your money. Neither does Laura. All we want is to save her son's life. I mentioned him, didn't I? A baby? Eighteen months old. He's going to die without a bone marrow donor. And you could be the one he needs. Instead, you're trying to kill his mother." Mitch leaned forward until his face was inches from Farley's. "I promise you this. If either of them is harmed, I *will* kill you."

Farley's breath deepened. "I wanted to scare her off. But I don't deal in physical threats. And I don't kill women."

Mitch felt like throwing the words back in the man's face, but his gut instinct told him Farley was telling the truth.

Which was worse than putting him back to square one. He was not only dealing with a killer. That killer was unknown.

LAURA CURLED UP on the couch, buried beneath a thick quilt. But nothing could warm her. This coldness was deep inside, unreachable.

As she watched, Alex played with the puppy, the two now inseparable. From the kitchen, she could hear Mitch rattling pans as he cooked dinner. He had sent Mrs. Plummer home when he returned, and she had to admit she was relieved.

"Soup," Mitch said a few minutes later, carrying in a steaming bowl.

"I'm not very hungry."

"There's always room for soup," he told her, his eyes filled with worry.

Unreasonably, she felt the need to reassure him. "I think that's Jell-O."

But his charming grin was nowhere in sight. "I'll feed Alex."

Mitch didn't bother to put Alex in the high chair. Instead, he tucked him into his lap and patiently fed him, not seeming to mind when the food spattered on his shirt. After Alex was full, Mitch washed small hands, then played with her son until he wriggled free and wandered off with Pal. Once Alex was out of earshot, Mitch met her gaze. "I don't think David Farley was behind either of the attempts."

"You saw him?" she asked in surprise.

"I had no choice. Someone tried to kill you today."

"And you really don't think it was him?"

"The first time I saw him he tried to pay me to back off. Or rather, make you back off. But I don't believe he was prepared to kill for what he wants."

"Someone was," she reminded him.

"I think it's connected to what happened thirty years ago. And David Farley was just a kid then."

"Then who?"

"I don't know. That's why I plan to unravel the rest of the secret. No matter what it takes."

"But you said someone had gone to a great deal of trouble to keep it hidden...maybe even murder."

Mitch nodded, his face, his manner, grim.

She glanced down, fearing what she was about to put on the line, aware she had no choice. "This has become too dangerous, Mitch."

"You aren't ready to give up?" he questioned in a shocked, disbelieving voice.

"I'm not." She took a deep breath, trying to keep the fear at bay. "But I can't ask you to keep putting yourself in danger."

"That's my decision."

"But you could be killed!"

"And if anything happens to you or Alex I'll die inside anyway."

Instantly she was ashamed of her suspicions, her short-sightedness. And she was caught by the intensity of his confession. Could he really mean those words? "Oh, Mitch…"

He crossed the room and knelt beside the couch. "God, you're a stubborn woman."

She laid her head against his shoulder. "Not nearly as stubborn as you."

He eased her face back. "This could be rough, Laura. Rougher than what we've dealt with so far."

Laura realized her smile wasn't quite steady. "That's why I hired the best."

"Believe," he told her quietly.

And she did. Deep in her heart she recognized that this man was exactly what he said he was. And she knew he was good and kind. And that if he would have her, she would spend the rest of her life wondering how she had been lucky enough to find him. And so for now she listened. And believed. And prayed her heart wouldn't betray her once again.

CHAPTER TWENTY-THREE

MITCH'S STREET CONTACTS jiggled, wriggled and choked out the information. Information that made pieces of the puzzle fall somewhat into place.

To his surprise, Mitch learned that Farley was a completely self-made man. He hadn't inherited a penny of the capital he had used to start Farley Industries. It made Mitch understand why the man was so protective of what he'd accumulated.

It also made Mitch wonder where the money had come from.

Again his street contacts twitched and spun. And they shook loose the most valuable information of all—names. Names he was tracing.

The apartment was hushed, the quiet broken primarily by the click of his fingers on the computer keyboard.

Laura crossed the room and paused beside him. "Alex is asleep." She laughed softly. "As is Pal and even Morgan." She had pulled the cover over the birdcage so that the parrot wouldn't waken Alex.

"Mmm," Mitch mumbled, scanning the computer screen.

"What're you doing?"

"Dissecting," he replied, caught up in the search.

"Anything interesting?"

"Very." Momentarily he abandoned the keyboard. "What would you say if I told you James Farley opened his first business within a year of your birth?"

She considered this. "That it's quite a coincidence."

"And suppose then I told you his closest associates, all now powerful people, also founded their businesses in the same time frame?"

"More than a coincidence. Did someone die and leave them fabulously well off?"

He was afraid someone had—in theory. Baby Gateley, to be precise. "What if I told you there was no inherited wealth involved?"

She frowned. "That would be an absolutely amazing coincidence. Too amazing to be believed."

He nodded, enjoying the way her mind clicked so quickly, and so in sync with his. "That's what I thought, too. So I've called in a lot of favors."

"Favors?"

"With street contacts, former cops, their snitches. If we can learn what happened with Barbara Gateley, the baby switch, the empty grave…"

"Then maybe we'll find out the truth and be able to save Alex," she concluded.

"Exactly."

Laura hesitated. "Do you think we can really learn what happened thirty years ago? They've had a long time to cover their tracks."

"True. But they didn't hide everything. Remember, we found the handwritten journal." Then what he'd said hit him.

Picking up his jacket, he pulled the crumpled file from the inside pocket.

"What's that?" Laura asked.

"Your file. A little worse for wear, but definitely safer than in my office. I want to look at the photocopies of the journal again."

"Do you think we missed something?"

"Maybe. I still don't have the doctor's name. It's one of the missing pieces. Probably the biggest piece. And Mary Jo Westien, the most reputable contact I know, says there was no Dr. I. Edwards."

Mitch smoothed the copied pages, going immediately to the entry on Laura's birthdate. He read the familiar information, noting that the nurses' names were ones he was currently checking. Then he straightened up in the chair, checking and rechecking what he'd just read. "It's not Edwards!" Mitch nearly shouted with excitement, keeping his voice down only because of Alex. "It's Edmonds!" He studied the paper closer. "And the initial is L, not I. It's L. Edmonds. We've been looking for the wrong guy!"

"Is this going to make a lot of difference?" Laura asked.

"If you were part of an illegal adoption, the doctor's role is pivotal. Typically, that's the point of contact. Of course, not always. But this was so well executed, so well hidden, it makes me think there were several people involved."

"But wouldn't that make them more vulnerable? I mean, more opportunities for leaks."

"Not necessarily. With enough people in the right places, information can be easier to hide."

She sat down suddenly. "We're close, aren't we?"

He expected elation, not the stunned trepidation in her face. "Laura?"

He could see she was pulling herself together with great effort. He could also hear it in the forced brightness of her voice. "I mean, wow, we're getting close!"

She put her arms around his neck, hugging him. But he knew the nuances of her body well now. And she couldn't quite disguise the faint trembling or the desperation in her embrace. Smoothing her hair, he comforted her, wondering why the assurance was needed.

THE GATELEY second cousins were not a match. It had been a distant chance; still, Laura had held hope. And now that was gone. Mitch was continuing his search for more Gateleys, and Ellen was renewing her efforts to remember any other relatives.

If only they had the results of Barbara Gateley's DNA testing. Then they would know if they were on the right path, if she was in fact Laura's birth mother. But because the tissues were held by a government agency, they were being processed at typical government speed. The speed of cement, in her opinion.

Meanwhile, because Mitch had stirred up more questions; he had also intensified his probe into James Farley's past, including the backgrounds of his closest associates.

Nevertheless, Laura was worried. She sensed that as Mitch delved deeper, he was risking more than he was letting on. While she desperately wanted answers, she also didn't want Mitch to die finding them. And surely, if someone had killed once, then tried to kill her, Mitch was not invincible.

But he wouldn't listen to reason. Stubbornly, Mitch insisted on continuing the investigation. Even when she had urged him to stop until they were certain Barbara Gateley was her mother. It couldn't be much longer until they had the results of the testing.

Mitch, however, was determined. Especially since Alex had weakened. Laura had railed against all the signs, not wanting to believe that Alex could be worsening so rapidly. Yet she sometimes wondered if Mitch's concern mirrored the fear in her own heart for her son. Often, she found him watching Alex as the baby slept, his worry undisguised.

Mitch offered his strength, yet she felt she should offer equal support. She had seen the bleakness in his eyes when he thought she wasn't looking. Could he have truly grown to care so much for her son?

Mrs. Plummer harrumphed, catching her attention. "I guess I'll go now."

Laura turned. "I'm sorry, Mrs. Plummer. I know you must think I'm ignoring you. But I've had so much on my mind lately."

"It's all right." The older woman hesitated, her expression tinged with unhappy acceptance. "Actually, you haven't had much need for me lately."

Laura gestured at the rooms around them. "Mitch feels it's safer if we stay inside. I'm aware that makes it difficult for you. But we still need you."

Mrs. Plummer's face didn't brighten. "Do you

really think Mr. Tucker has everything under control?''

Of this Laura was certain. Mitch, on the other hand, hadn't been certain confiding in Mrs. Plummer was wise. Laura had insisted, though. ''He has only our best interests at heart.''

Mrs. Plummer closed her eyes briefly. ''I lost one child. It was decades ago, but I remember exactly how it felt. I don't want to lose another.''

Laura took the other woman's hand, realizing the baby-sitter was old enough to be her mother, and at the moment her eyes were filled with a mother's concern. ''We aren't going to lose him, Mrs. Plummer. I'm going to make sure of that.'' Then what she'd just said hit her. She was still resisting. ''Actually, *we're* going to make sure of that. Mitch and I.'' Hope flared even as she said the words.

Mrs. Plummer finally left, still brimming with concern. Laura wondered again about the sad demise of the woman's child. Needing affirmation of her own, she walked over to Alex's crib and studied him as he slept. Issuing yet another silent prayer, she was struck again by the belief that somehow he would be all right.

Just then she heard the key at the door, and turned to see Mitch enter. Even though he maintained that the apartment was safe, she still worried.

Mitch's gaze traveled across the room and he strode forward. ''Is something wrong?''

She touched his arm, calming his apprehension. ''No. Just watching him.''

Mitch exhaled, then pushed back at already disheveled hair. ''Good,'' he replied, bending to pick up an ecstatic Pal, who licked him with obvious affection.

As they walked away from the crib and into the kitchen, Laura saw something disturbing in his face, emphasized by weary lines of fatigue. "Mitch, how about you? Is something wrong?"

He shook his head. "Not exactly. Just the more I learn about Farley and his associates, the more concerned I become."

"His associates?"

"It's a pretty close-knit circle of friends. And they all have interests in one another's businesses."

"Is there something wrong with that?" she asked.

"No. But it's yet another coincidence."

"And there are already too many coincidences," she concluded.

"Exactly." He managed a tired smile. "And they've gone to a great deal of trouble to keep their association conccalcd. Which makes me wonder why, if everything's aboveboard."

Laura studied his face. "But there's something else. Something you're not saying."

He had reached for a mug, but surprise stopped him. His gaze searched hers and then he sighed. "Yeah."

"Tell me. We're in this together you know."

Another arrow of surprise flitted through him. "Someone hit the office again."

Panic struck without warning. "Were you there?"

"No. And this time nothing was destroyed. Just a search. A very thorough search."

"Thank God you weren't there!"

But he still looked troubled. "That's not what bothers me. I think they're watching me."

She moved closer. "Oh, Mitch!"

"Don't worry. They didn't tail me here. I took several subversive routes."

She couldn't resist glancing over at Alex's crib. "I want *all* of us to be safe. That includes you."

Mitch waved away the words. "It's my job to protect you."

Laura tried not to let the hurt show. "Your job?"

He grasped her arms, pulling her closer. "My job as a man, Laura. Not a detective. Not even as an ex-cop. Can you understand that?"

She wanted to. Desperately. "What are you saying, Mitch?"

As she watched, a struggle played out over his face. "I don't have anything to offer you. Or Alex. I haven't even found the answers you both need."

Words and emotions locked in her throat. She longed to tell him that her suspicions had been laid to rest, that maybe even some of her own scars were healing. That together maybe they could both change. But he hadn't asked her to change. More important, he hadn't offered to change. It was one thing to be concerned about her, about Alex. It was another for Mitch to discard his lifestyle.

Yet somehow, she managed to smile, to fight past her desire to ask. "You'll find the answers, Mitch. I know you will."

Was it disappointment she glimpsed in his eyes? Or did his gaze simply mirror her own?

Before she could decide, he turned away. "I have a lot of work to do tonight."

"What about dinner?" she questioned, hearing the quiet despair in her own voice.

"Guess I don't have much appetite."

Laura understood completely. She'd just lost her own.

CHAPTER TWENTY-FOUR

MITCH WENT TO the office. One, his watchers expected it. Two, he had to escape Laura. He couldn't stare failure in the face any longer.

Still, he used caution opening the door. It seemed very empty without Morgan's squawking greeting, or Laura trailing him to query his methods, to push him.

He sank into his chair, appreciating the familiar creaking sounds. He considered making some coffee, then discarded the idea. His stomach was already too bitter.

Reaching for his keyboard, he glanced at the computer screen, which was in saver mode, the background dark. A new message crawled by in bright-green letters. A message he hadn't programmed. A message that chilled his blood and nearly stilled his heart: Drop the Investigation. Or the Child Will Disappear.

ALTHOUGH TERRIFIED, Laura moved quickly and efficiently alongside Mitch. His SUV was loaded with Alex's things along with a few of their own. While Mitch had packed his computer, disks and files, Laura had collected the box of papers and diaries that had belonged to Barbara Gateley. The bird and dog were installed in the rear of the vehicle.

Now Mitch was practically grilling Mrs. Plummer. "You understand. Once we move, if you come with us you may not be able to return home until this is over. And we have no idea how long that will be."

The woman to her credit didn't even hesitate. "I understand."

"If you're still all right about driving Laura's car, we'll follow you to your house so you can collect your things," Mitch continued. "I don't want Laura's car left here to possibly be traced. And, Mrs. Plummer, if you lose sight of us, don't worry. But if you sense anything is wrong, that someone may be following you, drive immediately to the police station." He handed her a slip of paper. "Here's the address of the nearest precinct."

She nodded, getting into Laura's car with jumpy movements.

Once inside the SUV, Mitch turned to Laura. "I still don't like taking her along. But at least this way, if anyone tails us you'll be with me in case we need to make a quick getaway."

"She's a woman alone," Laura pointed out. "If they trace your apartment, it's reasonable to believe they could trace her, as well. It's not fair to leave her in a vulnerable position."

"I agree with you there. I just don't want anyone knowing where we're going."

Laura turned to him. "Where *are* we going?"

"Randy and I owned a cabin just outside of town, not all that far from his precinct. When I started the business, he gave me the start-up cash and I signed over my half of the cabin to him. He contends that it's still half-mine, but my name's not on any of the papers, and hasn't been for years. So the cabin can't be traced to me. We'll be safe there.''

''Is it isolated?'' she asked, trying not to be afraid.

''Somewhat. But Randy's going to be sending patrols by.''

She couldn't stifle the next question. ''You're sure you can trust Randy?''

''With my life,'' he replied shortly. Then his gaze cut over to meet hers. ''But I don't blame you for asking. We have to question everyone and everything. From the most casual encounter, to the mailman, to the neighbors. We can't take anything at face value.''

''Mitch, what are we going to do? We can't stop the investigation or Alex will surely die. And if we don't, someone could, could…'' Unable to voice the horrifying thought, she covered her mouth.

''That's not going to happen,'' he assured her grimly. ''I won't let it happen.''

Again she was overwhelmed by this man. His willingness to risk his life for them.

First they detoured by Mrs. Plummer's house. She packed a bag in record time. Clearly, she had grasped their sense of urgency.

Back on the highway Mitch drove rapidly, but he made sure Mrs. Plummer could keep up with him. When he veered off the main road, as promised the route grew more remote. Then, like a deep aqua jewel, the lake appeared around the bend. Mitch made a succession of turns, passing an occasional home. Finally he pulled into a driveway.

And Laura could only stare in surprise. Although the homes they had passed were nice, some even impressive, she had expected a rustic cabin of small proportions.

Instead, a huge, two-story cedar-and-stone house soared amid ancient tall pines.

Laura faced Mitch. "This is your *cabin?*"

He was pensive, not grinning as he once might have. "Yeah. I designed it."

"And you traded it for your business? For the office you have now?"

"Prime business property is expensive," he explained. "So is getting a business off the ground. And until I had my setback, I'd planned on building an office complex on my property. But when my funds dried up, so did my financing. You really didn't think the little office I have is worthy of that land, did you? If things had worked out, it would have been demolished by now."

So that was what had happened. It made sense. The small pond, the beautiful sloping land situated close to downtown. It was the perfect spot for a dazzling office structure. And she thought he'd hit the height of his ambition. How could she have been so wrong?

Laura continued to stare at the house as Mitch got out of the vehicle and opened her door. As he did, Mrs. Plummer pulled into the driveway. Mitch lifted the garage door and motioned for the woman to park inside.

Then he returned to Laura's side. "Randy came

by and checked the house," he told her. "And the security system is operational."

Still, she noticed that Mitch kept a constant watch on his surroundings as he quickly unloaded the car and parked it in the garage.

Once inside, Laura could scarcely believe the house. The main-floor ceiling met the roof. And a loft ran around the entire perimeter. An immense stone fireplace dominated one wall, rising up to meet the roof, as well. And everywhere Laura looked, she could see oversize windows. Great, soaring windows that didn't simply invite the outdoors in. They demanded.

Disbelief kept Laura silent as Mitch led her through a gourmet kitchen and adjoining dining room. Double doors opened into a huge master suite with an equally incredible fireplace. "This leads to a smaller bedroom," Mitch was explaining. "I thought we'd put Alex in there and Mrs. Plummer upstairs."

"Fine," she mumbled, still trying to take the place in and not succeeding very well.

Mitch disappeared and she heard Mrs. Plummer walking upstairs. Mitch had put the parrot and puppy in the main living area and Morgan was shrieking at Pal, who was barking madly in return.

Laura smoothed the hair back on Alex's forehead. "Come on, punkin, we'd better check to see what's going on." Since Mitch had told her about the message on the computer screen, she hadn't been able to release Alex other than to put him in the car seat. She still felt the need to hold on to him, to assure herself that he was safe.

Entering the living room, she saw that Mitch had things under control. Morgan's cage was hung on what looked like a special hook for just that purpose. And Pal was following Mitch, nipping at his heels affectionately.

Despite the danger, Laura couldn't get over this house that Mitch had never even mentioned. Accustomed to his neglected apartment and messy office, she just couldn't fathom him creating this exquisite structure. She noticed the handsome furniture. "Since you designed the house, did Randy buy the furniture?"

"Not at the time." Catching her puzzled look, he explained. "I designed and built the furniture. But when Randy bought me out, I threw in the furniture, as well."

It hit her what he had sacrificed to start his business. Obviously, he had loved this place. His heart and soul was in every detail.

And now the business he had traded it for was at stake. Yet he had concentrated solely on her case, to the exclusion of any new clients. Watching him now, in this place, she realized what a sacrifice that truly was.

Her throat, tight with emotion, remained closed. A man of charm and substance. Was it possible?

Mitch finished checking all the windows. "Everything's secure. There's only one rear entrance—patio doors. But they have a rolling metal cover that works electrically from inside, making them virtually impossible to breach. And the blinds lower the same way—electrically. So no one can see in the house, especially at night. Also, all the windows and doors are connected to the security system and the alarm sounds at the police station.''

She nodded, before managing to find her voice. ''It sounds like we'll be safe.''

He met her gaze. ''Trust me, Laura.''

She was very close to doing just that. But she wasn't sure how to tell him. Or if he even wanted to hear those words.

''YOU DELIVERED the message?''

The voice on the other end of the phone shook. ''I told you I did!''

''You're getting overexcited.''

''Don't tell me how to react! I'm not some errand boy of yours. You can push Phillips and the others around if they'll let you, but I know all the secrets. And don't you forget it.''

''We need to meet.''

''Meet?''

''Yes. All of us. Tucker and the woman are becoming too dangerous. I've heard talk of the DA conducting an investigation on that empty grave.''

There was silence on the other end of the phone.

''And you know what that means.''

''If this gets out, we'll all be ruined.''

''And facing prison.''

''That can't be allowed to happen, can it?''

The sigh over the phone was loud. ''I'll set up the meeting.''

''Immediately.''

This time there was no hesitation. ''Immediately.''

THE FIRE CRACKLED as though welcoming him home. It had been a while. Mitch had used his injury and stay in the hospital as reasons not to return to the house. But they were just excuses. Even though Randy had insisted the money was only a loan, that the house was still half his, Mitch had felt differently.

He still did. He had put so much of himself into the house it had been difficult to sell. It was the closest thing to permanence he had ever allowed himself. And yet it had slipped away.

As he watched Laura enter the room, he wondered when she, too, would slip away. With the events now put in motion, it would be soon. And he was powerless to stop them. Besides, he wouldn't jeopardize Alex's chances for anything.

So there was no crossroads, no decision. They would find Alex's donor. Then the child and Laura would fade from his life. But it was what he knew, the pattern he had known since his own infancy.

"He's finally asleep," Laura told him, coming to sit beside him on the great, overstuffed couch. "He and Pal and Morgan have been a literal three-ring circus."

"It's another new environment."

"Yes. But kids adapt pretty well. Sometimes even better than adults."

"True."

Laura sighed as she relaxed against the couch. "Thanks for building the fire in the bedroom, as well. I rocked Alex in there. The fire was soothing for him. I think it helped get him to sleep. Then it was easy to take him in the other room and put him in the crib.''

''Mmm.''

She studied his expression. ''You're worried, aren't you?''

Mitch leaned his head back, enjoying the dance of flames against the rocks. ''I'd be lying if I said no. Farley and his associates are powerful men. If we're endangering them, they won't hesitate to act.''

''By act,'' she responded slowly, ''you mean get rid of us, don't you?''

He nodded. ''I'm afraid so. I just checked the house again, lowered all the blinds, and we're safe for now. I'm not saying this to frighten you, but so that you'll be aware, and careful.''

It was her turn to nod. ''You don't have to worry about that.''

That was where she was wrong. Laura was his concern, she and Alex. And right now he wanted to chase the shadows of fear from her eyes. So he changed subjects, veering away from the frightening. ''You know, this is a pretty great fire.''

She smiled. ''Yes, it is.''

''Shame to waste a great fire like this.''

She tilted her face up toward his. ''A real shame.''

''Mrs. Plummer is safely upstairs, isn't she?''

Laura smiled. ''The poor thing was so exhausted she probably conked out the minute she hit the bed.''

Mitch draped one arm around her. ''I guess you're right. Maybe she isn't so bad.''

"Does this have something to do with the fact that she *is* conked out upstairs?"

"Exactly."

"It's not a glowing recommendation, but today, I'll take it." Her hand curled within his. "Do you suppose it's crazy that I feel incredibly safe here…with you?"

Something deep inside warmed at her words. He tipped her chin, gently turning her face so that their mouths could meet. It was just a tender kiss.

At first.

One that was a simple connection, a reaffirmation.

But the warmth kindled. And grew. Laura was supple within his arms, curving her body to fit against his. Mitch knew he should pull back and take his emotions with him. But he could feel the trembling of her body, the tender caress of her hands as she traced the lines of his face. There was something different in her touch, almost as though she were memorizing his features…the moment.

"Oh, Mitch!" she whispered. And he could hear the plea in her voice.

Responding to that need, he lifted her in his arms and carried her through the open double doors of the master suite, pausing only to shut them.

Mitch set her on the side of the bed.

When Laura made a move toward the buttons of her blouse, Mitch stayed her hands. "Let me."

With careful deliberation, he knelt beside the bed. First, he slipped off her shoes, cupping his hand beneath the tender instep of her foot.

Laura wore stockings and he knew from previous experience that she favored garter belts, which he thought were incredibly sexy. Especially when she had on a plain tailored blouse and casual checked skirt as she did today. Because beneath the simple garments, her lingerie was stunningly sheer and feminine.

Sliding her skirt upward, he unfastened one garter, hearing the murmur of her indrawn breath when he slowly rolled down the stocking, his hands following the curvature of her leg. When he repeated the procedure with the other stocking, she began to tremble. And he knew it wasn't fear that made her quake beneath his hands.

Pulling her up with him, he unfastened her skirt, allowing it to slip free. Then he took painful care with each button of her blouse. By the time it opened, he could see the gentle heave of her breasts responding to the rapid beat of her pulse.

Again his breath caught at her loveliness as she stood only in her brief lacy underthings. She seemed even lovelier because she seemed so unaware of her beauty...and its effect on him.

After dispatching his own clothing, Mitch joined her on the bed, feeling the gentle indentation of the mattress. Through the panes of glass above the drapes, moonlight poked its way into the room. Persistent moonbeams that played across Laura's skin as though seeking the finest to illuminate. The silver rays combined with the flames from the fire, also dancing over them.

Mitch sought her mouth, craving the taste he knew he would never tire of...never forget. Then he trailed kisses over her chin and down the incredibly soft skin of her throat. She sighed in pleasure when the kisses continued.

He unfastened the solitary catch at the front of her bra, capturing her breasts. When he reached the last scrap of lace, she shuddered beneath his touch.

Then her hands were reaching for him, caressing his shoulders, running over his chest, exploring the tender skin of his inner thighs, making him nearly jolt beneath each enticing touch.

"Mitch," she whispered again.

And again he sensed there was more she wanted to say. But when the words didn't come, he closed his mouth over hers, sealing it with the words still lodged in his heart.

And when they came together, he knew it was more than the fit of their bodies. It was the fit of their hearts, now thundering together. He could feel the desperation in their caresses. And for the first time, he didn't know if the desperation was his. Or, remarkably, hers.

CHAPTER TWENTY-FIVE

OCCASIONALLY GLANCING through the huge windows, Laura sorted through Barbara Gateley's papers. Although she didn't yet know for certain whether Barbara was her mother, in her heart she believed it was true. And it made Laura feel close to her to read her diaries. To delve into the mind of a woman who had loved her child—despite the outcome.

Because Laura knew how it felt to fear losing a child. She could almost imagine the devastation of a realized loss.

After Mitch had left to meet with one of his contacts, Laura had spent the morning reading the diaries. Alex was unusually quiet, but Laura guessed it was because of all the unsettling moves first to the apartment and now to Mitch's "cabin."

As she read, Laura kept hoping she would run across something, anything, that would convince James Farley that he had nothing to be afraid of by listening to her. Although she had received a generous inheritance from her parents, Laura didn't think she could convince Farley that she wasn't interested in his money based solely on her bank account. Not when Farley had millions.

So she kept reading. And hoping that somewhere

in all these pages, Barbara Gateley had confided her suspicions about what had really happened to her child.

Scouring the diary from the year she was born, Laura was disappointed to find nothing resembling what she was seeking. She was so discouraged she almost put the box away. But the remaining diaries beckoned to her.

She retrieved another one dated many years later. Close to the end of that diary, Laura nearly put it back in the box. Then she decided to continue reading so that she could shelve the book, forget about it and then research another diary.

But it was in one of the final pages that she found it, the entry she had been seeking:

People will think I'm crazy if I pursue this. Sometimes I think even Ellen does, although she never says it. But it has been so many years now she must tire of hearing about my baby. And I've heard all the reasonings, all the logic. Everyone has said that it was my medication or my intense desire to believe what I wanted to hear. But I know in my heart that's not true. I heard my baby girl cry. It was a healthy, lusty cry, not one I imagined. So I know she couldn't have been stillborn like they said. For some reason, they lied. All of them. Even Brady. They wanted me to believe she never breathed. But she did. She breathed. She cried. And my arms have been empty ever since. I want my daughter, the child they ripped away from me.

A solitary tear rolled down Laura's cheek as she felt this woman's agony. Perhaps her mother's agony.

But she also realized she had struck gold. Gold that even James Farley would be forced to recognize. Brushing away the tear, she ran into the other room. Quickly, she dug through the papers on the desk, at last locating the one naming Farley's associates. Scanning the list, she spotted it: Hugh Brady. It couldn't be another coincidence. Heartened, she dashed into the kitchen.

"Mrs. Plummer. I have to leave. I shouldn't be long."

The other woman frowned. "Is that safe?"

"I think so. Mitch said we would be safe here until he returned, so you and Alex should be fine." She checked her watch. "Another patrol should be by within half an hour. Just make sure you deadbolt the door behind me and double-check that the security system is engaged."

"Alex isn't looking well," Mrs. Plummer said, fretting.

"He's ill. He's bound to look pale."

"You'll be careful, won't you?"

Laura smiled reassuringly. "Of course. And I'll leave my cell phone so that you'll be sure to have phone service here."

Mrs. Plummer looked slightly alarmed. "We have a phone."

"In the event anything happens to the regular phone, I would feel better knowing you have the cell phone."

"What if Mr. Tucker calls. What should I tell him?"

"That I've found proof to show Mr. Farley and that I'm going to his office."

Mrs. Plummer still looked concerned. "Shouldn't you wait for Mr. Tucker?"

"I'm hoping that Mr. Farley will feel less threatened if I approach him on a one-to-one basis. And I think he'll talk more without a detective in the room." Laura picked up her purse, retrieved her cell phone and set it on the counter. "I shouldn't be long."

Ignoring Mrs. Plummer's disapproval, Laura slipped the diary into her purse. It was her turn to accept some of the danger herself. Constantly putting Mitch on the front lines while she hid behind him wasn't fair. She was ready to confront the man who was surely her father. And this time she would make him listen.

MITCH THANKED the snitch in the language he understood—money. But he was truly indebted to the former cop the snitch had connected him with—a cop who had been on the police force thirty years earlier. A cop who remembered more than was wise to know at that time.

There had been a high-level cover-up and Farley had been smack in the middle of it. Farley had put his money behind the mayor and the mayor had made certain no dirt was connected to Farley. And the cop told Mitch what he'd guessed all along.

Back in his car, driving toward home, Mitch

flipped open his cell phone and dialed the cabin, reaching Mrs. Plummer.

"But she's not here, Mr. Tucker. I told her not to go, to wait until you got here, but she—"

"Where did she go, Mrs. Plummer?"

"To meet with that Mr. Farley."

He braked, then whipped the car around. "James Farley?"

"Yes, I believe so. At his office. I told her not to go," she repeated.

"If she calls before I reach her, tell her *not* to go into his office."

"Oh, I doubt she'll call. She left her cell phone here."

Mitch held the phone away from his ear, cursing lowly and violently.

"Mr. Tucker!" Mrs. Plummer's anxious voice reached him.

"Keep all the doors locked. Don't let anyone in. I don't care if someone tells you the house is about to blow up. Do you understand?"

He could hear her gulp, despite their less-than-perfect connection. "Yes…I understand. I will guard Alex with my life!"

And she would, he realized. With furious speed he dialed Randy's office, knowing he needed help. As Mitch raced toward the financial district where Farley's office was located, he cursed every red light, every car that dared loiter in front of him.

Mitch briefed him on the situation and Randy agreed to meet him at Farley's office, along with several uniforms for backup. Mitch prayed they would arrive in time.

Although it seemed to Mitch that it took him forever to reach the Farley Building, he arrived there
in record time. Spotting Laura's car in the garage,
he saw that it was empty. Which meant she was
inside. Alone. Facing men who wanted to kill her.
She had walked into a trap. And she didn't even
know it.

LAURA WAS NERVOUS. She knew she was on the
side of right, but it didn't make the task any easier.
And she wasn't sure it would make Farley any more
receptive.

Clutching her purse to her side, she walked down
the corridor. A discreet sign indicated that Farley's
office was at the end of the hall, no doubt behind
the huge double doors. Most of the offices in the
building belonged to Farley employees. She guessed
her half brother had his office here, as well.

She wondered if it was on this floor, a floor dedicated to executives. Farley's right-hand men. She
was surprised that it had been so easy to gain access
to the area. The guard had stopped her, but when
she had given her name, he made a phone call. And
then she was admitted. Was it too much to hope that
James Farley had had a change of heart?

As she passed the other formidable wooden office
doors, she scanned the names on each. Then she
paused. Hugh Brady. Could that be a coincidence?

Before the thought fully formed, the door opened.
A well-dressed gentleman stood on the other side.
"Miss Kelly?"

"Why, yes."

"Mr. Farley is expecting you."

She glanced down the hall. "But I thought his office was down there."

"Due to the confidential nature of the meeting, he felt it was best to meet in here."

"Oh." She supposed that made sense. Perhaps he felt the fewer people who saw her, the fewer questions. She stepped inside.

The man pointed to an inner door. "Through this way, Miss Kelly."

Passing through the next door, she saw a man seated behind the desk. But it wasn't James Farley. She turned back to the first man. "Where's Mr. Farley?"

But he had turned around and was clicking the lock in place.

Uneasily, she stepped back. "I really think you should let Mr. Farley know I'm here."

"I don't think that would be wise," the man behind the desk countered in a shaky voice.

"Who are you?" she demanded.

The first man moved aside nervously. "It's not important."

"Are you Brady?"

He attempted a smile. "And what do you know of Brady?"

"What my mother wrote about you in her diary."

Perspiration dotted his forehead. "She didn't know when it was wise to quit."

Laura backed up another foot. "You honestly don't think you can get away with this again, do you?"

He looked uncertain. Just then the phone buzzed. The first man snatched it up and listened.

"It looks like your boyfriend couldn't stay away, either."

She gasped. The last thing she had wanted to do was endanger Mitch.

The man unlocked the door. "No sense making it difficult for him." But his trembling hands betrayed the bravado of his words.

Laura could hear the outer door opening. "No, Mitch! It's a trap!" she screamed.

But he still pushed open the inner door, his gaze going to her, then resting on the two men, both of whom pointed guns in his direction.

"Why couldn't you stay away?"

"You must be Brady." Mitch then turned his gaze to the man behind the desk. "And Stanton."

Stanton spoke, his voice raised in fearful anger. "I told you he was dangerous."

Laura could scarcely contain a sob. "I'm sorry, Mitch. They waylaid me before I ever got to Farley's office. I'm such a fool. I shouldn't have come here."

"She's right," Brady agreed. "But you both knew it was only a matter of time. You've poked your noses in where you don't belong. You left us no other recourse." His eyes were chilled. "So you'll have to be eliminated."

Laura gasped.

"Couldn't stand anyone knowing the truth about your dirty little secret, could you, Brady? I think Laura deserves to hear the entire story." Mitch kept his eyes trained on the men. "Farley, Edmonds, Stanton, Brady and a few of their closest friends operated a black market baby ring. They stole babies and sold them into adoption. But then Dr. Edmonds got an attack of conscience. However, the rest of the men had plenty of money by then. Enough to cover up Edmonds's murder.''

Horrified, Laura stifled her gasp.

''But also by then they had stolen plenty of babies. In fact, Laura, you're probably one of them.''

Brady smirked. ''And she fetched a tidy sum.''

Laura managed to find her voice. ''Did James Farley know what you'd done?''

''No. It was my idea. The mother of the baby we had arranged to be 'adopted' got cold feet and ran out on us. And we needed another one fast. Farley made no secret of the fact he didn't want his bastard. So we didn't think he needed to know the details of how we procured the baby. You were out of the way. That's what counted.''

''What if he had known?'' Laura countered. ''Maybe he would have stopped you!''

''You're a dreamer,'' Brady snorted. ''Farley was up on every other detail of our business. He was the one who convinced Edmonds to go along with us. He made enough money to start Farley Industries with his profits. Don't kid yourself just because he didn't know the particulars about you. Farley wasn't only in this as thick as the rest of us—he was the mastermind.''

''So you say,'' Mitch countered, his voice still cool.

Laura marveled at his calm. They were facing death, yet he acted as though they were having an academic discussion.

Brady's jaw clenched and his fingers tightened on the gun. "Make no mistake, Tucker. Farley may be going soft because he's getting older, but you and the girl are loose ends we can't afford. We got rid of Edmonds and the Gateley woman. You don't think we're going to let the pair of you stand in our way?"

Suddenly, the door crashed open, the splintered wood shocking them all. Brady and Stanton froze when several policemen, guns drawn, burst into the room.

Limp with relief, Laura sagged into Mitch's arms. "Thank God! I thought we were goners."

"You didn't think I came in without calling for backup, did you?" Mitch responded.

She swallowed, her fear and relief colliding. "I...didn't know." But she did know that despite his words, he had risked his life for her. And now he deserved the truth, the entire truth about how she felt. The trust she wanted to place in him, her hopes for a future that included him.

His cell phone rang, a loud, insistent ring. "It can't be the cavalry," he joked. "They're already here." He listened for a moment, all humor draining away, before handing her the phone.

"Yes?" she asked, wondering who could be calling.

"Laura, it's Mrs. Plummer. Alex is worse. I've called the ambulance and we're heading to the emergency room at St. Luke's Children's Hospital."

Stricken, Laura leaned again on Mitch. But he was already pulling her from the room. He stopped only long enough to tell Randy where they were headed. And then they raced out, hearts in hand, hoping they hadn't uncovered the truth just to find it had been in vain.

THE ANTISEPTIC SMELL of the hospital only worsened Laura's fear. Alex's physician, Dr. Fletcher, had met her as she ran inside. He had assured her that they were doing everything possible, but he admitted the prognosis wasn't good.

Looking at Alex's tiny body lying so helplessly in the sterile, white-sheeted bed, Laura had completely broken down. Sobbing, she had allowed Mitch to lead her back to the waiting room. He had cradled her until the tears stopped. Now he was a quiet source of strength.

She accepted the coffee he brought, but then stared at it, clinging to the warmth, wondering if she would ever be warm again.

"It's so unfair," she railed again, sopping the coffee into the trash can. "Why couldn't I be a match? I'm his mother!"

"I understand how you feel," Mitch replied quietly.

Confused, she lifted her gaze. "What do you mean?"

"I was tested shortly after I took the case, just on the off chance that I might be a donor. But no go."

Incredibly, overwhelmingly touched, she fought the tears welling in her eyes. He was beyond doubt the most generous, caring man she had ever known. To be so willing to give of himself to a child he hadn't really cared about at that time...

She flung herself into his arms and clung to him,

praying for the life of her child, for a future they could all share.

And he accepted the embrace, their hearts aligned, their love sprouting its fragile new branches.

THE WAITING ROOM was growing quieter. Mitch and Laura sat together on a scratchy couch, their hands entwined. Their hopes focused solely on Alex.

Glancing up, Laura saw her aunt Rhoda hovering at the doorway.

Seeing that Laura had spotted her, she approached, her voice quiet, stricken. "I got Mrs. Plummer home okay. Even as she went inside, she kept insisting she would rather be here. The poor thing. I think she's reliving the time when she lost her own child."

"She was exhausted," Mitch commented, exhausted himself. "We know she cares. But she needed to get some sleep."

Rhoda looked from Mitch to Laura. "Can I get something for you two? Some dinner? Coffee?"

"No," Laura answered for them both. "I'm afraid my nerves couldn't take any more coffee."

"And we don't have much appetite," Mitch added.

Rhoda perched on the edge of the couch beside Laura. Her head was bent, and her eyes didn't quite meet Laura's gaze. "Laura, you have to believe that your parents never knew anything about this stolen baby business. They believed your adoption was perfectly legal." She twisted the handles of her purse in a nervous fashion. "If anyone's to blame, it's me. I was the contact. My lawyer told me he could cut through the red tape, the endless waiting lists. Your parents were older and the agencies kept turning them down. And I thought that would be a way for them to have the baby they wanted so much. But I didn't know anything about the babies being stolen!'' She paused, her expression remorseful. ''I did question where they found the mothers, but I told myself there were plenty of unwed mothers who wanted to give up their babies. Maybe that's what I wanted to believe. And, God help me, I've wondered about it over the years when I've heard stories. But I purposely turned a deaf ear, not willing to believe yours was that kind of adoption. Leonard Stanton was a lawyer and a good friend. I never guessed he would be involved in something so despicable.''

Rhoda took a deep breath, finally meeting Laura's eyes again. ''The fees sounded expensive, but Leonard told us that was to pay for the mother's medical and living expenses. It sounded reasonable. It was important that she had the best care, the best doctors. And your parents wanted you so very much. Please don't blame them for what happened.''

Laura took her aunt's hands. ''I don't. They never gave me any reason to doubt their love. They were victims, as well. I know this isn't the legacy they would have wished for me.''

''No, dear, it isn't. Still, I feel so terrible—''

''For no reason, Aunt Rhoda. You thought you were helping. And you didn't know the truth.''

''No. But when you started this search, I wondered. And I should have told you then. But I was so afraid you would blame your parents, discount their love.''

Laura wished Rhoda had come forward sooner. But it really wouldn't have mattered to the ultimate outcome. ''Thank you for telling me this. I suspected as much, but I feel so much better knowing the truth.''

Eyes bright with tears, Rhoda hugged her. ''I promise. Nothing but the truth in the future.''

It was a promise Laura wanted to cling to, one she hoped she could believe in.

CHAPTER TWENTY-SIX

THE HOURS PASSED, broken by the sound of the hospital paging system and the click of vending machines as they issued countless cups of coffee. A major car accident involving several vehicles brought in a slew of patients, and for a time the waiting room filled with anxious relatives. But then the condition of the victims was upgraded to stable and the people filtered away.

Still Mitch and Laura waited. There was no sleep for either of them. Instead, they took turns checking on Alex as he lay in the intensive care unit.

When soft footsteps approached, then hesitated at the doorway, Laura thought her heart would stop. Looking up, she feared the worst.

But nothing had prepared her to expect David Farley.

She stared as he approached.

"Laura?"

"Yes?" To her own ears, her voice sounded rusty and unused.

At her side, she could tell that Mitch was alert and on guard, but she was glad that he was letting her handle the encounter.

"As you might imagine, I heard about what happened in our building today. It was difficult to miss with the cops there and all the news media. I confronted my father. He didn't know what Brady and Stanton had planned. He was shaken—in a way I'd never seen before. We talked.'' David paused. ''I'm sorry I didn't listen to you before. Having been approached by dozens of people only after the Farley money, I wasn't prepared to learn I might really have a sister.''

''And now?'' she asked.

David glanced down, obvious torment on his face. ''I didn't know anything about the baby ring until today.'' Again he paused. ''I do want to make amends.''

''Amends?'' she questioned.

''Yes. I want you to share in Farley Enterprises, your inheritance.''

Laura opened her mouth to throw his offer back in his face.

But David spoke first. ''And I want to share my bone marrow. That is, if it's a match.''

Laura gasped.

Mitch steadied her before turning to Farley. ''Are you on the level about this?''

David Farley flinched, then straightened his shoulders. ''Can we talk to the doctor now?''

''Yes!'' Laura gasped out the reply before nearly choking on a sob of relief.

As they left the waiting room, Laura reached out and took David's hand. ''Thank you.''

He met her eyes, his own filled with remorse. ''I'm sorry it came to this. That I didn't offer before.''

''You're here now. That's all that counts.''

Together they headed out of the waiting room to locate the doctor, who promised the lab would work around the clock to test the match, making it top priority. Luckily, they were located in the same city as the M. D. Anderson Cancer Research Hospital, the premier cancer research facility in the world. A center that would do its best to save a young child.

Mitch kept his arm around her shoulders, shoring her up. And as they spoke to the doctor, she could read Mitch's thoughts as easily as if he spoken them aloud. He feared she would count on this too much. Every other potential donor had not been a match. This one, too, could fail.

Meeting his eyes, she squeezed his hand, mouthing a single word. "Believe."

IT WAS their mantra, through the long hours of the night, the following day and into the dawn of the next.

And when Dr. Fletcher entered the waiting room, they both leaped up, wondering if their belief had worked.

The doctor smiled. "I've heard of eleventh-hour reprieves, but this one's nothing short of a miracle. We have a match."

Laura felt tears of joy and hope flow down her cheeks as Mitch grabbed her and held her close. When he finally released her, she could see her reaction mirrored in his eyes.

"We're not out of the woods yet," Dr. Fletcher warned. "We have a long surgery ahead of us." However, he softened the words with a smile. "But I think your faith is finally being rewarded."

Laura buried her face against Mitch's shoulder. "It's nearly over. Can you believe it?"

HE COULDN'T. This was what he wanted. A conclusion to the case that meant Alex would live, provided the operation went well. And Mitch could feel only gratitude that David Farley had found his conscience, that the beloved little boy now had a chance.

But as he held Laura in his arms, Mitch wondered if it might be for the last time. He was about to regain his freedom, to shed any shackles, any responsibility. Why did that make him feel so bereft?

As did imagining life without Laura and Alex. Without family ties. Ones that didn't bind, but showed him the joy of commitment. Ones Laura didn't believe him capable of. But this *was* their family found.

So he held her close. And savored the moments, knowing they were numbered.

MITCH'S CELL PHONE RANG, startling him out of a troubled sleep. At his side, Laura was instantly alert, lifting her head from his shoulder.

He answered the cell phone, listening, nodding, then listening again. Finally, he spoke. "Thanks, Randy. No, it's not too late. It will be welcome news." He clicked the phone off, looking down into Laura's anxious eyes. "The DNA results are in. They're conclusive. Barbara Gateley is your mother."

Her face crumpled. "And she died trying to find me."

He pulled her close. "Overprotectiveness runs in your family. Seems you almost died trying to save Alex."

A smile surfaced through her tears. "Can you think of a better cause?"

His heart constricted. "Nope."

"Laura?"

Hearing the doctor's voice, they both leaped to their feet. "How's Alex?"

"He's doing well. Came through the surgery like a real trooper. He's in Recovery right now, and he'll be in Isolation for quite some time, but you can see him in a short while."

"Thank you," Laura told him in a shaking voice, unable to believe this incredible blessing.

Mitch grasped the man's hand in a firm shake. "We can't thank you enough."

The doctor returned the handshake. "This is the best part of my job."

As he walked away, Laura felt the tears of joy slide down her cheeks, but she didn't bother wiping them away. "Oh, Mitch. It's what we've prayed for, hoped for. I almost can't believe it. But you kept telling me to believe, to trust. It was so hard for me. I didn't think I could. But you kept standing beside me, making me believe."

He reached out to stroke the curve of her cheek. "I was where I wanted to be."

Emboldened, she met his gaze. "Will you be there for me always? When I falter? When I need your arms around me?"

"I love you, Laura. I think I've loved you since the day you stormed into my office and demanded

I give you my best. For you, I can be that person, the one you believe I am.''

"I believe in a man with a good and true heart. A man who risked his life for me…for my child. A man I can trust with my life…and with my heart. I love you, Mitch Tucker. In a way I've never loved before.''

Around them, the hospital stirred, the paging system bleating out messages that echoed in the hallways, the vending machines clacking with the sounds of coins dropping.

But neither Mitch nor Laura heard the bustle or clatter. Eyes focused only on each other, they signaled silent promises. Their lips met, another tender promise. One of a new beginning.

EPILOGUE

"WHAT ARE WE DOING HERE?" Mitch asked as they stood at the door of the cabin.

Laura's eyes were bright, but he couldn't decipher the mystery in them.

"Isn't this the sort of place you want to bring your new bride to?" she asked, smoothing the folds of her long, silk wedding gown.

Just watching her took his breath away. He wondered if it would be that way always.

It certainly had that morning at their intimate wedding. As intimate a service as possible when the groom had a mother, five sisters and an ex-partner-best friend. Naturally, Laura had wanted both her aunts, Rhoda and Ellen. And of course Mrs. Plummer. And their little star, Alex, who had served as the tiny ring bearer in a tux identical to Mitch's. But the biggest surprise was David Farley, who stood proudly on the bride's half of the church.

Still, they had managed to escape before the reception had completely wound down. But Mitch couldn't imagine why Laura had insisted on coming here.

Although truth be told, he would have gone anywhere for her. In fact, their celebratory trip with

Alex to Ireland was already scheduled. But that was after the honeymoon.

"Laura, I made reservations at the Warwick."

"And I canceled them," she confessed without apparent remorse.

He glanced at the cabin door. "So this is our honeymoon escape?"

She smiled. "You do have a key, don't you?"

"I keep one on my key ring," he admitted.

Seeing her expectant look, he reluctantly slid the key into the lock, hearing the click as the tumblers slid into place.

"You still haven't told me why we're here."

She reached into the tiny silk purse she carried, and pulled out a small box, which she handed to him.

His brows rose in question.

"Open it," she urged.

He untied the solitary ribbon and looked inside at a neatly folded paper.

"Read it," she encouraged him.

He scanned the paper, realizing it was a deed. To the cabin. "I don't understand."

"It's my wedding gift to you," she replied softly. "I could see how much this house meant to you, how much of yourself you put into it. It should be yours. And now it is."

"I can't accept this," he protested. "It's a wonderful, touching gesture, but I can't let you do this. It's too much."

Her eyes brightened. "You gave me the ultimate gift—the life of my son. It's something I can never repay. Even if I try from now until forever. I'll always be in your debt, trying to show you how much you mean to us. How much you will always mean to me.'' Her fingers stroked his face. ''Don't you know by now? You're my white knight.''

Mitch pushed the door open wider, then swept her up into his arms and carried her over the threshold. ''From now until forever, eh? I may be able to think of a few ways.''

Her laugh was soft, seductive. ''A few?''

''At least. Because you're mine forever.''

''Forever,'' she echoed. And her laugh was lost in his kiss. And the kiss was lost in the love they shared. A love that would tie them together for all time. Two spirits so different...brought together by chance, forged by fate and sealed by love.

CELEBRATE VALENTINE'S DAY WITH HARLEQUIN®'S LATEST TITLE— *Stolen Memories*

Available in trade-size format, this collector's edition contains three full-length novels by *New York Times* bestselling authors Jayne Ann Krentz and Tess Gerritsen, along with national bestselling author Stella Cameron.

TEST OF TIME by **Jayne Ann Krentz**—

He married for the best reason.... She married for the only reason.... Did they stand a chance at making the only reason the real reason to share a lifetime?

THIEF OF HEARTS by **Tess Gerritsen**—

Their distrust of each other was only as strong as their desire. And Jordan began to fear that Diana was more than just a thief of hearts.

MOONTIDE by **Stella Cameron**—

For Andrew, Greer's return is a miracle. It had broken his heart to let her go. Now fate has brought them back together. And he won't lose her again...

Make this Valentine's Day one to remember!

Look for this exciting collector's edition on sale January 2001 at your favorite retail outlet.

HARLEQUIN®
Makes any time special ™

Visit us at www.eHarlequin.com

PHSM

#1 *New York Times* bestselling author

NORA ROBERTS

brings you more of the loyal and loving, tempestuous and tantalizing Stanislaski family.

Coming in February 2001

The Stanislaski Sisters

Natasha and Rachel

Though raised in the Old World traditions of their family, fiery Natasha Stanislaski and cool, classy Rachel Stanislaski are ready for a *new* world of love....

And also available in February 2001 from Silhouette Special Edition, the newest book in the heartwarming Stanislaski saga

CONSIDERING KATE

Natasha and Spencer Kimball's daughter Kate turns her back on old dreams and returns to her hometown, where she finds the *man* of her dreams.

Available at your favorite retail outlet.

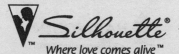

Where love comes alive™

Harlequin proudly brings you

STELLA CAMERON
Bobby Hutchinson
Sandra Marton

in

MARRIED IN SPRING

*a brand-new anthology in which three couples
find that when spring arrives, romance soon
follows…along with an unexpected
walk down the aisle!*

February 2001

Available wherever Harlequin books are sold.